# WEDNESDAY'S BOOK

# WEDNESDAY'S BOOK

REBEKAH ISERT

# Contents

*vii*

For Mitzi—
The prettiest kitty in all the land.
Also for everyone else—especially Jesse, Sarah, and Mom.
Sorry the cat got the first dedication. In my defense, this book wasn't supposed to be published until 2022.

# PROLOGUE

I am human.

Prickles and sticks, held together by mud made from the falling snow squished in between my toes. The viscous mixture pushed into my undercoat, taking the cold and sending it in spikes straight into my bones.

I needed to get somewhere dry. My thick coat was now saturated by mud and snow from my escape. I wouldn't last long without shelter.

My whiskers twitched, and my ears pricked up. I could hear the scratching of squirrels hiding in their dreys, curling up with their families against the bitter cold. I could smell the fresh pine, interlaced with a wood fire nearby.

A fire...

I closed my eyes momentarily, trying to remember anything I could. I could remember toes—my human toes—warmed by the flames in a dim room. A cup of something in my hands. Human hands.

I am human. I didn't know my name. I didn't know where I was, or where I had come from. But I was human. I was.

The trees parted into a clearing that was bigger than the world itself, a beautiful white house with lots of windows almost blending in with the falling snow but for the golden light emitting from the porch. Yellow meant warm. Warm meant safe.

I meant to set off. One wet paw stopped, my body freezing at the *prospect of going out into the open. It would be exposed. Who knew what would carry me off? A hawk? A fox? Would they be out in the storm?*

*The wind howled a long mournful moan, sending the flurry of snowflakes sideways. I shivered. At least I would be low to the ground. Perhaps if I stayed low enough, nothing would see me.*

*I would be safe.*

*I had to get to that...*

*What was the word again?*

*House.*

*What people lived in.*

*What I lived in.*

I am human.

*Get to the house.*

# I

# IN WHICH THERE IS A MISSING GIRL AND I FIND A CAT

I fought the urge to rub my forehead as I looked down at the smiling face in the photograph.

Odell Richardson. Age thirty-three. Profession: ballet dancer. Missing since August twenty-third.

I looked up at Mrs. Richardson, who was dressed in some sort of fur coat, clutching the black whatever-it-was in her hand as if it were a life preserver and she was out to sea with no land in sight. She looked everywhere but me, looking more and more uncomfortable the longer I didn't say anything.

"I understand that your daughter disappeared one night after practice?" I said, laying the photograph down on the table. She looked up at me, her eye contact a refreshing change, before nodding and looking down again.

"Yes," she said. "She was with her friends. Giselle Carabosse and

Seigfried Handel. From what Giselle was able to tell me, they'd gone to some bonfire with the dance company—they'd just wrapped Sleeping Beauty. Odell wandered off by herself, which...I'm sorry Mr. Orris, it's just not like her. She's never been outdoorsy. I'm surprised that she'd even be out there, even for a company bonfire."

"This was by Henley Mill?" I said.

She looked down again. "Yes," she replied.

I looked down at the file that she had handed me once again and shook my head. "You realize that it's been almost two and a half months since she's disappeared?" I asked. She nodded.

"That's why I came to you," she said quietly, "The police have suspended their investigation. They think...Well, I think they think she's dead."

I shifted. "Is that what they told you?" I asked seriously.

She shook her head."No," she admitted. "But they called off the search. Their reasoning to me, though, it seemed...odd."

"Well, often when the police have no leads—"

"They didn't say there were no leads," she corrected me. "They said they had exhausted all avenues that they wanted to pursue. That...well, that means magic, doesn't it?"

We sat in silence for a few moments pondering the reality of that statement. The police weren't cowards, but there was no official magical branch. Only the few magic sensitive humans or whatever changeling or half-elf who wanted to be in the justice system joined—though whether they disclosed their status as such varied greatly. She sighed, and shook her head. "Mr. Orris, I know the odds. At this point... It's December third. If we can't find her alive...and safe... I'd just like something to—" She looked down again, eyes full of tears. I pushed the tissue box toward her.

She didn't have to finish her sentence. If I couldn't find her alive, then finding her body was the next best option. I looked up at the window. It was getting dark.

"I'll take the case," I said quietly. "One way or another, I'll find her."

She looked up at me, face solemn. "Thank you, Mr. Orris." Then, standing, she pulled another tissue from the box. I stood as well, extending my hand. She took it.

"Call me Trillion. If you could sign the releases of information, the contract, and request that the case file is sent over from the police station by the end of the week, that would be helpful," I said. "Also, if you have any questions or if you think of something that might help, please give me a call anytime."

She nodded again. With our business concluded for now, I showed her out and then walked back slowly to my desk, deep in my thoughts. Missing people were hardly my favorite types of cases. Most often they turned out just fine, but every so often...

I sighed. It was time to head home. It was already snowing outside, and the road back to the house was going to only get more slick from here on out. Packing up the the file I'd started and my computer in my satchel, I grabbed my car keys and headed out.

The ride home was thankfully not as eventful as I had anticipated. Twenty miles out of the city, the asphalt had kept enough of its warmth so the roads were only wet. If the amount of snow falling was anything to go by, however, it wouldn't last.

My phone beeped as a call came in. I looked down at the car display.

Konstantin.

I pressed the button. "Any word?" I asked, not waiting for him to speak.

I could practically hear Konstantin frown. "No. Whatever spell Rothbart is using to hide his identity, the trail's old and it's going cold fast."

"Where did you lose it?"

"After the Councilwoman's office, it led to some housing complex near downtown. I lost it altogether in the alleys near the Metropolitan Theatre," Konstantin said uncomfortably. My eyebrows drew together.

"Did it really?" I said quietly, glancing over at the briefcase on the passenger's seat. "How very interesting."

"How so?" he asked.

I smiled grimly. "The mother of the missing ballet dancer—Odell Richardson—contacted me today. She wants me to look into Odell's disappearance."

"Did she go missing near the theatre?" Konstantin asked, confused.

"No," I responded. "But she worked at the Metropolitan." The man on the other end of the line was quiet for a moment.

"Think they're related?" he finally asked.

I frowned and shook my head. "I don't know," I admitted, turning my car up the long driveway. The snow didn't look that deep yet. Small mercies.

"The Councilwoman is part of both The Aggregate and Domovoi," Konstantin reminded me. "If it is magic related, it wouldn't be too much of an ask for the daughter to know about the disappearance, or to know which of her friends have that sort of power."

"Except there's not enough purity in the Domovoi line to make someone go missing by magical means," I said. "As for the dancer... I don't know. This smacks of something extra to me. To the mother as well."

Konstantin snorted. "I dare you to tell the Councilwoman to her face that there's not enough purity in her line to do serious magic," he said.

I frowned and shook my head. "Thanks," I said wryly. "But I'd like to keep my thumbs."

"She's never publicly done anything like that," Konstantin said.

I smiled ruefully. "Clearly you didn't know Stanislava a century ago."

I could practically hear Konstantin smile. "A bit before my time, that. Well, I'm going to sniff around here a little longer and see if I can get some other sort of lead. Maybe Rothbart's left the notes to his diabolical plans somewhere," he said hopefully.

I snorted. "Probably not," I said. "But one can only hope."

"Do you want me to talk to anyone about Odell?" Konstantin asked. "Since I'll be around the theatre?"

"Not just yet," I said, pulling up to the garage and pressing the button. As I watched the door go up, something small and mud-brown crept under the door, and snuck around the wall. A cat? I edged the car forward, watching the small creature carefully as I drove in. "I'd like a better handle on the case before I start scaring people off."

"Most people don't know I'm associated with you," he reminded me.

"I agree," I said, turning off the car. "But people do remember if they get asked the same questions multiple times in a row."

"Fair," Konstantin replied. "Well, good luck."

"And you," I added. "Get inside soon. The storm is supposed to be getting worse in the next couple of hours. I don't anticipate I'll be back in the city for the rest of the week. If you can track something down, fine. If not, get inside."

"That bad?"

"We'll be getting a white Christmas," I confirmed. "Holly told me she has a bed for the night if you need one."

"I'll get by," Konstantin said. "You know I can't rest if I'm not at home."

"Well, then, get done soon, and get there."

"Yes, sir," he said, and hung up. I hit the garage door button, and the door started to scroll down. I looked closely for the small animal that I'd seen creep in. I'd far surpassed any fear of animals. If it had left the security of the forest surrounding my home, it was going to be looking for shelter or warmth due to injury or the inclement weather.

I could shelter, and I could also provide first aid.

I stepped out of the car as the garage door finished closing, but I could tell by the eye-shine beside the refrigerator in the corner that I wasn't alone. It was almost definitely a cat—a tiny one, but not a kitten. Brushing my hair over one shoulder, I knelt down and held out one hand.

"Hello, precious," I said softly. "What are you doing here?"

There was a weak little meow, and in the dim light from the night light set into the wall, I saw it walk, or rather shake, toward me step by step. It was covered in mud, and seemed to be soaked to the skin. Wherever this little feline had come from, it wouldn't have lasted long outdoors. Not on a night like tonight.

"C'mere, kitty," I said, accessing the tiniest bit of magic that I could. Just to help it trust me. Just so I could handle it and get it out of the cold without contracting rabies. It was resistant at first, body angled away from me as if to run, and yet it kept on sidling forward.

"Come on, sweetheart," I murmured. It stretched out its neck and sniffed my fingers. Then, wobbling forward, the small cat bunted its muddy head against my palm.

"There we go," I said, stroking my thumb across the slick spikes of the fur on its head. "Yeah, I'm not so bad, huh? Do you think you want to come inside?" Reaching back, I opened the door to the house, the low-lying hall lights illuminating the indoors in a warm, dim yellow. The little cat shrank back a bit, and meowed a little when I picked it—her—up, but didn't struggle as I carried her into the house.

# 2

# IN WHICH I NAME A CAT AND SUSPECT A VARIETY OF PEOPLE

At least she was clean now. I looked over the top of my file at the cat sitting by the fireplace, head low, back firmly facing me. She was already mostly dry—helping it along with her raspy tongue, but I was definitely Being Ignored.

I examined the scratch on my hand, grateful that I couldn't catch rabies. There weren't too many physiological differences between elves and humans, but immunity from some diseases was a definite perk. And, for whatever my body couldn't handle, I had Morfi's It-Just-Sucks Wound Balm. Despite the name, it did the job.

If only it could soothe the injured feelings of cats.

"You know you were filthy," I murmured primly, turning the page of the case file. "Don't act like you would have licked yourself clean."

There was a low, rolling, clearly annoyed meow, but the little cat didn't turn around, staring squarely into the fireplace. I smiled. I needed to figure out what to call her. She was a bit thinner than I liked, and didn't look like she was accustomed to being outside. I'd keep her until the roads to the city cleared up, and then I'd take her to the vet. Until then, though...

I honestly probably shouldn't have taken her in. It wasn't that I didn't want to, or that I didn't know how to take care of her—I'd kept up-to-date on my veterinary license on purpose. I simply couldn't become attached to her, no matter how much personality she had, or how adorable it was when she was ignoring me.

But I couldn't just call her 'Little Cat' while she was here. I watched her for a moment longer. Nothing came to mind. I'd already had a Princess and Missy Miss. She didn't seem quite so uppity. More just annoyed.

Or embarrassed.

I glanced at the calendar. Wednesday, December third. I couldn't name her December in good conscience. Wednesday, maybe?

"Hey, Wednesday," I called down at the cat. Her ears twitched, and I smiled. Good enough for now.

Cat now named, I looked down at the file again. Odell Richardson. She was one of the soloists at the Metropolitan, graduated from the University of Utah. She was good, there was no denying that. But why would she have disappeared? More importantly, in a disappearance case, why had the police suddenly declined to investigate?

Odell's mother was right—it usually indicated magical involvement. I sighed. Whatever I was looking for I doubted that I would find evidence of it in the company that she was in. Going by previous run-ins with the Metropolitan Ballet, most of them seemed to be of magical descent, but as far as I knew, there wasn't anyone in the dance company that was currently registered in the American Association of Sorcerers.

Come to think of it, given what I knew of dancers and their habits, I doubted that any of them would have time to study sorcery on the side, let alone become proficient or powerful enough to make someone disappear.

"So what would the police have found?" I murmured to myself. "Unless someone in the company was born to it. Carabosse is an old family. Maybe Giselle has a stronger gift than she realized?"

I sat in silence for a few moments when I felt a slight shift on the sofa, and then a soft paw on my knee. I looked down at the little tabby and smiled.

"Am I forgiven?" I asked. She meowed a little in response, but then stepped further onto my lap, circling once before settling down on my legs. I scratched her head, much softer now without the mud, and continued studying the case until my phone buzzed. I picked it up, frowning.

"Konstantin?" I asked.

There was a gruff huff of air, before a slight crackle of static. "Trillion," he said, "just calling to let you know I got to shelter."

"Holly?"

"No, I made it home, just in time. We've already gotten a foot. I'd be surprised if you get out before the end of this week," he said.

"It wouldn't be the first time," I said. "Thank you for letting me know. Did you find anything at the theatre before you left?"

"Nothing definitive," he said. "The magic trail went cold for sure, but I'm still trying to figure out whether or not it's just because Rothbart hasn't been there, or simply hasn't used any magic lately."

"He has to be using some sort of magic," I disagreed, "or we would have spotted him by now. And we know that he hasn't left the city, either." I snorted. "Unless he's finally gone straight—"

"That man is so crooked that if he swallowed a nail, he'd spit up a corkscrew," Konstantin said flatly. I laughed. Wednesday's head jerked up and she glared at me in response.

"Sorry," I mouthed at her. She yawned and laid her head back down.

"I don't doubt it," I admitted. "I guess we're no further along than we used to be." I thought for a moment. "You said earlier today that his magical trace was somewhere downtown?"

"Yeah, some apartment. I'm not sure whose."

"Could you find out?" I asked. I heard the pause.

"It'll have to wait until the snow stops," he said. "And you know I hate office buildings."

"You could call," I suggested gently.

"Waiting on hold is worse," Konstantin grumbled. "You owe me."

"Considering how much I already owe you, Konstantin, I'm surprised you'll let me add more to the ledger," I said.

I could almost see the devilish curl at one corner of his mouth. "Well, I'm saving up for something big," he said.

I smiled as well, absently running my hand over Wednesday's back. "I dread the day," I said smartly. "Hey, you live near Henley Mill, right?"

"Yes, only about a mile away."

"Think you could make it there if it's stopped snowing by tomorrow afternoon?"

"I know I could. You thinking you'll snowshoe out?"

"I was thinking snowmobile, but more or less," I said. "I'd like to take a look at the area where Odell disappeared, but I need your expertise."

"Think sorcery is involved?"

"I don't know for sure. Not yet," I said. "The police seem to think so, but I'm not sure how they came to that conclusion. I'll have to dig deeper. It'll be better once I get the police file."

"Fair," Konstantin said.

I sighed. "Well, take care of yourself. Stay warm."

"Already done," he said, and hung up.

I looked down at Wednesday. I could tell she wasn't quite asleep yet—her body wasn't relaxed fully, and she was still in a position where she could get up in a hurry. Still, it wasn't as if I could just stand up. It was practically a cardinal sin to kick a cat off your lap if she'd deposited herself there. But I had work to do. Something about this wasn't sitting right.

"Okay, Wednesday," I said. "Since you're my captive audience—hopefully not literally—let me tell you a story. Maybe you'll have some insight."

She didn't move.

"So, once upon a time, there was a man whose name is Rothbart. He's a pretty bad man. He's a half elf—I'm a full elf, by the way, it's probably why you've trusted me so quickly, with the exception of the bath— and he's been cursing people up and down the United States, with more than a couple of fatalities.

"The regular police won't do anything because he's a half-elf sorcerer, and so they contacted my father. He's pretty important in the elven world. Father has...invited me to track him down. I've been here near the city for the last fifty years or so, but I've been following Rothbart everywhere. Earlier this year, he found his way here to the city, and disappeared. We thought we'd lost him until today—as you probably heard in the garage—when we found the last trace of him at the theatre."

Wednesday seemed to look up at me with interest and shifted so she fit in the crease between my arm and my chest, head resting on my shoulder.

What a weird cat.

I needed to talk, so I kept talking.

"I'm not sure where to go from here. He's almost addicted to using magic—to travel, to hide his identity, to influence people. I doubt that he's gone off it, but there's...no trace of him." I shook my head. I pulled in my chin to look down at her. "Any ideas?" I asked.

She didn't respond. Her body was relaxed now. She must have gone to sleep. How she was comfortable, I had no idea. I sighed.

"And then I've got my missing girl, who for some reason the police don't want to investigate. That points to magic, but in the two pages that I've got about her life from her mother...she led an ordinary life for a ballerina. Wake up, train, dance, perform, go home. Seems to be happy, loves her job, and then poof. Bonfire. Gone."

I shook my head.

Wednesday lifted up her head and chirped in my ear softly, as if to tell me to be quiet. I smiled and patted her gently.

"Okay, okay," I said, "I'll worry about it tomorrow."

# 3

## IN WHICH I ARGUE WITH A CAT AND FLEE THE PREMISES

I don't know where people got the idea that magical creatures don't sleep. Yes, my metabolism was amazing, yes, my body was still youthful at over two thousand years old, but the secret of my success was a good, solid eight hours each night, and that was the case for almost every other elf, shapeshifter, and sorcerer that I had ever met. Tapping into the magical world, whether by birth or by study, gave you power and helped you live longer, but it only went so far if you weren't willing to take care of yourself.

I woke up to a wall of tabby colored fur. Since I wasn't in the habit of redecorating in my sleep, and there was an uncommon weight on my chest, I was willing to guess that there was a cat there.

"Wednesday," I rumbled, spitting cat hair out of my mouth. "Wednesday, get up."

There was a soft burr, and I felt the mound of cat shift a little.

"Get up," I said. The bundle shifted.

*No.*

I blinked. Staring up at the ceiling, my eyebrows furrowed. I had to have imagined it. The small female voice in my brain...

"Wednesday—"

*Go away.*

Nope.

"I can't. You're laying on my neck," I said.

The furry mass curled up tighter. *Warm.*

"I know. But I have to get up. If it's done snowing then I've got to go somewhere," I said, trying to process the fact that I was talking to a responsive cat.

Well, sort of responsive, at least.

*Snowing.*

"I can feel sunlight."

*Dreaming. Still night.*

"It is not!" I protested, wondering if I was correct. I reached up to move her off of my neck, and paused as I felt the barest pinprick of a claw. Rolling my eyes, bidding my unscarred chest goodbye, I quickly reached up and plucked her off.

*Lifting! Not allowed lifting!* Wednesday's indignant thought was punctuated by a yowl, which died rather quickly as I set her down where I had just sat up. Feeling the warmth of the patch that I had just left, Wednesday stared up at me, thoroughly miffed before curling up once more beside my pillow.

"Crazy cat," I said, rubbing a hand over my face, and looking out the window. Despite evidence to the contrary, Wednesday was right—it was actually still snowing outside, the brightness caused by the sheer whiteness of the snow. Time to check the weather, then.

Leaving Wednesday to take advantage of my absence, I made my way out into the front room and flipped on the television. Unlike most of the elvish population—even in these modern days—I had no problem integrating modern technology into my life. Any help was help, especially in my line of work, and if Wednesday speaking to me was any indication, it did nothing to dampen magic like everybody feared.

The weather channel was on, like normal.

"—The low pressure system seems to have halted over the city, pressing to the north. We expect snow for the next twenty-four hours, with another twelve inches expected. The highways will continue to be plowed, but the Maryland Department of Transportation has informed us that they will not be able to get to registered private drives until the snowfall stops. We recommend that residents stay home as much as possible for their own safety."

I stared at the weather lady, my lips pursed in displeasure. Not that I couldn't technically get anywhere where I wanted to go, but I tried to be smart as much as possible, and wandering out in the middle of a snowstorm just didn't seem to cut it. I thought about Wednesday, long fur caked in so much mud that I hadn't been able to tell what color she was. She'd been lucky to get here when she did.

There was a small chirp behind me. I turned to see Wednesday's small frame walk through the bedroom door. The soft whisper of a translation entered my head.

*Food?*

I looked down at her. "Hungry?"

She looked up at me disparagingly. *Yes. Said want food.*

Wow. I looked down at her, eyebrows pulled together. "I think I need a please or something," I said. "I do not help impolite cats."

I never thought I would ever say something like that in my two millennia of life. Wednesday looked up at me, her large green eyes blinking once.

*Please or something.*

I blinked. "Rude!"

She didn't respond, but swished her tail and walked away. Shaking my head, disbelieving that seven pounds of fluff thought she could order me around—and was uncomfortably correct in that assumption—I turned to the pantry. I kept an emergency supply for exactly this type of scenario, and I pulled out a can of cat food. Cracking it open, I scooped out half onto a plate and placed that on the ground at my feet, just as she jumped up onto the counter.

*Where food?*

"Down here," I said, tapping the plate. There was a soft fwump as she landed on the ground and came over to sniff at the plate.

*What.*

"What what?" I asked. "It's cat food."

*Cat food.*

"Yes, cat food. You had it last night," I said, standing and walking over and opened the fridge. Pizza leftovers. I smiled, and pulled the box out of the fridge.

*Cat food.* Wednesday's voice was disdainful. *Cat food.*

"Yes," I said, pulling two pieces out of the box and putting them on a plate. "Cat food. For you. The cat."

She looked up at me, as if genuinely shocked and more than a little disturbed. She meowed, a hurt chirp.

*Not cat.*

"Yes, you are," I said, putting my plate into the microwave and choosing a setting that vacillated between making my food lukewarm and molten lava. "Despite being well-spoken for a feline, madam, from the tip of your glossy whiskers to the tip of your fluffy tail, you are one-hundred percent cat."

*Am human.*

"Not from where I'm standing," I said. "Eat your food."

*Wrong.*

"Eat your cat food, Wednesday," I said, a little more sternly.

*Not cat.* Her voice was plaintive, and an accompanying meow punctuated her remark. The microwave beeped. Not sure how to re-

WEDNESDAY'S BOOK · 19

spond to the cat, I reached into the microwave and subsequently burnt my hand on the plate which was now roughly the temperature of the sun.

*Want pizza.*

"I'm not giving you my pizza," I said sharply. She sat down and looked at me, tail twitching back and forth, clearly displeased. Instead of using her words, she meowed. Loudly. "No!" I said. She meowed again, longer and louder. I was going to pass this cat off to the local rescue nonprofit as soon as I possibly could, I thought, stalking into the dining room. She followed me, her drawn out meow bouncing with each step.

"No. Go eat your food!"

*Want pizza.*

I turned to her, "Look, Wednesday, you might think you're a human, but you have a cat stomach. If you eat pizza, you're going to be sick."

Her expression darkened, and she sat, her fluffy tail swishing around dainty paws. She didn't seem to have an argument for that.

*Cat food nasty yuck gross. Fish.*

I closed my eyes and exhaled slowly. I looked down at her. "Fine," I said, "If you can turn into a human right now, you may have pizza."

The fluffy tail swished, and an annoyed, defensive tone came into her voice. *Can't.*

"Like I thought," I said, turning away.

*Not time.*

I raised an eyebrow, turning back.

"Oh really?" I asked. "And what time would that be?"

Silence.

*Don't know. Not now.*

"Uh huh," I said. "Well, if you figure it out, let me know, will you?"

*Yes. Then have pizza?*

I sighed. "Fine. When you turn human, we'll have pizza."

She swished her tail again. *Good. Will eat yuck food now. Pizza later.*

"Don't complain. The 'yuck food' will help your coat, and provides you with all the amino acids you need," I called over my shoulder, before sitting down at the table and biting into my lukewarm pizza. My own pizza. Cat-free.

I'd won.

So why did it feel like I'd lost?

I shook it off. The cat was a cat. If she'd been an enchanted human, I would have been able to feel the enchantment. I frowned. Or at least, I hoped so.

Maybe I'd bring Konstantin around to check.

I felt equal draws to smile and grimace at the prospect. As valuable as my friend was, the longer I could go without traumatizing the little cat, the better. If I was wrong, though...

I wasn't, though. I was not wrong. All cats thought they were humans. All of them. It was practically a required part of their personality. Besides, the regular cat mannerisms were all there—the tail twitching, meowing, sleeping on my face... All there. Literally the only reason why I was even questioning it was because she said she wasn't.

And because she was speaking.

Was that normal? I knew some elves with the talent to speak with animals. I'd never had it before, at least not beyond telling moods and diagnosing internal complaints, but perhaps it depended on the animal. I'd had a lot through the years. Maybe I'd just never been listening properly.

Father would know.

I was reaching toward my cell phone on the table before I finished the thought, and froze right after I did, hand hovering over it. Then I put my hand back at my side.

He would know, but I didn't need to ask.

Wednesday was a cat.

I looked over at her accusingly, leaning over her cat dish, tail swishing every couple of seconds. I heard echoes of some very fake gagging noises from the cat's direction. I would have been worried, except I could clearly tell they were in my head.

"Stop it, Wednesday," I said. "You're fine."

*Better with pizza.*

I rolled my eyes and didn't respond. Instead, I looked out the window. The snow was slowing down. Henley Mill was only three miles away. I pulled out my phone. Only light snow for the next three hours. If I took the snowmobile, I'd be able to get there in twenty minutes and have a good look around.

I glanced back at Wednesday, and caught the tail-end of a withering look.

Time to call Konstantin.

# 4

## IN WHICH I INVESTIGATE A RAVE AND RECEIVE A DINNER ORDER

The cold air whipped against my face as I revved the snowmobile a little faster. It was cold, but not as unpleasant as it could have been. The snow had all but stopped, at least for the next little while. I could see the path through the woods, and that was all that mattered.

Technically, the old mill was on my property. I owned over two thousand acres of forested land around my house, but the mill was right on the edge, backed up right next to the state park to the south. The rules were simple, and I had posted them on the property in plain sight: You could have bonfires and parties, as long as nothing but the bonfire burned, and any and all traces of humanity were cleared up, except for the fire pit.

I'd only ever had to ban someone once, right when it opened. He was sixty now, and still didn't like me much. Of course, that was probably because he'd turned from a college party-goer into a recalcitrant drunk, but there wasn't much I could do about that anyway. Not that my actions had ruined his life or anything—he was a CEO of something or other now.

I saw the wheelhouse before I saw the clearing, and just above the rumble of the engine heard the faint gurgle of the half-frozen mill creek just beyond. A moment later, I burst into the clearing, sending up a spray of snow as I slowed the machine to a stop.

A man walked out of the trees, hands stuffed into the pocket of an old tan coat that he wouldn't throw away, and a subdued smile on his face. "Trillion," he said, shaking his long brown hair out of his face as I turned off the snowmobile.

I smiled and reached out my hand. "Konstantin," I said. "Made it home all right, I see."

Konstanin's smile turned wolfish and grabbed my hand, his grip strong. "Always," he said. "And yourself? You look a bit...harried." He paused. "You smell like cat."

"I don't want to talk about it," I said firmly, looking around the clearing. I saw Konstantin pull in his chin, but he didn't comment.

"So?" he asked, motioning around us. "Old Mill, under a fresh blanket of snow? Anything you want me to find in particular, or just look for magic?"

"Anything you can tell me," I said. "There were a couple of fall bonfires since the one where Odell disappeared, so I wouldn't rely too much on individual smells. The trace of magic that would be required to make someone disappear—"

"Should still be lingering around," Konstantin finished. "Anywhere I should start looking in particular?"

I shook my head. "Not that I know of. That's what bothers me—no one seemed to notice that Odell was gone until later when she didn't show up for work. There were at least twenty people at that party, but from what I've been able to find out only two of the girl's friends—Carabosse's daughter, and some dance company member—ever gave statements."

"Ah, the joys of partying," Konstantin said ironically. "Inspiration for living alone like nothing else."

"Tell me about it," I said, thinking of the ridiculously vocal cat currently stashed away in my house. Konstantin closed his eyes, tilting his head upward toward the sky and inhaled deeply. As he did, his frame started to change, a bright spot of magic in a suddenly dull landscape. Giving him his privacy, I turned toward the mill house, only turning back when I heard the panting of a dog.

Shapeshifter that he was, Konstantin—now in his alternate frame of an enormous Irish Wolfhound—chuffed a little in the cold air, and started padding toward the creek. Following him, grateful that I could walk on top of the snow rather than sinking down into it, we made our way over to the creek.

Konstantin circled the clearing twice before heading off another direction—over the bridge that headed into the state park. I swiftly followed him farther down the path than I would have anticipated. After sniffing around for a moment longer, Konstantin paused, and rippled back into human form.

"There's a trail, then," I said.

Konstantin looked up the path through the woods and then back to me. "Yes. Stronger than I would have thought, under the circumstances," he said.

"What does that mean?" I said, frowning.

"I mean," he said, "that your dancer disappeared almost three months ago, yeah?" I nodded. He motioned down the trail back toward the mill with his chin. "This is only a week old. Whatever came through here... Whatever was practicing magic like that, it was recently."

I looked at him, my expression hard, but not directed toward the shapeshifter. "Does it originate at the clearing where you stopped before?" I asked.

He paused, and shrugged a little hesitantly. "Yes and no," he said. I frowned, but didn't say anything. Konstantin continued. "The clearing has the imprint of strong magic, far stronger than the magic along the trail, but it's much, much older. That large imprint *does* seem like it's from the time that the girl disappeared, and is related to the trail. At the very least it comes from the same source."

I thought for a moment. "Why would it go off into the woods, then?" I asked. "Or did it?"

"I couldn't tell you. I'll keep on working it out. Unless whatever it was that left the trail left and came back again, there should be an imprint of where it was staying in the meantime."

"No one reported anything out of the ordinary to me," I said in wonder, looking around the clearing. "If the enchantment happened on my property, the wards should have been tripped."

Konstantin looked around the clearing again, lips pursed. "That I can't answer for you. I will say, though, I've smelled this magical trace before."

I looked up in interest. "Really?" Konstantin nodded. "Where?"

He shook his head. "I can't remember. I've been running down so many magical leads on Rothbart, I can't place it."

"It's not Rothbart, though?" I asked.

I expected him to give me a dirty look, and he did, but shook his head anyway. "No, it's not. I would have told you immediately," he said, his voice rather huffy. It reminded me of another animal—one who had a human complex.

"Fine," I said. "When you remember, let me know?"

"I wouldn't know who it belongs to," he cautioned me. "I haven't run down any of the other scents."

"No matter, it hasn't been important until now," I said, reassuring.

The snowfall had started to pick up again. Konstantin's head rose once more, and he took a deep breath in. "You'd better get home, the wind is going to start soon," he said. He paused, the ghost of smile playing around his mouth. "You sure you don't want to tell me why you smell like a cat?"

I was tempted to roll my eyes in exasperation. "Just a rescue. I'll be taking her to the shelter once the snow clears."

"You sure? They usually don't get under your skin like this. Is she hurt, or—"

"She's fine. Just very...communicative," I said. To put it mildly.

Konstantin smiled and shook his head as we made it back to the mill. "That's the trouble with cats, man. They give you their opinions whether you ask for them or not."

I couldn't help but laugh. "And I suppose you're a dog person?" I asked. He laughed. The magic around him started to ripple, and he spoke just before he shrunk down into his dog form.

"What gave me away?"

Once changed, he burst into a run, heading away from the clearing in the direction of where he lived. Following his lead, I made my way back to the snowmobile, and headed for home.

The snow was falling thick and fast by the time I got home. I could see Wednesday pacing in the front room windows as I drove up, mouth opening wide in a meow when she saw me. Apparently there was a range with how far her voice carried, even in my head, because I couldn't hear a word.

Small mercies.

Driving the snowmobile into the shed, I covered the vehicle and locked it up before heading inside through the garage. As soon as I was through the side door, I could hear Wednesday meowing through the door into the kitchen. The translation flowed through my mind in sharp, punctuated phrases.

*Let me in! Let me in! There is a closed door! Let me in!* Shrugging off my big coat, and stepping from my boots into my indoor shoes, I crossed the garage, and opened the door during a particularly piteous *Let me iiiiiiiiinnnn!*

"Hello, Wednesday," I said, opening the door. Swarming through the door, she pushed herself against my leg, meowing loudly.

*You are back. Good,* she said. Then, before I could do so much as lean down to pet her, the little cat turned around, her tail high, and trotted through the kitchen. Closing the door to the garage behind me, I followed her into the kitchen.

*It is quiet when you are not here. I do not like it. I cannot open the cold box door. I have no thumbs. I am annoyed I have no thumbs. Also the handle is too high. You should get a low handle for your cold box.*

"It's called a refrigerator," I said, watching her go. "And you are speaking in complete sentences." She looked up at me, and the tip of her tail swished.

*Yes. I have practiced. I am human. I remember fast.*

I sighed and looked down at the floor, pinching the bridge of my nose, and nodded. "Okay."

*Also, I see your nasty can food for cats. There is one with a bird on it. I request the bird.*

It took me for a minute to realize what she was talking about. "You mean the chicken flavor?"

*Ah. Chicken. This is an acceptable offering.*

"You can remember the word 'offering' but not 'chicken'?" I asked incredulously. She thought for a moment, blinking once.

*Some words come nice. Some hard.*

I frowned. Of course a cat would know the word 'offering'.

"But we have half a can of salmon left," I said. She looked up at me and meowed, long and nasally. No translation came through.

"Was I supposed to understand that?" I asked.

She looked at me disparagingly.

Ah. No translation necessary.

# 5

## IN WHICH THERE IS MORE UNDIGNIFIED FLEEING AND I FIND SOMETHING ODD

*T*he sun is out. I want to go outside.

"No."

*Why not?*

"Because I said so."

*I do not like that reason. You keep using it.*

"Because you're still not going outside!" I said, looking down at her. Her ears twitched, the white of her chin standing out as she meowed.

*But it is pretty. The sky is blue. Why can I not go outside?*

"Because I said so." I turned back to my work.

*You keep using that reason. I have been inside for four days. I do not like it.*

"Fine." Placing the folder that I held in my hands onto the table, I turned back to the small cat. "It's because I need to take you to the vet, I have no way to contain you, and I'm not able to let you out to go frighten the neighborhood birds."

Wednesday looked up, her big green eyes the exact image of innocence.

*I would* never *frighten the birds.*

"Right. Just like you would never get into the kitty treats, or lick the butter, or use the table as a launchpad to get onto the chandelier," I said.

She blinked up at me. *Well, if you are going to get personal—*

"Wednesday, I'm not arguing about this. I am the hum—er, elf. I am the elf. What I say, goes," I said. She stared at me for me a moment, her tail flicked back and forth, and with a scowl she turned away and prowled over to the window to stare through it. "The silent treatment?" I asked sarcastically.

*You said you did not want to talk.* Her voice was terse, and one ear flicked.

I sighed. "Fine, I'll go into town and get a harness so we can go out."

*A harness for whom?* she asked suspiciously.

For the first time, I realized I was going to be the one who had to put it on her. Well, she was going to have to deal with it.

"You," I said. "It's the only way you're going to leave this house."

She hunched her shoulders and didn't turn back to me, only her tail twitching back and forth. *Good luck with that.*

I looked over at her, but didn't say anything else. I tried not to feel cowed. I wasn't cowed! I was the biped in this relationship. And an elf besides. I was at least two thousand years older than her, and at least....well, a lot bigger and stronger.

"Don't make me use my elvish persuasion on you," I said. That did earn me a look, bitterly sarcastic.

*What, like you have been doing?*

I refused to be pegged by a feline. Wednesday or not, I tried to let animals do what they were going to do as much as possible. She should appreciate that. I was about to open my mouth to fire off something disparaging about her attitude when my phone rang. Grabbing it savagely, I pressed the green button and held it up to my ear.

"This is Trillion," I said curtly.

There was a short pause, and then a cautiously cheerful voice chirped on the other end. "Hello, Mr. Orris, my name is Rachel," the Department of Transportation representative said. "We just wanted to let you know that your drive has been cleared."

"Oh," I said, struggling to moderate my tone. "That's...wonderful. Thank you for letting me know, Rachel."

"You're welcome, Mr. Orris," she said. "Please let us know if there's any way that we can assist you in the future!"

"I will," I said, and then disconnected. I looked over at the cat by the window. "Well, it looks like your harness days are nearly upon you. I'm going into town." Standing up, I walked toward the kitchen, taking my keys out of the dish on the counter.

*I will come.* Wednesday's voice was accompanied by a sharp meow as she moved to follow me.

I laughed harshly. "That is *so* not happening," I said.

She followed me, her meow sharpening into a yowl. *I will come!*

"No way!" I said. "With all the trouble you've been, the last thing I need is to get indicted for leaving my cat in the car on a below-freezing day."

*I have a coat,* she said, her tone indicating that I should already know this.

"If it were up to me," I said, "I'd bring you just so you'd stop bothering me. But unfortunately, it's against the law, and I don't feel like getting a mark on my record because of you. You're not coming, and that is the last thing I'm going to say about that."

*Is this the point where you run away because you cannot win?* she asked.

I glared down at her. "No, this is the point where I leave like I was planning on doing anyway. I don't run away from supercilious cats."

*If that is what you prefer to believe,* she said acidly, sitting down on the floor, her fluffy tail swishing back and forth. *I am sure I would never be able to dissuade you.*

I resisted the urge to growl in response, and swiftly exited the house.

I had never thought of myself as vindictive, but my first stop as I entered the city was the cat rescue to buy a harness and more cat food. Vanessa, the attendant at the counter looked at me as I glared at the obnoxiously colored harness with vicious pleasure. It was loud. It was orange. She would hate it.

It was perfect.

"You doing alright, Trillion?" Vanessa asked, her voice a little cautious.

I looked up. "Yeah, I'm fine," I said.

She smiled. "Could've fooled me. You find another one?"

I nodded, an uncomfortable smile crossing my face. "You could say that."

"Feral?" She asked. Then she looked down at the harness and tipped her head to one side. "Then again—"

"No, she's not feral. Just... annoying," I said, sighing. Then, realizing this could potentially be construed as odd, I glanced up at her.

Vanessa, however, only nodded sagely. "Tell me about it. I've been fostering a cat for the last two weeks. Ugh. Little thing totally thinks that it's a human, meowing at me like it's responding." She lowered the barcode scanner. "Come to think of it...maybe she is. Anyway,

I haven't fostered for a while, so I'm getting back into the swing of things. Sometimes I'm not sure whether I'm fostering the cat, or the cat has taken me hostage."

My purchases rung up, I paid, then smiled. "Vanessa," I said, "resign yourself. We've totally been taken hostage."

She grinned. "Keeping her, then?"

I laughed. "Not if I can help it."

Exiting the store, still laughing a little, I threw the bag with the cat food and the harness into the passenger seat and headed over to the office. I wasn't surprised to see Konstantin's car. I was surprised to see a police squad car parked out front. Looking over, I caught sight of the identification number on the vehicle and groaned.

This day just kept on getting better.

I sat in my car for a full minute, debating on whether I wanted to see Officer Farragut or go another round with Wednesday. It was a tough call.

I got out of the car.

Climbing up the stairs to the office, I hear Konstantin's low voice speaking to a much higher voice, hearing the peaks of his statements through the door. As I approached, Farragut's words became understandable.

"—Richardson only gave permission for Orris to receive the file. Much as I would like to, I can't just give it to some unnatural—"

"I'm here, Farragut," I said, sighing as I opened the door. The desk jockey came into view. Long since relegated to paperwork, the rail thin man looked up at me over the spectacles that were quickly sliding to the end of his nose. Walking toward him, I watched him push his glasses up his nose and held out my hand. "File."

"I have a release—"

Reaching into my jacket, I pulled out a pen, signing the papers as I spoke. "I'll sign it. Then, provided you're done insulting my business partner, please leave." Finishing with a dot at the end of my name, I stared down at the officer expectantly. He looked up at me, eyes narrowed.

"Look, Orris, if you think for a minute that I appreciate the fact we're just handing this over, you've got another—"

"Officer Farragut," I said calmly, "if your office did not have such a reluctance to deal with any case that was remotely involved with magic, perhaps you wouldn't have so many unsolved cases. Which would, in turn, cut down on the need for the 'unnatural' ones to do the work for you."

"But—"

I shifted slightly and he stopped. Stepping up to Farragut, towering over him by several inches, I looked down my nose at him. "Leave."

"But—"

I frowned, leaning in just a little closer. "Now."

Farragut, seeming very reluctant to look away from me while I was close, glanced from me to Konstantin, who had shifted and drawn the officer's attention. Perhaps he thought he was being overtly threatened. The shapeshifter raised his eyebrows momentarily, and then wiggled his fingers in a cheeky wave. Huffing, Farragut turned on his heel and beat a hasty retreat, nearly running into the door before stumbling through it. Opening up the file, I seated myself on the edge of the front desk and started glancing through the file.

"You know," Konstantin said mildly, "I'm really glad that he's not on the streets."

"As much as the Commissioner isn't comfortable with magic," I said, "he's no fool."

"He keeps on sending Farragut to deliver files," Konstantin pointed out.

I smiled. "True, but Farragut knows when he doesn't have the upper hand. He's unlikely to start a physical altercation."

"You're thinking of Tomlin, then," Konstantin said.

I smiled again, a little whimsically. "I am," I said. "He is also, by the way, now relegated to desk work. And not involved in any magic-related cases, so I've been informed."

Konstantin inhaled to laugh and winced instead. "Have you not gotten rid of that cat yet?" he asked.

I looked up and sniffed my jacket. I couldn't smell anything. "Not yet. I'm taking her to the vet tomorrow to make sure she's okay to go to the cat rescue. Why?" I pulled my lapel up to my face again. Maybe it was just a dog thing?

Konstantin smirked. "You sure she's a cat?"

"*Yes*," I said, trying not to sound sulky.

"Whoa," Konstantin replied. "Why does that sound like I'm not the first person to ask that question?"

I frowned. "Because whatever magical...whatever she and I are on, I can understand her. Like, full sentences, arguing over whether or not she can have pizza, or why it's a bad idea to climb my curtains." The possibility bloomed in my mind, and mentally I said a sad goodbye to the billowing white chiffon. "Oh, Mother of the Fairies, the curtains."

Konstantin studied me carefully. "You sure you can't make that visit to the vet today?"

I looked up at him, clearly displeased. "We've already argued once today. Do you think I'm going near her with a harness for another—" I checked my watch "—sixteen hours?"

Konstantin blinked. "Don't you usually use a blanket or something?"

I winced, and stared past him. "I...thought this would be more dignified for her."

Konstantin pulled in his chin and shook his head. "Trillion. She's a cat."

"Of course she is! But she talks! Constantly! It's like being followed around by a radio that I can't turn off that's obsessed with birds and getting into stuff that she shouldn't!"

"That kind of sounds like a toddler. Do you know how old she is?"

His tone was decidedly too gleeful. I raised my eyes to him, my expression dead.

"Unless I want a new set of piercings and an understanding of cat profanity, I have decided that the best way to get her to the vet is a harness."

He pointed his pencil at me. "Cat carrier."

"Wednesday has a problem with control, Konstantin."

"'Wednesday'?" he said. I frowned at him. He smiled back.

I pointed my own pencil at him. "*You* are enjoying this far too much," I told him.

He shrugged. "You're usually so on top of things. It's nice for something to take you by surprise for a change," he said.

I glowered. "If you weren't one of my best friends, I'd—"

"Fire me," Konstantin said sweetly. "Except for my impeccable sense of smell and my keen investigative skills."

"Speaking of which," I said, flipping through the folder, "I know you haven't looked through this, but any idea why there aren't any photos in this case file?"

Konstantin frowned and walked over toward it. "That's weird," Konstantin said. He pointed to the corners. "It doesn't look like there were any, either. No staple marks."

"Why would the police not have pictures of people of interest? Just scanning this I see two names come up over and over—the friends, Giselle Carabosse and Siegfried Handel. Why wouldn't there be photographic evidence or even reference photos?"

"Maybe they weren't people of interest? If there's evidence clearing them, then it's probably further in the file."

I nodded in response, but I wasn't happy. Not with lack of the pictures, not with any of it. This wasn't just a dropped case due to magic—the more I saw made it seem like not much had been done on this case at all.

I needed to figure out why.

# 6

# IN WHICH WEDNESDAY SUFFERS A GRAVE INJUSTICE AND THE QUADRUPEDS UNITE

"Here, kitty, kitty, kitty," I said, holding the harness behind me.

*What is that?*

I jumped as I heard her suspicious tone behind me, and I twisted around. As much as I hated things sneaking up behind me, I was grateful that I could at least tell what direction she was coming from, even if it was all inside my head. Holding the harness aloft in my hands, I tried to hide my guilt as I held it out to her.

"It's, well, it's a harness. I was going to take you out today."

*Take me where?* The suspicion had not lifted, and as she sat, the tip of her tail twitched.

I looked down at her. "To the vet. I have to make sure you're healthy and you don't belong to anyone."

If her face could have scowled I would have have been scorched by a doozy. *I am healthy! I am human! I do not belong to anyone! You will not take me to the vet!*

I sighed. "Wednesday, if you are a human, then tell me your name."

Forget scorched. If looks could kill, I never would have existed.

*You know I do not know my name. I have forgotten.*

"Then how do I know you're human?"

*How many other cats do you talk to?* she demanded. *You cannot communicate with animals, this much I know!*

"And how's that?"

*I can hear the flies. And the wolves. And the bobcats. They tell me they cannot speak to the elf in this house. You do not understand them, they say. And me—they do not treat me as one of their own. They tell me that I am unnatural.*

"When did you meet a wolf?" I hadn't seen any tracks lately. Normally they weren't a problem, but I hardly wanted them to get used to coming close to the house.

Wednesday's tail swished. *When I was in the forest. At first it wanted to eat me. Then it did not.*

Knowing Wednesday's personality, that could have been for a variety of reasons. Still, if she was telling the truth...

What in the world was I thinking? Leaning down, I quickly clipped the harness around her. She looked down at it.

*A harness?*

"Glad you know what it is," I said, clipping the leash to the back loop.

She looked up at me in disbelief. *Surely you are not serious.*

"I'd rather not lose you as soon as I get you on the street."

*At this point I would have thought you would be relieved.*

I sighed. "No, I'm legally responsible for you now."

She looked up at me, insincerity dripping off of every strand of fur. *Aw. Poor thing.*

"If you don't behave, I'm going to tell them you're feral at the vet's office," I said.

*And what does that mean?*

"They'll sedate you," I said smugly.

She blinked in horror. *I—it—what—you will not!*

"Better shore up that dignity now, precious," I said, "because I have a feeling neither of us are going to enjoy this very much. Oh wait." I looked down at her. "Maybe I'm lying."

*I will smother you while you sleep*, Wednesday said darkly. *I will shed on everything. I will lick every stick of butter that you own!*

I narrowed my eyes at her. "Two words: Feral. Cat."

The drive from the vet's office to Orris Investigations was dead silent. I wasn't sure whether it was because I had gone deaf from all the yowling that had gone on in the office, or whether Wednesday was finally so put out that she had stopped talking.

Either that, or they'd removed her vocal cords.

The... magical... ones.

We pulled to a stop at a red light, and I looked over at her, both paws on the door, looking out the window.

"I hesitate to ask this," I admitted, "but are you okay?"

She didn't respond. Her ears didn't even twitch. Only her tail jerked back and forth like an angry snake, following a potential victim.

That was me.

"Much as I probably don't need your input, I would actually like to know that you still have your vocal cords. Mental... or physical," I said, my voice trailing off, looking over at her. One angry ear twitched.

*The light is green.*

I looked up, just as the car behind us honked. Sighing, I pressed on the gas, easing the SUV forward through the intersection. I followed the streets to the office, pulling into the parking lot. Konstantin's old beat-up Saturn was in its parking spot already. Turning off the car and opening the door, I reached over to pick Wednesday up.

*If you pick me up, you will lose both your hands,* she said acidly. She walked across my lap and jumped down out of the car with an injured air, leaving me to simply grab the leash and my bags and follow her.

Surprisingly, she didn't need any direction toward the agency.

"What, can you read now?" I asked, my voice most likely insultingly impressed. Sure enough she looked up at me, and then up ahead. *I have always been able to read.*

"You couldn't remember the word for chicken."

*I was adapting to verbal language. I have been a cat for as long as I remember.*

"Because you *are* a cat," I muttered under my breath, making it to the top of the stairs after her. Wednesday paused at the door and looked up at me.

"What?" I demanded.

*Open the door, please,* she said.

I looked down at her. "Oh, you know that word now?" I asked.

She narrowed her eyes. *I can forget it in a hurry if it makes you uncomfortable,* she shot back sarcastically. Rolling my eyes, I reached forward and pushed the door open.

"Ah, Trillion," Konstantin said. "I was wondering when you'd get here. And you brought the cat."

*He smells like wet dog.*

"Hush, you," I said, looking down at Wednesday. Konstantin looked from me to the cat and then back again.

"You weren't kidding," he said. I scowled at him, and then closed the door behind me. Unclipping Wednesday's leash, I hung it and my coat on the coat hanger by the door, before turning back to my partner.

"You have no idea."

"She gone to the vet yet?" he asked.

A very loud silence filled the room as Wednesday turned to stare at us, fire and brimstone flickering behind her eyes.

"I'll take that as a yes," Konstantin said, hunching. I shook my head, and watched Wednesday wander into the other room before turning back.

"Is it unusual that I'm legitimately worried about being smothered in my sleep?" I asked in a low voice.

Konstantin looked at me and laughed. "And you wonder why I'm a dog person," he said, sliding off his desk. I rolled my eyes, and walked back over to the bags that I'd left by the door. Konstantin picked up the file off of his desk before catching a view of me opening up a can of chicken.

"What are you doing?" he asked.

"Hopefully extending an olive branch," I said. Konstantin frowned. I straightened and sighed. "I told Wednesday that they wouldn't be doing anything invasive today at the vet. Just a normal checkup."

"And?"

"Do you know how they check cats' temperatures?" I asked.

Konstantin winced. "You didn't forget."

"I've never heard *any* animal scream so loudly," I said guiltily. "I'm not entirely sure all the staff made it out alive. They might have just retreated to bury their dead."

Konstantin peeked into the bag on the floor. "Put out both of the catnip toys, and don't make eye contact for the rest of the day," he said.

"For real?" I asked uncomfortably.

He raised both eyebrows. "Do you want to wake up tomorrow morning?" he asked in a whisper.

I grimaced, and then nodded. "Fair enough," I said, breaking open the packaging for the toys, and rubbing a bit of extra catnip on the bed.

"Not too much! You'll make me giddy, and she'll think you're trying to drug her," Konstantin whispered.

I made a face. "I can live with that," I said.

He looked at me skeptically. "Can you, though?"

"Whose side are you on?" I demanded.

Konstantin straightened up and shook his hair back grandly. "I will always reach out to help a fellow quadruped," he said.

"Should have figured," I grumbled.

*I like the dog man,* Wednesday said from the doorway, making me jump. *He smells odd, but he is good.* I looked up at Konstantin, dead inside.

"Congratulations," I said dryly. "You have a new friend." Konstantin flashed me a grin. Reaching down toward Wednesday, he offered her his hand. Game, Wednesday came over and sniffed it.

Then she looked up at me. *Why are we in this building?* she asked. *I thought you said we were going home.*

"We are, Wednesday, in a bit. This is my job."

*Standing in a building, talking to a man who smells like dog?*

"That is... surprisingly accurate," I admitted. "It's like I told you the other day. We're trying to find a missing girl. She—what?" I looked over at Konstantin, who was grinning.

"Nothing," he said unconvincingly. I looked down at Wednesday, who leapt into my lap, and then back at Konstantin.

"Can you not hear her?" I asked cautiously.

His grinned widened, if that were possible. "Not a peep."

I sighed.

"I sound like a crazy person," I concluded.

Konstantin nodded. "Yes. Does that sound any different than normal, I don't—ow!" I punched him in the shoulder. Wednesday chirped in annoyance at the movement, digging her claws into my thigh.

"Ow, ow, ow," I said, pulling the little cat into my arms. She wiggled to escape.

*No lifting!*

"Well, no clawing!" I responded, putting her back down on the floor.

Konstantin looked at me seriously. "Violence is bad for you," he said.

I sighed. "Tell me about it," I said, rubbing my leg. "Now, tell me what you've found. You said on the phone you had something?"

*When did you speak to the dog-man on the phone?* Wednesday asked.

"While you were..." I looked down at her, seriously wondering if I should actually bring up having taken her to the vet again. Since the answer was absolutely not, I shrugged as casually as I could. "You know what? Never mind."

"Coward," Konstantin said.

I scowled back at him. "I have over two thousand years of experience not dying," I said. "It's called self preservation." I motioned to the case file in his hands. "What did you find? Either case."

"Still not a lot," he admitted. "Rothbart's trail definitively ends at the theatre. As for the apartment building, I haven't been able to get in to track the scent. I haven't been to city hall to get permission, either. It's a high rise, though. The odds of my picking out a single name from the roster is next to nothing." He showed me a picture of the apartment building. It was in the higher income sector of town. Nothing too posh, but definitely someone who had money.

"Interesting," I said.

"I thought so," Konstantin said. "As for your missing girl—I spent some time at the Old Mill trying to track down the scent, and it's the weirdest thing. It's like I know the scent, but where it is or what magic was used, I just can't put my finger on it."

I shook my head. "A man who cannot be found and a girl who has disappeared. I hate missing persons cases." Wednesday jumped up into my lap, head butting into my hand as I reached up to stroke her fur.

"Then why do you keep taking them?" Konstantin asked. I smiled sadly, and scratched the little tabby's chin as she purred.

"Because the only thing worse than being dead is being lost."

# 7

## IN WHICH I BUY FAR TOO MANY LINT ROLLERS AND BRUSH A CAT

I was gone from the house most of the next day. Konstantin had better things to do than to get a permit to enter an apartment building, and I needed time away from Wednesday's needling. She'd gotten into an uncomfortable habit of sleeping on my chest or neck, and it seemed like no matter what I did, I was surrounded by fur.

Everywhere.

I was breathing it. I was eating it. I was pretty sure most of my clothes had a second layer of insulation with how much was flying around the house.

After spending three hours at City Hall, filling out every form that Ms. Linda from Permits could throw at me, I headed straight to the grocery store for lint rollers.

All of them.

The clerk—named Izzy—looked at me with a little bit of trepidation as I heaped my twenty-seven jumbo-sized lint rollers onto the conveyor belt. "Good afternoon, um... sir," she said, staring down at the sticky appliances.

I looked up at her evenly. "I have a new cat."

That the shelter couldn't take.

It was overbooked.

In December.

Wasn't it the season for new pets?

"Um, I don't know, sir," she said quietly.

I blinked. Had I said all that out loud? I sighed. "I'm sorry, I just... seem to be a little overwhelmed with my new duties," I said. "And the flipping thing is shedding everywhere."

"Long hair or short hair?" she asked.

I looked up. "Pardon?"

"Your kitty. Do they have long hair or short hair?" she asked.

I blinked. "Well, long," I said.

Izzy perked up a little bit. "Have you tried brushing them?" she offered. I looked at her for a couple moments. The idea of me getting Wednesday to stay still long enough for me to brush her was laughable, but at this point it was that, or I attempt to shave her.

I seemed to have a better probability of survival with the brush.

"Where do I... get one?" I asked.

She smiled mercifully. "If you have a minute, I can grab one. We carry my favorite kind for my cat," she said.

I looked at her for a moment, but then nodded. "Sure." Smiling, she practically skipped away on her customer-service high, and returned quickly with the small pink brush. Plopping it on top of my skyscraper of lint rollers she quickly rang up the remainder of the items, and turned back to me.

"That'll be $142.57," she said. I handed her my card, wondering

at the inflation on the humble lint roller. Then, gathering my purchases I headed out to the car. As I climbed in, tossing the bags onto
the seat, I felt my phone buzz. I pulled it out.

"Mrs. Richardson," I said, answering the phone. "How have you
been?"

There was a sigh. "I've been better," she admitted. "Sorry for missing your call earlier. Do you have any news?"

"Not yet," I said. "I've been working on building the case from
home, but what with the snow and everything, we just started most
of the legwork today. We're following a couple of leads."

"I see," she said, her voice a little wary. "Mr. Orris, Trillion, I hate
to bring this up, but I have to admit that I simply don't know very
much more than the case—"

"Don't worry, Mrs. Richardson," I said. "We know that you're as
much in the dark on this as anyone else. However, I did have a couple of questions. I know that the police searched your daughter's
apartment. Is there a possibility that I might do the same?"

There was only the slightest of pauses. "Well, of course. I'm sure I
have the key somewhere."

"I don't have the file in front of me. Could you remind me of the
address?" I asked. I heard the rustle of paper on the other end of the
line. Did she not have regular contact with her daughter?

"I think it's... Ah, here it is. Number 1107, 726 Appian Way. So,
midtown, south side. Right by the theatre."

And nowhere near the apartment that Konstantin found.

"And you said you had keys?"

"I can drop them by the office tomorrow," she offered.

I smiled, even though she couldn't see me. "Perfect," I said.
"That'll do fine. Konstantin should be there if I'm not."

"Good. I'll be sure to put the address and building code on there
so you can get in. The landlord knows me—I'm still paying for it.
Just in case—well, I'm paying for it." Her voice went a little quieter.

I pressed forward to relieve the pressure of the somber moment. "Good. Well, I won't keep you, unless you have any other questions?" I asked. I could almost see her shaking her head.

"No, but thank you," she said. "Goodbye."

"Goodbye," I returned, and watched my phone to make sure she hung up. I sat there, thinking for a moment, before driving over to the office.

Konstantin looked up hopefully as I entered. "What, no kitty?" he asked, disappointed.

"No, she's at home. I figured she had enough excitement for the week," I said.

Konstantin sniffed. "And going by the smell of Handy's Lint Roller glue in the air, you needed a little time to breathe something other than fur, I'm guessing," he said.

"Well, good thing I never keep any secrets from you," I said, scowling. Opening my briefcase, I handed him the permission slip signed by the city. Being the unofficial magical sector of the police had its benefits, but it was a far cry from actually having a badge. Not that magical beings had anything against joining law enforcement. We just... didn't.

"Here's the permit to enter the building to search for magical residue. They take threats like Rothbart pretty seriously, apparently. Well, once I showed them my charge papers."

"Oy. That bad?" he asked.

"Linda was very determined to know that I wasn't some sort of miscreant."

Konstantin grimaced. "Bless Linda and her justice loving ways," he said.

I raised an eyebrow. "You've met?" I asked.

He shrugged. "I've heard rumors. Mostly I ask for Maggie. She's nicer," he said.

"You couldn't have told me this before I went into the hall?"

"As you so often remind me," Konstantin said sweetly, "some things are better learned by experience."

I glared at him for a moment, before smiling despite myself. "Mrs. Richardson is bringing by the keys to Odell's place tomorrow. Do you want to go over it, or should I do the once-over?"

"I'll be casing the Rothbart apartment," he said. "Do you expect any magical trace?"

I walked over to the case board that Konstantin had been constructing over the last few days. "I'm not sure. Honestly, as far as I've been able to tell, she hasn't had her hands in anything magical at all. I'll do a sweep tomorrow and if I can't find anything, I'll have you come take a whiff."

Konstantin gave me a wolfish grin. "You gonna take the cat?"

I looked up. "Why would I take the cat?" I asked incredulously.

He shrugged. "I don't know. It just seemed like something that she would like. She likes you, you know?"

I did not. She slept on my face. If that wasn't attempted murder I didn't know what was.

"Explain," I said.

Konstantin shrugged. "If she was a stray or feral, you shouldn't have been able to catch her as soon as you did, or bathe her, or anything. She *definitely* wouldn't be sleeping on you. Not to mention that she probably would have run away by now. Not to mention the fact that you can talk to her."

"Yeah, that confuses me, too," I said. "I don't have the gift of animal speech. I'm a healer—what's up with that?"

Konstantin shrugged. "No clue. I bet your dad would know."

I stiffened, and dropped my focus down to my paperwork. "No thanks. I'll try and figure it out on my own." Konstantin didn't respond. Father and I had a particularly strained relationship. Not necessarily due to any disregard for the other, our temperaments were simply vastly different.

As was our way of dealing with problems.

I frowned, and turned to the board. There was the picture of Odell in the center, her smile radiating above the list of facts we knew about her. To the left was Mrs. Richardson. To the right were the names 'Giselle Carabosse' and 'Siegfried Handel'. Next to their names, a little further out, was a list of people—ballet company members.

"Do we have *any* pictures at all of any of these people?" I asked.

Konstantin looked displeased. "Just what I've been able to find on social media. I was going to start printing things off tomorrow, but turns out the whole company was pretty camera shy—their principal dancer especially. Giselle Carabosse."

"Well, considering who her family is, I suppose I shouldn't be surprised. I'll have to go interview her," I said.

Konstantin grimaced. "Better you than me," he said.

I pulled a face, and tapped Handel's name. "What about Siegfried?"

Konstantin pulled out his phone, pressed a couple of buttons, and handed it to me. I scanned through the social media page. Pictures of a handsome man smiled back at me. I noted the date as Konstantin spoke. "Nothing since July. It's kind of weird. He used to post almost every day, pictures of the dance company, doing Facebook Live and Instagram videos, and then all of a sudden, around the twenty-sixth...nothing. Not even a 'taking a break from Social Media' post."

I frowned. "And he still went to work?"

"As far as I can tell. I haven't looked into it too much, but he is still featured on the Met Ballet's website as a soloist. He hasn't disappeared, just gone dark."

I bowed my head and rubbed my eyes. "And nothing more on Rothbart?"

"No. I'll trace the building tomorrow, though," he said. I sighed and rubbed my face again. Konstantin looked over. "You okay? You seem more tired than usual."

I nodded. "Yeah. Probably just oxygen deprivation from having a cat sleep on my face."

"I'm telling you, she just loves you!"

"Well, I hope we can find a healthier option for both of us before I lock her in a cupboard or something."

Konstantin laughed. "She'd never let you forget it."

I cast him a dark look. "It might just be a risk I'm willing to take."

We worked for a little bit longer, matching faces to names on Facebook and Instagram profiles before Konstantin looked up at the clock. "It's a quarter of six, Trillion. I should probably head back before the driveway gets icy."

I nodded in agreement. "Sounds good. I'll continue this at home. Let me know if you find a picture of Giselle. It's weird that her biography link on the ballet site is broken."

"Will do. Anything else for tonight?" he asked.

I shook my head. "No, we'll let it sit. Not much more to do, anyway, until we examine Odell's apartment and talk to the dance company."

"Fair," Konstantin said, pulling on his oversized coat and shaking his hair back over his shoulders. "Goodnight, then."

"Goodnight," I echoed. I intended to stay a couple more minutes, trying to figure out the shockingly bare police report that I had been handed. It was as though they had done the bare minimum—talked to her friends, searched the Mill, and searched the apartment—and then flatly refused to do anything else. Upon further inspection, there were statements from each member of the dance company—some thirty-two people, both present and absent from the party, all of whom said Odell was acting a little strange, but nothing that would have made her a flight risk or suicidal. None of them were more than a couple of sentences long, which was probably why no one had seen fit to notice them before.

Her closest friends—Giselle and Siegfried—had been the most verbose of these, also completely rejecting the idea that she had run off on her own.

*She was always the most steady of people,* Giselle's statement read. *I can't imagine that she would go haring off at a moment's notice, let alone during the middle of a party. Something surely must have happened to her.*

What that might actually be, however, or when it came to knowledge about who might have done it, Giselle was clueless.

I stared at it a moment longer before giving up for the night. It wasn't going to do me any good to wear myself thin trying to figure it out. If my two thousand years of life had taught me anything, it was that all things revealed themselves in time. Some things came faster than others, but I would be patient. I could wait.

It was dark in the house when I got to it. I didn't see Wednesday sitting two feet past the swing of the door and nearly jumped out of my skin when her soft voice broke the silence close by my feet.

*You have no routine.*

"Stars above and Earth beneath!" I exclaimed breathlessly, jumping to the side. The bags slid to the floor as I pressed my hand to my chest, trying not to end two thousand years of reasonably good health with a heart attack. After a moment, I fervidly kicked the door shut behind me and stalked into the kitchen. There was a purring chirp as Wednesday greeted me audibly, rubbing up against one leg before sticking her nose into the bags.

*You shop a lot. And you have bought... a brush?*

"Yes," I said breathlessly. "The clerk said it might help with the shedding. Plus, now that I think about it, I don't want you getting matted. Your fur is long."

*I have an effective grooming routine,* she said primly. *I am not convinced I need it.*

I flipped on the light. Wednesday blinked up at me with distaste. *Is your night vision so bad that you must use such bright lights?* she complained.

I sighed, pulling my coat off. "Give it a minute, Wednesday. You'll adjust. You've been shedding a lot, that's why I got the brush. Man, it's cold in here. Did the heating go out during the day?" I asked, wandering through the house toward the thermostat. I couldn't see any windows or doors open, not that I would have opened any a quarter of the way through December. Weird.

The power hadn't gone out. The house was solar powered, but out here on the East Coast, I had a backup system simply because it could be clouded over with only rare patches of sun for weeks, like it had been since the beginning of the month. Wednesday trotted in front of me.

*The heating is fine,* she said simply. *I have been practicing being a human.*

I looked at the thermostat, which was still set to seventy degrees, not really paying attention to what the cat was saying. I checked the current temperature. Sixty-five. Had something poked through the roof? I didn't see any damage. What was going on?

"Oh, yeah?" I asked absently, staring at the tiny display. "And what does that entail?"

She didn't answer right away. Or for a couple of minutes. I flipped through a couple screens of the thermostat, finding nothing. Blast. I looked down.

She seemed to be studying me. Her tail swished. She still didn't answer. I kept staring. Her tail flicked back and forth again. She was not happy.

"What?"

*You are not interested. I will not tell you. I wish to be brushed. I will lay on the couch while you check your television for news.* With a long swipe of her tail, she turned grandly and paraded toward the living room as if my sole obligation was to take care of her.

Infuriatingly, since I had brought her into my home to do exactly that, I didn't have much of an alternative. I sighed, following her into the living room. Snagging the remote on my way past the table where I had left it, I flicked the TV on as I detoured into the kitchen. There, I grabbed the little pink brush and one of the lint rollers from the bag.

*What is that?* Wednesday asked from beside the counter. I looked down at the violent shade of pink.

"It's a brush?" I said.

*No, what is* that? I looked down at the lint roller in my other hand.

"The lint roller?"

*Its name is Handy's. Why is that?*

"That's the brand. The...company that made it. It's sticky, and it picks up the fur you leave behind. It's everywhere. That's why I got the brush."

Wednesday looked around, as if the idea that she shedded had never occurred to her.

*You leave behind your hairs,* she pointed out, narrowing her eyes at my own long blond hair.

I nodded. "And I also use a lint roller to pick up my hair," I said. "That is, when I need it. Most of it gets caught up in the vacuum."

She stared at me, not understanding. *Vacuum?*

"It's a cleaner that uses suction. I'll show you tomorrow. Come on, to the couch."

*I think I have changed my mind. I want to smell the lint roller.*

"You can do that on the couch."

*But I want to smell it* now.

I tried not to roll my eyes, but failed miserably. Then, leaning over, I offered the lint roller for her to smell. She sniffed it, made a face, and then turned away, making a beeline over to the couch.

Okay then. Following her, I sat down beside the place she now considered 'her spot' and put my feet up on the ottoman. Then, holding up the brush, I resigned myself that I was about to groom a cat.

# 8

# IN WHICH WEDNESDAY EXPRESSES HER EXPECTATIONS AND WE EVALUATE A KITCHEN

T *ake off the leash.*
"No."
*Take off the leash.*
"No, Wednesday, we're in public. Hush."
*Hush? You hush. You are speaking to a cat that no one else can hear while you walk with her down Main Street on a leash. No one walks cats on leashes. No wonder people think magic users are crazy.*

"Main Street is two blocks over, and you're the one who whined all morning because you hadn't been out since I took you to the vet."

*I did not.*

"Your exact words were 'You never take me anywhere'."

*So you are taking me to a crime scene?*

"No, I'm taking you to our missing person's house. She disappeared from the Old Mill. Also, I didn't want to leave you in the house when I don't know why it's getting cold," I said. Shifting the leash to the other hand, I took the key out of the envelope that Mrs. Richardson had provided. Using it to open the outer door to the apartment building, I allowed the fluffy cat inside first.

*I was not cold. I have a coat.*

"Yes, well, it's irresponsible of me to—" One of the doors in the hallway opened, and a young woman in a red beanie appeared. She looked from me to the cat, and a small smile crawled up one side of her rosebud mouth.

"Cute cat," she said, moving past me, hoisting her bag up onto her shoulder. I opened and closed my mouth and finally stuttered out a 'thank you' long after the door had closed.

Wednesday's tail swished. *Please tell me you do not normally act like that around women.*

I looked down accusingly. "I refuse to take relationship advice from a cat."

*That was not a relationship. That was not even a normal person to person encounter. That was embarrassing.*

"You're a cat. You can't feel embarrassed," I said, walking down the hallway.

*Well, color me impossible, because it is happening.* Her voice was frank and matter-of-fact in my head, and I tried not to scowl as I walked to the elevator and pressed the call button.

"Stop talking," I said irritably. "If you talk, then I want to respond, and it's not normal to be talking to one's cat."

*Oh, please,* she said. *Most people cannot keep themselves from talking to their pets. In those cutesy little voices, too.* She paused. *Come to think of it, it is annoying.*

"I don't talk to you like that," I said, leading her into the elevator.

*I know,* Wednesday said thoughtfully. *That is what I meant.*

I looked down at her, frowning.

"I do not speak to anything or anyone in a cutesy voice," I said. "You're not special." The elevator dinged, and the doors opened. She walked out, tail lashing from side to side.

*Clearly,* she said, her voice injured.

I sighed. "Not like that."

*No, no, I get it,* she said. *You would only deign to speak that way to the truly deserving, like—like babies and* dogs.

I couldn't win. I couldn't. I knew that, and yet I still just had to open my big fat mouth.

"No, I mean out of the seven billion people, and at least two billion pets in the world, I would not talk to a single one in a baby tone. Plus, wouldn't you find that condescending and super annoying?" I asked, coming up to the end of the hall where #1107 should have been. It stopped at #1105. I looked at the door.

*The number you have on the paper is at the opposite end of the building,* Wednesday said helpfully. *I read it on the sign that we passed by the elevator. You were busy telling me that you don't speak to anyone in a special tone.*

"And you couldn't have interrupted me like usual?"

*I have been trying to improve my manners.*

"Since when?" I asked, my patience snapping. She looked up at me and meowed loudly. I waited for a translation. Nothing. In the next second, I could have sworn that fluffy tabby face smirked as she turned to walk in the other direction. Feeling the gentle tug on the leash I sighed and followed.

Sure enough, Number 1107 was clear at the other end of the

building. Inserting the key into the lock, I twisted, hearing the tumblers turn. Good. I'd gotten the right door. I pushed the door open, and Wednesday went into the room in front of me, mentally expressing a noise of disgust.

*This place smells wrong.*

"Well, no one's lived in it for three months, so it's bound to smell a little musty," I said, flipping on the lights. Sure enough, the smell of dust and stale air filled my nose. Wednesday made another disparaging noise.

*I did not say uninhabited. I said wrong,* she corrected me.

I looked down. "What's the difference?" I asked.

She looked up and sniffed the air. *Something died here.*

That got my attention. I looked down, a mixture of disgust and deep concern crossing my face. "What? Can you tell?" I asked, off balance.

Wednesday looked up at me and blinked. *Yeah, like a mouse or something,* she said casually, walking further into the room to the end of her leash, waiting patiently for me to follow.

"Not cool," I said.

*You are very tense. I think you need a better sense of humor,* she said airily.

I frowned. "Very funny. If I let you off the lead line, can I trust you to not get into anything that will kill you or ruin the case?"

Innocence sparkled through the room like a baptism of glitter.

*You doubt me?* she said, her eyes twice as large as normal, the teeniest 'mew' escaping her mouth.

I sighed, and unclipped the leash. "I'm going to regret this," I said to myself. Then, to her, "If I find you eating anything, relieving yourself on anything, or laying on anything not meant to be laid on," I paused. "Or hiding, or scratching or—"

*Okay, okay,* she said, trotting toward the kitchen. *I will observe, not interact.*

"You'd better."

*Keep your hair on.*

"Excuse me?" I demanded toward one of the rooms—the kitchen, going by the tile. No response. Sighing, I turned to look around. I wasn't sure what I was going to find. I wasn't even sure what I was supposed to be looking for. There was apparently, just something... here. Something that would have convinced the police that they wanted nothing to do with this case.

It didn't look like there was much that had been touched or taken away. There was no evidence in the police report that anything had been taken from her apartment. I went through everything meticulously—the magazines, the small arrangement of books in the shelves, and the newspaper on the table.

It was dated August twenty-first. There was a small exposé-type article on magic-keepers and Rothbart in particular, his picture accompanying the article. Konstantin had written it, to keep everyone on their toes. It had been almost three months. We probably needed to do something similar soon. If only we could give out something more than simply 'caution, crazy person in the vicinity.' At least three months ago we'd had a strong magic trace through the city.

Now we had a dead end at a theatre. The same theatre where our mystery girl had disappeared. I honestly hoped that it was a coincidence. If Rothbart had gotten his claws into Odell, the odds of finding her in one piece, if at all, diminished greatly.

I sank down onto the couch. Nothing out here. I steepled my hands, fingers pressing to my lips as I thought. If I had been thinking at the time, I would have taken care of him for good the last time that I had seen him. But that would have had consequences of its own.

I couldn't win.

*There is no food here!* Wednesday's voice came from the kitchen, shaking me violently from my thoughts. Lifting my head in alarm,

I hustled into the next room, scooping her up. She yowled in response, all four legs spreading out wide, trying to gain purchase on something.

*No lifting!*

"You said you weren't going to eat anything!" I said, moving back out into the front room. She squirmed and twisted, and I caught her by the back of the harness, holding her out at arms length, confident that the padding in the jacket-like apparatus wouldn't cut into her. She stilled, and then glared at me, feet dangling.

*I did not eat anything—there was no food!*

"Then why were you looking for it?" I demanded.

*There is always food in the refrigerator-cold box!* she said, as if it were the most obvious thing in the world. *Why is there no food? Or did someone take it? How long has this missing girl been missing? Why did she have no food?*

I stared down at her. It was...a surprisingly valid question. As much as I believed in the police as a generally helpful entity, at least as far as non-magic things went, cleaning out the fridge seemed a step outside the norm.

But I wasn't taking Wednesday back in there. Frowning, I set her down, and pointed at her.

"Sit there. And stay," I commanded. Sulkily, she sat, tail curled up around her, the tip twitching back and forth, staring up dolefully at me, head lowered.

*I had no intention of eating anything.*

Ignoring Wednesday's protest, I pulled out my phone and dialed my partner as I headed into the kitchen.

"Trillion?" Konstantin's voice was a little fuzzy over the phone. I looked through the kitchen. The refrigerator door was closed, so were all the cupboards. The counters and surfaces were covered in a thin layer of dust, but otherwise, no crumbs, no food, nothing out of place. What was—

"Trillion, if you pocket dialed me, I'm going to howl into your phone until you start attracting beagles. What's going on?"

"Sorry," I said, putting the phone up to my ear. "I was just wondering—does it say in the report whether any of the rooms were cleaned or anything?"

There was silence for a moment. "What?"

I opened the fridge. Nothing. Not a jug of milk, not a stick of butter. Not even a left behind moldy onion in the vegetable crisper. The freezer told the same story—a half-empty ice cube tray, and a healthy layer of frost. Quickly stepping over to the pantry, I opened it. There was a sealed plastic bin of pancake mix that, if the nibble marks had anything to say about it, had been unsuccessfully targeted by mice. I suddenly realized that Konstantin was still on the phone.

"Sorry, it's just weird. I haven't searched the whole house yet, but the living room seemed normal, if a little sparse. Coming into the kitchen, though, there's no food anywhere. Not in the fridge, not in the freezer, not in the pantry," I said. "Everything is spotless, apart from a thick layer of dust. Could someone from the Crime Scene Cleaners have come in and cleaned everything out when she went missing?"

"Usually it's the family members in a case like this," Konstantin said. "I could call Mrs. Richardson, and ask if she's been by to clean. Anything in the garbage? Though, I'm not seeing in her file that Odell ate out much, if at all. She seems to be your regular make it yourself, eat in, stay healthy kind of girl."

*There is always food in the fridge*, Wednesday said from the door. I pulled the phone away from my ear and glared at her.

"I told you to stay in the front room," I whispered furiously.

*You don't understand—there is always food in the fridge!* she said insistently. I sighed.

"Maybe some people don't live up to your standards, Wednesday," I said. "Some people could just not cook for themselves."

*She has books for cooking,* Wednesday pointed out, walking across the kitchen to the counter. Jumping up onto the counter, leaving itty-bitty paw prints behind, she walked up to the books and sniffed them. *She has used them.*

"Wait, wait, wait," Konstantin said. "You brought your pet cat to a crime scene?"

*The dog man thinks this is a crime scene,* Wednesday said triumphantly. *I told you.*

"She is not my pet, and this is not a crime scene," I said stiffly to both accusers, purposefully neglecting to mention that this was all Konstantin's idea in the first place. "This is simply the residence where our victim lived. Odell disappeared from the Old Mill."

"As far as we *know,*" Konstantin pointed out. "But I'm looking through the reports, and...no. It's actually mentioned in the *very* short police report how spotless it was in the kitchen."

"Why does that feel significant?" I said thoughtfully. Walking over to where Wednesday was, I reached out and patted her head with one hand as I pulled a cookbook out with the other. Holding the spine to the counter, I let the book drop open to its most opened page.

I would have been able to tell anyway. The grease spots, wrinkles from water splashes and random bits of food stuck to the page were enough to make it easily identifiable.

"Roast herbed chicken, with a written-in recipe for...focaccia bread. And grilled asparagus," I said. "We have a healthy eater."

"Makes sense," Konstantin said. "She's a professional dancer. She would need a balanced diet to be competitive and healthy. I've been researching the Metro Ballet—they are really, really strict about keeping their dancers healthy."

"So, if she's a big health nut, it makes sense that she cooks for herself," I conceded. "The old home-versus-take-out thing. So... why is her kitchen so clean? When did the police search her apartment?"

"Two weeks after she went missing."

I blinked, bemused. "What?"

"Yeah. The more I read into this case, the more it just makes me sad."

"So anyone could have come in and cleaned the kitchen?"

"Theoretically. Not a ton of dust would have settled in two weeks, though. Maybe she just did a deep clean and got rid of all her food?"

I sighed, looking around. "Maybe. But if she was the one who did...why? Why then? What if it wasn't...her? What then? What was in here that made that much of a difference?"

Konstantin was quiet for a moment. I shook my head, cognizant of the fact that he couldn't see me.

"I'll keep searching the apartment," I said.

Wednesday burbled in her throat. *I told you—there is always food in the fridge.*

I sighed, and looked up at the ceiling, wondering if what she said would ever make sense.

Leaving the kitchen, knowing now that there was nothing for Wednesday to get into, I walked through the living room again to the bedroom. It only took one look around the room to know I had found exactly what I was looking for.

# 9

## IN WHICH WE MAKE A DISCOVERY, RESULTING IN UNEXPECTED CONSEQUENCES

"That's... a lot of sorcery text," Konstantin said, scratching the top of Wednesday's head. He watched as I loaded book after book into the boxes he had brought from the office. Pushing the seventh box from the bedroom using my foot, I looked between him and the cat and shook my head.

"Nice to know who does all of the heavy lifting around here," I said wryly, scooting the box a couple more steps forward.

"I carried the boxes and the trolley up. Besides, Wednesday needed some tender loving care," he said, scratching her chin. "She seemed agitated when I came in."

Probably because she was still repeating herself over and over about the fridge, and I'd long since stopped listening, but I didn't say that.

"I wouldn't let her play with the dust bunnies," I said instead, marking the box with a big '7' and setting it by the trolley for the next trip downstairs.

Wednesday meowed in response. *No, it is because you are deaf and rude,* she shot back, her tail swishing.

Konstantin smoothed back the fur on her head. "You know, Wednesday, those aren't the best for you. Plus, if you get too dirty, Trillion's just going to have to give you another bath."

I heard her voice clearly, deep and serious, even though Konstantin kept on talking, and I was clear in the next room. *If you attempt to bathe me again, I will make sure you never see January.*

She reminded me of someone, but I couldn't quite place who. I didn't respond, but made a deferential if sarcastic nod that I was pretty sure she couldn't see instead. Then I loaded up the trolley, and took it down to the car.

Konstantin needed to get a look around the place anyway, and he could take the next load down while I finished up in the apartment. As I waited in the elevator, my phone beeped. A text from Mrs. Richardson. I read my question and then her answer.

*Mrs. Richardson, it's Trillion Orris. Did you go to Odell's apartment before the police searched it back in August?*

*Trillion, not into the asparagus. I went and knocked, but when I didn't get a repose, I called the police. They went in first. I didn't want to disturb anything.*

Another text came in.

*\*\*apartment.*

And another.

*\*\*response. Sorry, autocorrect.*

I smiled grimly, and then slid my phone back into my pocket.

So, it wasn't Mrs. Richardson who had cleaned the kitchen. Which meant it was undisturbed by anyone that we knew.

There seemed to be four options. One, Mrs. Richardson was lying and she had gone in. Unlikely.

Two, the police had cleaned it for some reason. That wouldn't have made sense, though, unless they were trying to cover up who had done this. But they didn't cover up magic related crime, they just backed off.

Third, Odell could have cleaned her apartment, and then faked her disappearance. I doubted it. I was no expert, but if I was planning on leaving and never coming back, I didn't think I would have taken the time to clean my house first.

Fourth, whoever *was* responsible was covering something up.

I liked that one the least, but until I found something else that adequately explained anything, it was also the most likely.

Blast it all.

The trip back upstairs seemed shorter than I remembered—probably because I didn't get lost—and I walked in to Konstantin holding Wednesday in one arm, walking around the kitchen. He was opening up cupboards with his free hand, when he wasn't busy scratching the cat's head.

"It—what?!" I exclaimed. I glared at the small cat, galled. "You threaten to remove my hands if I pick you up, and yet he can carry you around the apartment?"

She blinked slowly. *You have not earned it,* she said simply.

My mouth dropped open. "I took you in! I bought canned chicken cat food because you don't like salmon. *I let you sleep on my face!*"

*And you complain about all of those things,* she said.

I glared at her, trying to think of a decent response. "Because you're inconvenient," I finally said.

She sniffed, the tip of her limp tail twitching from side to side.

*So are you, yet you do not hear me complaining about it. I have told you approximately a million times that I am human, and yet you treat me as though I was a know-nothing quadruped with the brain capacity of a canine. What is forty-five times fifty-four?*

"What does that have to—"

*Two thousand, four hundred and thirty. What is the capital of Belize?*

"Belize City."

*Wrong, it's Belmopan,* she said. *It changed after a hurricane wiped out Belize City in 1961. Why would a cat know these things?*

"Well, you're a remarkably well-read cat," I said stiffly. "I would imagine that at least some—"

*I went to university, Trillion!* she exclaimed furiously. *I have two degrees! Why would I remember going to school if I was not human?*

I stood there, speechless and fuming. Konstantin, completely oblivious to what had just occurred between the two of us, looked at me.

"...Did you just get owned by a cat?" he asked.

*Yes,* Wednesday responded smugly, clearly aware that I was the only one that could hear her.

"No," I said. "She's making a point, but before I believe she's *human*, she needs to tell me what her name is. Humans have legal names, ones that are researchable so I can know who to search for. I can't help her unless I can work from the human angle as well. She can't do that, so no, I don't believe that she's human."

Wednesday's ears pricked up, staring at me, her eyes digging into me like lasers. She didn't respond. Her tail started to twitch back and forth, and she wiggled ever so slightly to where Konstantin got the hint to put her down. Then, walking across the room, she stopped in the doorway of the kitchen, back placed firmly to me.

*Uh-huh.*

"That's what I thought," I said, far too triumphantly. She didn't respond back, vocally, or through thought.

Konstantin gave me a weird, uncharacteristically severe look, and walked up to the cat. "Wednesday?" he said, reaching down to touch her back. She gave a small mew, much more hurt than I was anticipating. Konstantin looked up a me a little accusingly. I flashed him an annoyed, defensive glare. She wasn't human. She wasn't. She was a cat with a human complex. That was it. She could be as offended as she wanted, but that wasn't going to change anything.

Throwing a nervous look up at me, Konstantin took a deep breath, and melded into his dog form. The Irish wolfhound looked almost ridiculously large next to the dainty cat. Wednesday looked up, and then looked up again in a double take before she sighed and looked back into the kitchen.

*I suppose that makes sense. If you are going to eat me, go ahead. Life is already enough of a trial, I suppose it will not make much difference.*

I rolled my eyes. Oh please.

Konstantin chuffed, his breath moving the fur on Wednesday's face, and I could hear her response.

*I just don't know how to convince him. I've tried everything I can think of, and all I get is his preconceived notion that I'm just a cat, and flat refusal to hear anything that points away from that. Do you know how hard it is to fight against a curse when all you hear is that that's how it always was?*

Konstantin huffed again, and Wednesday looked down.

*I know. And I know I've got a good situation. I could be locked out in that old building in the woods again, after all.*

I looked up from where I was staring down at the floor. Konstantin must have asked her another question, because she looked away from him, her banded tail swishing back and forth.

*I don't know who put me there. All I know is I was there since the leaves were green. Cold air was a hint on a warm breeze, and the sun turned the dirt into deep patches of warmth. Then the warmth went away. I was lucky* to get out when I did. *The girl who brought me food stopped coming weeks before the snow came. I had to find food. Mice. Birds. Whatever came in.*

I didn't know quite when I stood, listening carefully, but before long I stood only a couple of feet behind them.

"Konstantin," I said softly. The wolfhound looked back at me, ears pricked up, head tilted to the side. I considered how to say what I was thinking. "What does she smell like?" Konstantin blinked and then looked down at Wednesday sitting there.

She looked at him long-sufferingly. *Go ahead. I have nothing more to lose.*

I sighed. Konstantin looked up at me, his canine expression unreadable, then turned back to Wednesday. At her nod, he buried his enormous nose between her ears and sniffed deeply. Wednesday's shoulders hunched in discomfort as the shapeshifter took in her scent.

Then we sat.

And sat.

And sat.

Then Konstantin shuddered, growing into his human form. Looking down at the cat, he held out his arms. Wednesday walked up to him, and jumped into them.

Cuddling her, he looked up at me and shook his head. "She smells like a cat, Trillion," he said quietly. Stroking Wednesday's fur, he kissed the top of her head. "Sorry, sweetie."

*Tell him it is not his fault,* she said, very subdued. I couldn't help myself—I relayed the message. It was silent for a moment, all of us staring at each other. Finally, Wednesday looked up at me, something dull and a little lifeless in her eyes. *If you want to take me to a shelter now, you can.*

I stood there for a moment, simply staring at the suddenly-spiritless little cat, caught flat-footed. Then I cleared my throat.

"Can't."

Wednesday's ears twitched. *Why not?* she asked, blinking her eyes, as if waking up slowly. I opened my mouth, and then closed it. Yes, why not?

"The shelters are full," I finally said. Then, apparently that wasn't enough to assuage my suddenly guilty conscience for those lifeless and dull eyes, because I shrugged defensively. "Besides, it's Christmas. I couldn't make you go stay in shelter for the holidays. You need space. You know, for now. We'll give them a little time to get a little room in the shelter for you."

*Really?* Wednesday asked, her voice a little disbelieving.

"Really?" asked Konstantin, his voice also a little disbelieving. "Don't you think that's cutting it a little—"

"It'll be fine," I said to both of them. "I have the room, and we've only got this case going on."

"No, I know you've got the room. And the time," Konstantin said. "I mean..." he trailed off, glancing down at Wednesday in his arms. "You know. Your thing."

*What thing?* Wednesday asked, looking between the two of us.

"She's a cat, Konstantin," I said, reaching out to stroke Wednesday's fur, feeling the guilt slowly diminishing. In its place, a small seed of discomfort pricked at my heart. "I'm sure it'll be fine. It's only for another couple of weeks."

Konstantin nodded, and held Wednesday out. To my surprise, she let me take her into my arms, and let Konstantin clip the leash onto her back. Settling down in my arms, she rested her chin on my forearm as we gathered the last boxes of books, locked the apartment, and left.

It was quiet on the way home.

# 10

# IN WHICH I DO LAUNDRY, MEET WITH AN OLD FRIEND, AND PLAY POLITICS

"Wednesday, get out of the laundry basket," I said, finishing folding another shirt. Wednesday burrowed herself further into it, all but her ears and back disappearing into the warm fabric.

*No.*

"Come on, I've got to get this done before dinnertime," I said, putting the shirt on the end of my bed, and tugging another out from underneath her. It came out with difficulty, and I had to disentangle it from three claws before I got it fully out.

*I don't understand why you have to fold your laundry the day you wash it,* she complained. *The rest of humanity lets it sit in the basket at least a week.*

"Well, I'm not exactly human, now am I?" I said sweetly.

She unburied her face from the fabric and blinked slowly at me. *You keep saying that. All I've seen to the contrary is pointy ears and an attitude,* she said smartly.

I smirked. "I could say the same about you, but in reverse," I pointed out. She didn't respond, one of her ears flicking. I smiled. "I'm older than I look."

*So, what, you're like 300?*

"That's a little young," I said. "I'm a little over two thousand years old."

There was a moment of silence.

*Oh.*

"Why?"

*No reason,* she said, burying her face back into the warm clothes. *You don't act your age.*

"Oh? And what do two thousand year old elves act like?" I asked.

She looked back up, blinking owlishly. *I don't know. I guess I would have thought they'd be less whiny.*

"I'm not whiny!" I said, pulling another shirt out from underneath her.

Wednesday stretched out long, kneading the fabric with long claws. *If you say so,* she said, flopping over onto her side and closing her eyes. After a few moments, she opened them again. *What's at dinnertime?*

I looked down at her. "What?"

*What's at dinnertime?* she repeated. *You said you had to be done before dinnertime. What's after dinner?*

"I'm going *to* dinner," I said. "I'll feed you before I go."

*Who are you eating dinner with? The dog man?*

"No, I'm going to dinner with Solange Bautista. She's a ballet dancer."

Wednesday stared at me for a moment before speaking. *Are you sure you can handle it? She is a woman.*

I frowned. "Ha, ha. For the record, I can talk to women. I've had two millennia to practice."

*Ah, well, at least you've tried. It must be an inborn thing, then.*

"Hey! I will not take criticism from a feline!" I said, yanking another shirt out from under her and rolling onto her other side.

She yowled in annoyance. *Better than humiliating yourself at dinner. What are you going to wear?*

"What do you mean? I'm wearing what I always wear," I said.

*You mean black on black? Do you want to seem like a serial killer?*

I shifted self consciously. "I think it makes me look nice," I said, a little defensively, looking down at my already all-black attire.

*You do look nice,* she conceded. *You also look like you could drink her blood at any moment.* I rolled my eyes, and pulled out another shirt, surveying the cat hair on it with distaste before hanging it up.

*Couldn't you at least wear like a grey shirt, or jacket?*

"Grey with a black shirt? Does that even go?" I asked, thinking of a grey suit coat my father had sent to me a couple of years before, before shrugging it off.

*Of course it does. Black goes with everything.*

"I'll think about it," I said, fully intending on forgetting about it the first chance I got.

*Not if I keep reminding you,* Wednesday responded. I paused for a moment, wondering if I had spoken out loud. No, I had definitely just said that in my mind.

*I can hear you, you know.*

No. I stared at her, trying to keep my mind blank and failing.

*That's not a word you should use in front of women and pets.*

"Don't tell me how to behave!"

*If you behaved properly I wouldn't have to.*

"I behave just fine!"

*I'll tell your mother you think that word is acceptable behavior,* Wednesday threatened.

"My mother is dead, thank you very much. I'm wearing the black. Get out of my laundry basket," I said through gritted teeth.

She stood, stretched, and then looked up at me with her big green eyes. *On one condition,* she said.

"You are not in a position to negotiate," I told her.

She looked at me narrowly. *Am I not? You are going to leave me unsupervised. Anything could happen.* I studied her carefully, pretending to not notice the claws digging deeper into my shirts.

"Fine. What do you want?" I asked.

*Leave the back door unlocked,* she said evenly.

I frowned and narrowed my eyes. "No! Why?" I asked suspiciously.

Her ears twitched. *I'm trying to grow thumbs,* she said, voice dry.

"Absolutely not," I said.

*Why not?*

"Because I said so!"

*But how will I ever* learn? she asked, her voice dropping into mock desperation.

"Try it on the inside doors," I told her unsympathetically. "I don't want to leave the outside doors unlocked while I'm not here."

*Who do you think is going to come in, the neighborhood raccoons?* she asked sardonically. *You live in the middle of nowhere.*

"Which is closer to somewhere than you might think at first," I told her, taking the stack of shirts that I had already folded and making my way to my closet. "I have my reasons."

*You mean Rothbart?*

I turned around, frowning.

"Where did you hear that name?" I asked her.

I received a simple blink in response. *You talk about him all the time. The dog man told me you were hunting him. I am confused. I thought you were a healer. A rescuer. Not someone who hunts.* Her voice was a little quiet. I looked down at the small tabby.

"Is it impossible that a man can be both?" I asked, sliding the closet door open, and placing my shirts inside.

*Not at once.* Wednesday's was more matter-of-fact that I'd ever heard it. *You'll love one more than the other. Which is it?*

I stepped into view and locked eyes with her.

"You tell me."

I locked all the doors before I left for dinner, leaving a couple of pieces of chicken out for Wednesday along with her regular dinner. Then, placing a blanket over the heating pad on the couch, and turning the television on so it wouldn't be too quiet in the house while I was gone, I left.

The cat was too perceptive for her own good. Her comments about hurting and healing had been something that I had been trying to ignore. Especially with the introduction of Odell's case and the puzzle solving that always accompanied this type of hunt, the gifts that I had been given—the innate elvish talents I had been born with—would set my brain working and my blood pumping. Over the centuries, I had honed them in their duality, learning to bend them to my will and control them like everything else in my life. But that flip side was always there, waiting for me to not pay quite enough attention. To be distracted.

Because, for all of her perceptiveness, Wednesday hadn't gotten it exactly right. I was a healer—a good one, too, gifted with insight and a heightened ability to learn. I'd spent hundreds of years studying my craft, first learning to heal elves, then other magical beings and humans, and then the animals around us. But the opposite of healer was not hunter.

It was killer.

The greens and reds of streetlights glimmered off wet asphalt as another snow shower let loose from the heavens. Frowning as I navigated through downtown, I hoped that Solange would be waiting for me inside instead of freezing in the slushy weather. Ten minutes later, as I stepped out of the car, handing my keys to the valet, I saw her cheerful smile radiating at me through the restaurant window.

"Trillion!" she said, her light Spanish accent trilling the 'r' in my name. "It has truly been too long!"

"Solange," I said. "You look more radiant than ever. Thank you for accepting my invitation tonight."

"Of course," she said, curly brown hair bouncing past smiling dark eyes. "Meeting my favorite elven prince at my favorite restaurant on my day off, how could I refuse?"

I smiled, held out my arm, and walked with her to our table. "You do know that my invitation wasn't solely pleasure," I said sometime later, after the main course was served. "I wanted your opinion on something."

"Oh?" she asked, looking up from her chicken. "And what would that be?" I shifted a little. Solange was not the type of person to take offense, but I didn't want to make it seem like I was taking advantage of her, especially after not seeing her for upwards of a year.

Even though I technically was.

"Word gets around," I said. "I'm sure you've at least heard rumors that I'm investigating Odell Richardson's disappearance."

Her smile shrank a bit, but didn't necessarily dim. Now, instead of a carefree smile, it was the intelligent smile of a player that had just come to the table.

"Yes, I heard," she said, her voice calming as she looked me directly in the eye. "I'm assuming you want interviews with the company."

"That would be nice," I said. She shook her head and looked down.

"Are you sure you want to rile the Domovoi like that?" she asked. "They're the ballet's main patron. Stanislava isn't one to let someone run over her turf and bug her family."

"I'm aware," I said, taking a sip of my water. "Which is why I want you to arrange an interview with her for me first."

She sat back in her chair. "You're not serious."

"I am. You're not Domovoi, you're Fada. You can be my go-between."

"Because I *want* to be the go-between between The Faerie Court and the Domovoi. Trillion, that's like mediating the Americans and Russians during the Cold War. No, thank you. I am a ballet dancer, not a hostage negotiator."

"I'm not representing the Faerie Court," I corrected. "Orrin Investigations. Besides, Odell didn't seem to be part of any faction of the Aggregate. It would solely be toward the Richardson investigation, and nothing else."

Solange leaned back in her chair, the dim light gleaming off of her soft, dark skin. "I wasn't aware that she was a magic user," she said.

I smiled. "I'm not sure anyone did except Odell," I said. "I haven't found any sort of evidence that she's had formal schooling for it, but there were over fifty magical textbooks in her apartment when we searched it."

"So the police are complicit?" Solange asked.

I flicked my eyes up. "They handed over the case without argument," I said, straightening my napkin. "Her mother brought us on."

Solange made a noise of approval. "I like Mrs. Richardson. She was Odell's most faithful fan. There at every one of her performances."

"Really?" I asked. "Even the one the night of the party?"

Solange shrugged. "I think so," she said, stabbing a piece of chicken and placing it in her mouth. Then she sat silent for a moment, chewing and thinking. "I'll talk to the producer of the show. Marya Leonidovna is one of Stanislava's closest friends. If there's any chance of the interview happening, Marya will be able to facilitate the meeting."

"Excellent," I said.

Solange held up a finger. "I'm not part of the Domovoi. I cannot guarantee that you will be able to meet with Stanislava. She is a very busy, very powerful woman, the Councilwoman," she said.

Taking a bite of my own food, I smiled and sat back. "I'm only asking for you to try," I reassured her.

Taking her glass of wine, she raised it to her lips and smiled. "Well, then," she said, "trust me to try."

# 11

# IN WHICH I STAY UP TOO LATE, AND FORGO A MYSTERY

I decided to swing by the office before I went home. The snow had slowed to a few flakes here and there, but the clouds hung like thick and heavy clots of wool just above the skyscrapers. Turning into the parking lot, I noticed Konstantin's car still sitting there, the lights on the second and third floors of our building illuminated. I frowned. Usually Konstantin was home by now.

Pulling into my parking spot, I made my way up the stairs to the second floor, unlocking the door and pushing it open. Konstantin didn't look up from his desk, his thick eyebrows drawn as he concentrated on the paperwork he was reading.

"Working late?" I asked.

"I thought you were at dinner with that ballet dancer," he said, pouring over the papers.

"We're done."

"Went badly?" he asked, still not looking up.

"She's going to reach out to get me an interview with Stanislava." I said, sticking my gloves into my pocket. He turned the page of whatever he was reading, his expression unchanging.

"Yeah, like I said, it went badly?" he asked, his tone the same.

"On the contrary. That was the whole point of the meeting." I walked across the room to my desk.

"But you'll actually have to meet with her if she says yes," Konstantin pointed out, finally looking up at me, eyes tired. "That doesn't sound like a win to me."

"Depends on the outcome," I said, not disagreeing. I thumbed through a few of the new papers that had appeared since I'd left, and then looked up at the case board. "I see you've finally gotten pictures of everyone."

Konstantin looked up at it as well. "Yep. The Metropolitan Dance Company from A to Z. Solange is down toward the bottom."

"And there is our friend Giselle," I said, tapping her picture. "And Siegfried." Both were incredibly good looking people. Siegfried's chiseled jaw and dark brown hair, combined with the dramatic pose, exhibited exactly why he was a principal in the dance company. Likewise, Giselle's long brown hair draped down her back as she looked back at the camera over her shoulder, a dazzling smile on her face in what could only be a publicity shot.

"No personal photos for our principals?" I asked. I preferred them. It was easier to get a feel for a person when I could see what they found important, and what they chose to ignore.

Konstantin sighed and shook his head. "No," he said, dissatisfied. "I've looked everywhere, short of asking the families for baby photos. As far as I can tell, neither of them have taken any photos of themselves, or allowed anyone else to, since August."

"Around the time of our disappearance," I said. Then I grimaced.

"Konstantin, I'm getting the sinking feeling that young Miss Carabosse is not nearly as innocent as I would like her to be."

"I didn't think you'd have that much of a vested interest," he responded.

"Yesterday I probably wouldn't have," I said, frowning. "But I just set up an interview with her mother."

Konstantin laughed at me. For a long time. When he finally wiped his eyes, he shook his head, and leaned back in his chair. "Serves you right."

"Better than starting a turf war," I said simply. "Particularly when none of it is my turf."

"Your dad would back you up if you really caused a stir," he said, helpfully.

I grimaced. "I have no doubt of that, but I'm trying to avoid his help if I can possibly manage it," I groaned. "Father wouldn't have to 'help' so much as 'take over'."

"Yeah..." Konstantin agreed. "Hey, speaking of ballerinas, I was able to go through the apartment with Rothbart's scent in it."

"Yeah?" I said. "Anything of interest?"

"Wouldn't report it if there wasn't," he said blandly. He nodded to the bulletin board. "Guess which of your ballet dancers lived in the building?"

I froze, and looked back at him.

"If her last name is Carabosse—"

"Ooh, bad news," Konstantin said unapologetically. "Fortunately for you, she moved a couple of months ago back to her mom's house. Six other members of the company currently live in the building, and three of those are on her floor. The trail is old though—a couple months at least. I couldn't definitively say whether she was there at the time, or where Rothbart went and why."

"Well," I said, uncomfortable at how disturbed I was at this, "that doesn't rule Carabosse out, then. If he chose to mess with her, he's going to become very uncomfortable as soon as Stanislava finds out."

"Unless he's trying to form some sort of alliance with the younger Carabosse," Konstantin said quietly.

I looked severely at him for a moment without speaking. "I don't like that theory," I said, discomfort twisting in my stomach.

Konstantin's face mirrored mine, then he looked up at Giselle's face on the bulletin board. "Me neither. Thankfully we can trust Stanislava to be too much of a power hog," he said. He perked up. "Maybe he'll ask, and she'll kill him for us."

"If only," I said, smiling grimly. Then I looked over at him. "You never answered my question. How come you're here so late? Usually you're home by now."

Konstantin grimaced. "Car died. Waiting for Bee. Thought I might work in the meantime."

I stiffened, and counted to ten before turning to look at the clock, frowning deeply. "What time does her shift end? Why didn't you tell me?"

Konstantin rolled his eyes. "It's almost midnight, Trillion. I didn't think you'd be in again. Usually it takes an emergency to keep you awake past ten."

I didn't want to respond to that.

"Anyway," Konstantin said, turning to his desktop and clicking the mouse, "Bee texted like ten minutes ago. If you leave now, you'll probably meet her in the parking lot."

Honestly, I'd rather meet her in a well-lit place. It wasn't as though I didn't like his sister—there wasn't anyone who exuded 'awe-inspiring' quite as much as she did— but I just wasn't sure whether she actually liked *me*.

Not in a romantic way, either. Just in general. She hadn't taken a swing at me, which was nice, but considering I'd never even seen her crack a smile, I wasn't sure that was saying much. If she had been overtly aggressive, or just a touch nicer, it would have been easier to know what to do. Under the circumstances, however, it was easier to simply avoid her entirely rather than to navigate that minefield.

"Oh," I responded, far too late.

Konstantin looked up from the computer. "Something wrong?"

I picked up a paperweight. "Do you think she's feeling particularly murderous today?"

"No more than usual, but if Konstantin doesn't get a new car, that might change," a rough female voice said from the door. I looked over. Bernadette Vorkowitz stood in the doorway, dressed head to toe in black leather, the color broken up only by the deep red of her lipstick and nails. The very image of a pharmaceutical technician.

"Hey, Bee," Konstantin said mildly, turning off his computer. "I'll be ready in a sec."

"I mean it. Get a new car, pup," she said.

He smiled cherubically at her. "Louisa's got a couple more miles in her, Bee," he said. "I'll have her towed to the shop and she'll be as good as new."

"Like the last three times since August?" she said flatly. "You can afford it, just buy a new car!"

"I won't abandon Louisa. Just because you buy a new car every other month—"

It was clearly time to go. Grabbing my coat, I waved to Konstantin as he protested to his sister and tried to slide out the door before Bee actually paid me any attention. It was that predator-like gaze. I didn't like it whenever she stared me down. I knew her shapeshifter form, and despite Konstantin's assurance of her control there was just something ever-so-slightly wild about her gaze. It put me on edge, like I was waiting for an attack, and the part of me that I had tried very hard to stifle whispered just a little louder when she was closer.

"Hey, Trillion?" she said, as my foot hit the wood flooring outside. Changing my wince to a smile before she had a chance to see it, I leaned back into the office.

"Yes?"

"Will you take him to work tomorrow?" she asked, pointing back at her brother with her thumb. "I'm not getting up at eight."

The likelihood that I was getting up then either was getting dimmer and dimmer, but I smiled and nodded all the same.

"Of course," I said.

"I'll call you!" Konstantin called from the coat rack. Bee's expression didn't change.

"Perfect. Have a nice evening," she said flatly, saluting sardonically with one hand as I closed the door. As soon as the door clicked shut, I heard her voice, now muffled through the door. "Konstantin, if you take any more time, we might as well build a campfire and sleep here for the night. Get moving."

"Keep your hair on, I forgot something."

The snow had started up again in earnest as I stepped out into the cold air. I took a deep breath, sweet and clean from the precipitation. Closing my eyes, I just listened for a moment, enjoying the quiet shush of the cars driving by.

Time to go home. Mocking as he'd been, Konstantin was right. I was not one to stay out or up late, and I could feel fatigue pulling at my bones.

The roads were empty but wet, reflecting the headlights from my car back at me as I drove out of the city. Similarly, apart from a couple of puddles, my driveway was clear, and I was able to get to the house without having to put my car in four-wheel drive.

Pulling up to the house, I frowned. There was a light on in the kitchen. I paused in front of the open garage door, peering at the light as it blazed happily out of the window.

I could have sworn I turned all the lights off. I knew I had left the TV on, and I could see the bright blue flicker as the weather channel played. Normally I would have left it on the news, but it tended to skew more and more toward the improbable lately, and the last thing I needed was Wednesday to become involved in conspiracy theories.

I sat there for a moment.

*Had* I left the kitchen light on? I could have sworn that I hadn't. I never left lights on at home unless I could help it—the last time being about four hundred years ago when I had rescued a baby goat and had left it in the kitchen because it tended to destroy things when it got dark.

Of course, it turned out that it destroyed things when it was light, too, and I simply hadn't realized that it didn't like being alone until it was too late. There had been nibble marks on the cabinets until the day I had moved out, shortly before the American Revolution. Thank goodness I'd had the sense to not use a candle. Magic had its uses, after all.

After a moment more, I pulled the car into the garage, parked, and entered the house.

My mouth dropped open. Every single cupboard in the kitchen was open, various pots and pans from the lower cupboards scattered across the floor. I stared at the disaster zone, wondering how in the world this had happened. Had someone come in? Had there been an earthquake? Had Wednesday made good on her threat of growing thumbs?

*Oh. You're back.* Wednesday's voice was remarkably unconcerned for the amount of destruction in the kitchen.

"What—what is this?" I practically gasped, my voice strangled as I indicated the mess around me. Wednesday walked into the kitchen, tail high and fluffy, and surveyed the damage with interest. After a moment of silence as she sniffed a couple of the dishes on the floor, she looked up at me, eyes big.

*It's messy in here,* she said, as if seeing it for the first time.

I looked around. "Well, yes. What I meant—did something or someone come in?" I demanded. "It looks like a bomb went off."

Wednesday looked around. *A bomb would have caused more damage,* she said sagely. *Besides, I didn't hear a bomb.*

"Then what happened?" I demanded.

She looked up at me and blinked. *Well, it looks like someone opened all the cupboards and pulled all the dishes out,* she said matter-of-factly.

"Did you have something to do with it?" I asked stiffly.

*I'm just a cat. I don't have opposable thumbs,* she said, looking up at me innocently. *How could I possibly open a cupboard?*

"Yes, well, you also talk to me. It's not like you're a normal cat."

*Your dog man seems to think I am, and he can smell magic,* she said defensively, her tail swishing in annoyance. *There must be some other explanation.*

I stared down at her, quiet for a full minute, lips pressed together furiously. It couldn't have been her. I knew that, but as I quickly made my way through the house, checking all the doors and windows—which were all locked—and going through the kitchen—where nothing seemed to be missing—I was drawing more and more of a blank.

It couldn't have been Wednesday. But who else could it have been? She was so small, even if she had stretched she couldn't have reached most of the cupboards, and yet all of them were open. Konstantin had smelled her—she wasn't magical. And yet... Could he be wrong? I'd never asked before. I'd never had to.

What was going on?

*Trillion?* Wednesday asked. *Are you okay?*

I looked down at the little cat, and decided to give up for the night. It was almost one in the morning. Whatever brainpower I had was gone, and it was only going to get more frustrating from here if I decided to figure this out right then.

"I'm going to bed," I proclaimed firmly to the slightly smug cat, pinching the bridge of my nose. "I don't have the energy for this."

# 12

# IN WHICH I HAVE TWO SURPRISING CONVERSATIONS

I woke up with Wednesday snugged up against my back, one of my arms and also one leg hanging off the edge of my bed. I blinked slowly against the bright sunlight coming through the window, squinting through the strands of blonde hair that fell over my face.

Something had woken me up. A buzzing sound vibrated rhythmically through the air, and I reached groggily over to my bedside table to grab my cell phone. As I reached, I overbalanced out of the bed, my head narrowly missing ramming into the bedside table.

I sat there for a moment, blinking confusedly at the phone in my hands, wondering how I got down on the floor. Then I looked down at the number.

'Restricted' read the caller ID. I looked at the time. Nine in the morning. Probably not a telemarketer.

Telemarketer? Was that the right word?

*Will you just answer the flipping phone already?* Wednesday's head picked up, fur slightly ruffled.

Blinking, I pressed the green button and held it up to one ear, clearing my throat. "Hello?" I rasped.

"Trillion, I heard you wanted to get in touch with me." Lightly accented English came through the phone, and my brain woke up the rest of the way in a rush of adrenaline.

"Councilwoman," I said, brain suddenly firing at full capacity. "How pleasant to hear from you."

"I highly doubt that," Stanislava Carabosse responded evenly. "I am a very busy woman, please skip the pleasantries and get to the point."

Shaking my head, I winced slightly and mentally scolded myself. I knew she wasn't one for small talk. "Very well. I would like to meet with you to discuss my investigating your ballet company in relation to the disappearance of Odell Richardson," I said. There was a short pause.

Short, of course, is relative. What was probably only about five seconds felt like five hundred years as I forced myself to remain calm while waiting for the Councilwoman's response.

As much as I disliked the reality of the situation, whatever decision she made, I had to live by it. There were three points of authority that she had over me—firstly, as main patron and owner of the Metropolitan Ballet she had a massive say over what happened to her ballet dancers. Secondly, as a councilwoman for the city, she was highly educated—both in politics and in law, neither of which were my forte. If I wasn't careful, there were a lot of ways that she could pin me down and negate my effectiveness in the city. Thirdly, and possibly most importantly, she was the head of the American chapter of the Domovoi.

Some lines you just didn't cross.

There were many factions of elves in the world, largely separated by geography and bloodlines. The Domovoi were primarily Germanic, French, and Russian. While I had traveled enough to know that it wasn't the case, many people thought the Domovoi were either tricksters, scheming toward your demise, or some sort of aberrant faerie that could be appeased by gifts or trinkets. That was no more true of them than of the Fada—the Spanish, Portuguese, and Moorish sector—the Kitsune of Japan, or The Faerie Court from my own native England.

Even if they weren't tricksters, the Domovoi were not to be trifled with. Stanislava had not become the head of their organization without some careful, perhaps morally dubious, maneuvering. It would not do to cause an inter-Aggregate incident.

Particularly because that meant that my father would suddenly be directly involved. Which, as galling as that would have been for anyone, would have been particularly humiliating for me.

One did not inconvenience The Faerie King.

Particularly with our history.

"I believe that that could be arranged," Stanislava said quietly. "On one condition."

Discomfort squirmed in my stomach. Shoving down the feeling I was about to lose my nonexistent first-born child, I kept my voice calm. "And what would that be?" I asked.

"Would you meet with me after your interviews and share your thoughts with me?" she said.

I stopped, free hand dropping into my lap as I stared blankly out the window. "Do you mind me asking why?" I asked.

There was a brief pause, and then she answered. "I have a vested interest," she said quietly. "I will explain more when we meet. I do not want to color your investigations. I fear there will be enough of that at the theatre."

"Do you mean that—"

"I will speak to you about this later," she said firmly. "Call me when you are done. I will have Violente clear my schedule when you have drawn your interviews to a close."

Running one hand through my hair, I vaguely realized that she had a very clear idea of when I was going to do this. "Very well, I agree. When am I allowed to go interview the dance company?"

"Their schedules will be cleared today and Monday. Please report any trouble you receive from the company. Please let them know—as I will—that if they do not cooperate, their jobs are at stake."

My mouth dropped open, despite my efforts to keep it closed. "I have to admit, Councilwoman," I said, "I am surprised at your willingness to help me."

"One of my dancers is missing, Trillion," she said stiffly. "We look after our own. If they are not willing to aid their comrades, they have no place in the company. I will wait for your call. Good day."

And then she hung up.

I sat there for a moment, looking down at the phone in utter bemusement, and then out the window in front of me. The sun was starting to peek up over the tops of the trees, as if unsure if it should be there. I smiled, feeling the rejuvenating rays soak into my skin, even through the window. I was far from being a plant, but I definitely felt a kinship to the small pots of green that seemed to perk up as much as I did at the sight of the celestial body. Maybe that was what had been so difficult about the last couple of weeks. Sitting there for a moment longer, letting the morning rays sink into my skin, I reluctantly rose. I had interviews to conduct, and I couldn't do them in a T-shirt and sweats. Standing, I turned to find Wednesday curled up into a tight, fluffy ball in the middle of the bed.

Sudden memories of waking up sliding off the bed rushed back into my head and I frowned down at her.

"Have you been like that all night?" I asked. She didn't respond for a moment. Was she still asleep? "Wednesday?" I repeated, poking the center of the furry ball. It moved. "Have you been there all night?" Eyes cracking open, she looked up at me without moving.

*Shhhhhhh. You have risen, but I have not.* Her voice was heavy with sleep. I sighed hopelessly and walked out of the room. After showering and dressing, I went into the kitchen to meet with the mess that I hadn't been able to quite take in the night before.

I looked around and shook my head. Now that I was a little more rested, I could apply myself to what was causing all this trouble. It wasn't likely that I had a sprite in my house—they usually hibernated in winter, and were usually only the size of a firefly—but in light of Konstantin's proclamation of Wednesday's normalness, such as it was, it was about the only option that I had.

But it was winter, and there had been no breach on my house wards. I frowned. The sprite could possibly explain the coldness in the house a couple of night ago as well. They could fly through glass window panes, but the way they did it brought in the air from the outside.

I put away the pots and pans, not being particularly careful about how loud I was. It was well past nine. Even though I was tired from staying up late the night before, Wednesday had probably slept most of the day before. She'd be up in a moment, begging for her breakfast before I left. Except...

Well, if there was a sprite in the house, it wasn't a particularly good idea to leave her at home. Whether for her or the sprite, I wasn't sure, but I wasn't willing to let my house to be the site of that particular battleground.

*What are you doing?* Wednesday said, walking into the kitchen on delicate paws, watching me as I closed the last of the cabinets.

"Cleaning up the mess from last night," I said. Looking down, I asked, "Are you hungry?"

*Yes*, she said, meowing to punctuate her words, *You did not feed me last night. You did not wake up when I tried to wake you up in the middle of the night.* She sat up and looked up at me piteously. *I thought you had died.*

"Oh," I said. "I didn't."

*You have my thanks*, she said in reply, her voice dropping into sarcasm.

I fought down a smile. "Well, I'll try to keep that going as long as possible."

Her tail swished. *Again, you have my thanks.*

"Awesome." So the cat didn't want me dead. It was faintly relieving.

Opening a can of cat food, I put the contents onto a plate and then placed it in front of her as she jumped up onto the counter.

"How do you feel about coming with me and hanging out with Konstantin at the office today?" I said, running my hair across her soft fur. She really was a beautiful cat. She wouldn't have any trouble finding a home once she was put up for adoption.

A small pang hit my soul, and I pulled my hand back swiftly, turning away to put my things in my bag. I rubbed my fingers together to get rid of the sensation. Enough of that.

*I feel fine about that. What will you be doing? Why can't I stay here?* she asked, looking up at me.

I pointed to her food. "Eat. I think there's something in the house, and if it's what I think it is, I don't want to leave you alone with it."

*What is it?*

"Er, a sprite, I think. It's like a little tiny—"

*I know what a sprite is, Trillion*, she said flatly. *It is not a sprite. They hibernate.*

"Then what is it?" I demanded. "Whatever it is, I don't want to leave you alone where it could... have consequences." Like destroying my house.

*I'm not sure what to call it*, Wednesday said musingly. *Not a sprite.*

I tried not to growl in response. This cat enjoyed wordplay far too much for something that was nonverbal. I wouldn't get it out of her unless I played her game, which I was suddenly in no mood to do.

"Well, whatever it is, I'm bringing you with me."

*Very well,* she said, licking the last bit of her plate clean. She jumped down as I rinsed off the dish and placed it in the sink, and headed toward the coatrack where her harness hung. She looked up at the orange apparatus in distaste and meowed.

*Hurry up.*

"I'm coming," I said defensively, looking around. "Bother."

*What?* Wednesday said, trotting back over.

"Where's my cellphone?" I said, reaching into my pockets.

She blinked at me. *Did you not have it five minutes ago?* she asked, her voice flat. *You're going to be late.*

"Just hold on!" I said. "I have to call Konstantin before I leave so he can be ready."

*What?* Wednesday said, *Why does Konstantin have to be ready? Is it a surprise? It is not my birthday.*

I looked down at her, finally finding my cell phone in the sel-dom-used cell phone pocket on my satchel. Funny, I didn't remember putting it there.

"You remember when your birthday is?" I asked. Her tail swished, and I got the distinct impression that she was annoyed.

*Perhaps,* she said. *Not that you believe me.*

"I might," I said, a brush of defensiveness coloring my words. "Are you withholding information from me?"

Another swish of the tail, and Wednesday sauntered back to the coat rack. *Would it make a difference?* she said as I clipped on her har-ness, *You and Konstantin haven't believed anything I've told you so far.*

"Well, the magical, enchantment-sniffing shapeshifter hound said that you were a cat, so..." I shrugged, opening the door to the garage, "not sure what to tell you there."

She didn't reply, instead trotting ahead of me to hop up into the car first. Once I'd backed out of the driveway, Wednesday stood up on her hind legs, paws against the window, leaving little toe-bean impressions against the cold glass as she watched the world go by.

*There is something wrong,* she said quietly. *I do not know what it is, but it is wrong that Konstantin smells only cat. I am human. Or at least I was. I do not know what has changed. Perhaps... it is permanent.* She didn't sound like she liked that idea at all, and at least in that context I didn't blame Wednesday.

I thought about it for a moment, and then decided to humor her. "Out of curiosity, what was the last memory you have as a human?"

She turned around fully and looked at me, waves of disbelief coming off her.

*You believe me?*

"Now, I didn't say that," I said, glancing over at her in warning. "But...if you were human, tell me about it."

She studied me carefully.

*You are not mocking me,* she observed.

"I'd like to think I know better," I responded.

Wednesday snorted. *You do not.*

"I do!"

*Prove it.*

"Didn't I just do that?" I said. "If you don't want to tell me—"

*I remember summertime,* she interrupted, turning back to look out the window. *I remember walking through the woods. And going to school. And a building. It smelled like chalk and... something.* She sat back down on the seat, the tip of her tail twitching back and forth. She stared forward, as if lost in thought.

"What is it?"

*I remember my mother. Not her face. But I know she was my mother,* she said quietly. *I... miss her. Her hugs. Home. I miss home.*

I looked over at her, staring at her long enough that I nearly missed the turn into the driveway and practically ran into the blue car slowing down in front of me. Wednesday chirped in annoyance as I slammed on the breaks and skidded around the corner faster than was probably legal or safe.

She was a cat, I reminded myself. Pull yourself together. Whatever these memories were, they couldn't be hers. Couldn't possibly be hers.

I pulled up in front of Konstantin's house. Wednesday put her paws up on the window ledge once more, pressing her pink nose against the glass, tail slowly dancing back and forth.

*You haven't said anything*, she said after a moment of quiet.

I looked down for a moment. "I didn't know what to say," I said.

She seemed to mull this over, turning back to me for a moment. *I understand*, she said finally, turning to face the window as Konstantin came out of the house. *I'm not sure what to believe either.*

# 13

## IN WHICH WEDNESDAY (DEBATABLY) WINS FAR TOO MANY ARGUMENTS

Konstantin opened the door to the car a moment later. Scooping Wednesday up into his lap, he slid into his seat and kissed the top of her head.

"Who's the prettiest kitty in all the land?" he said, scratching in between her ears. Wednesday meowed in response.

*That had better not be a hypothetical question,* Wednesday warned. I managed what felt like a fake smile and shook my head.

Konstantin looked between me and the cat. "Did I miss something?"

I shook my head. "Wednesday warns you against idle compliments, and confirms that she is, in fact, the prettiest kitty in *all* the land," I said. I paused. Had those words actually come out of my mouth? I frowned. Konstantin frowned, too.

"Did I come in in the middle of an argument or something?" Konstantin asked.

Slowly, I shook my head again. "Konstantin, I'm not—well," I paused for a moment, trying to think of the best way to phrase my question. "Have you ever been... wrong?"

Konstantin frowned at me like I was insane. "About what precisely?"

*Yes, about what, Trillion?* Wednesday piped up from Konstantin's arms.

"About... I don't know." How did I put this without giving Wednesday too much hope? There was something that bothered me about her statement earlier that morning. *Turned into a cat permanently...*

"That doesn't help me, Trillion," Konstantin said blandly.

I shook myself free from the statement. "Sorry, I mean, have you ever been wrong in identifying magical scents?" I asked.

Konstantin gave me a long, frankly concerned look. "Why?"

"It, well—Wednesday." I jerked out, eventually just going quiet to make the pain end.

Konstantin's concerned expression didn't necessarily change, but it softened around the edges. Slightly. "Not as long as I've been doing this professionally." Suddenly, he blinked, as if what I had said suddenly registered. "Why? Has something happened?" He looked down at Wednesday in horror. "Is she actually human?"

"I—well, *I* don't think so," I said, wondering if that was actually the case. "But..."

"But you might be becoming convinced?" Konstantin said. He

looked down at Wednesday, who looked up at him with enormous green eyes.

*No*, Wednesday said, remarkably pleasant for her words. *But I'm hoping with more evidence, I can jam the possibility into his minuscule brain.*

"Hey!" I said to her. "He can't even hear you."

*I'm aware.*

"*Hey*," I protested.

Konstantin laughed. "So the tenacious kitten is still sticking to the belief that she's a human, is she?"

"Or at least *was* human," I confirmed grimly. "She claims to have memories."

"Of?"

"Going to school. And her mother."

*And summertime.*

"Summertime isn't unique to humans," I reminded her. "I remember summertime, too, and I'm not human."

*In more ways than one*, she grumbled. I frowned at her, but pulled the car forward and back out onto the road.

"Who was your mother?" Konstantin asked her. Then looked up at me. Great, I was going to be a translator.

*I don't know her name. She had dark hair, and a nice smile.*

I repeated it.

Konstantin scratched his head absently, thinking. "Anything else?" he finally asked.

She chirped. *No.*

"She said 'no'," I said helpfully.

Konstantin nodded. "Cool. Well, if you'd like," he said, looking down at her, "you and I can do some more tests back at the office."

She looked up at him and blinked. *I'll think about it.*

I frowned up the road, glancing over briefly. "What? I thought you'd jump at the chance to prove me wrong."

"She said no?" Konstantin asked.

I glanced over at him. "She said that she'll think about it."

"Well, there's no pressure," Konstantin said to her. "I got an email notification last night of a possible Rothbart trail north of the city from Cradle Borrigan. Between that and sifting through the dance company's records, I have plenty to do."

"Leave Wednesday at the office when you go after Rothbart," I said. It surprised me a little, and Konstantin looked over.

"O...kay? How come? It's probably going to be just as old as the other trails that we've found."

"I don't want Wednesday mixed up with Rothbart. She didn't sign on for that," I said, looking over at Konstantin seriously.

*I can't sign anything,* Wednesday said flatly. *I can't even hold a pen. It's not like I'm scared. Besides, why would Rothbart go after a dog and a cat? I want to talk to someone at some point today.*

"Because I asked you both very kindly not to," I said, stopping at the first stoplight into the city.

*That's horrible reasoning. You can't tell me what to do.*

"Why not?" I demanded.

*Because,* she said smugly, *I said so.*

"That's not a good reason."

*It is the best reason. That's why you use it all the time. And,* she swished her tail, *in your own words it's the only one that matters. You're going to miss the turn for the theatre.*

I started, and turned my blinker on by instinct. Sure enough, the turn was right there, and I narrowly missed cutting another car off as I swerved into the turn lane.

"Stop talking to me!" I exclaimed, glaring over at the cat.

Konstantin looked over at me, bemused. "Are you okay?" he asked.

"I'm fine!" I hissed.

*Ha! Lies.* Wednesday interjected, settling down comfortably on

Konstantin's lap. *I make you sweat like a sinner in church, and you know it.*

I tightened my grip on the steering wheel and didn't answer. She was just trying to get a rise out of me.

And it was working.

Blast.

"Where did you even learn that metaphor?" I demanded finally.

Konstantin looked up. "It's not a metaphor, it's literally just a que— you were talking to the cat," he said, interrupting himself.

I swallowed, and looked over at him sheepishly. "Sorry," I said quietly.

Konstantin stared at me, clearly concerned. "Should we... talk about this?"

"No," I said definitively.

"Are you sure?" he prodded.

My frown deepened. "*No.*"

*Does that mean you're not sure?* Wednesday asked innocently. I resisted the urge to turn and glare.

"Fine," Konstantin said, almost unconcerned as we pulled up in front of the theatre. Parking the car and throwing the door open violently, I stalked to the driver's side back door. Wednesday stood on my satchel, tiny paws firm against the faux leather.

*Aren't you going to say goodbye?* she demanded.

I glared at her. "No."

*Why not?* She took a step forward, setting herself as though she weighed seven hundred pounds instead of seven.

"Get off my briefcase, Wednesday," I said, reaching for it. Striking faster than most species of snake, she reached out and bit my hand. Not hard, but enough that I had four tiny canine prints on my hand. I drew back, more than a little shocked. Her feline face seemed to form an impossible scowl as I rubbed the small bite mark.

*Tell me goodbye!* she demanded.

I scoffed. Her ears started swiveling back, and I sighed. "Goodbye, Wednesday," I said, rolling my eyes.

*That was a horrible goodbye,* she said, stepping off my satchel. *No wonder you're single.*

"That has nothing to do with it," I said icily. I should have picked my words better.

*Ah, so it's more than one thing. What a pity.*

I shut my eyes. "Goodbye, Wednesday," I said firmly, stepping away from the car, swinging the door closed. Before it slammed shut, I heard her cheerful voice call after me.

*Have a good day!*

I doubted it. Throwing a half-hearted wave at Konstantin, I took a deep breath, trying to let go of the frustration. The interviews would not go well if any of the dancers sensed any semblance of irritation or impatience from me. Besides, missing person aside, my issues really didn't have anything to do with any of them. I was just there to find the truth.

Shouldering the strap of my satchel, I strode into the front door of the theatre. A tall woman with grey streaked hair stood behind a desk, half moon glasses perched fastidiously on the end of her nose. She glanced up at me. Recognition danced behind those eyes.

"Ah, you're here," she said.

I narrowed my eyes, just slightly. "Do I know you?" I asked.

A slow, humorless smile curled up one side of the woman's face. "I am Marya Leonidovna Putoshevska. We have been expecting you, Mr. Orris," she said, grandly raising a hand to indicate a door to the side. We left the main entryway, stepping through the doors into a large auditorium. At least forty dancers lined the walls and barres, getting ready to warm up.

Marya Leonidovna looked around the room, and then over at me, her smile curling up the other side of her face into a dangerous smirk.

"Welcome to the Metropolitan Ballet."

# 14

### IN WHICH I GO HEAD TO HEAD WITH THE METROPOLITAN BALLET - OR - WEDNESDAY DISCOVERS TEXTING

"Thank you for letting me talk to you today," I said, sitting across from the dancer. She looked up at me, black hair pulled back into a bun, a tired look on her face.

Sitting up, a little straighter, Fumi Yoshikawa titled her head to the side and frowned. "Look, let's all save ourselves a little bit of time so I can get back to practice. Giselle's responsible for all of this."

I sat back, frowning. "You seem very certain," I said, a little taken aback by the dancer's candor.

Fumi shrugged. "What? It's not like I blame her. She and Odell had been at odds ever since Giselle was named principal at the beginning of this season. Not that Odell should have been surprised—Giselle's always been a better dancer," she said. "Maybe Odell crossed a line."

"So Giselle is to blame for Odell's disappearance," I summed up. "How, do you think?"

Fumi shrugged again. "I don't know. They were both at the bonfire that night. They went out walking with Siegfried around the mill," she said. "I don't remember seeing her after that, but there were drinks there, and the company was having a good time. Anything could have happened."

"Did you know that Odell was studying magic?" I asked.

Fumi drew her eyebrows together, as if she hadn't anticipated the question. "No," she said, a little quieter. More unsure. "No, I didn't."

"Do you know why she might have started?" I asked. Her eyes flicked up. According to our research, Fumi was human, but was distantly related to the Japanese faction of elves. Whether or not she knew that was anyone's guess, but Konstantin's sources could not be denied.

"No," she said, shaking her head decisively. She looked around, her face drawn in concern.

"Is there something else?" I asked. "Something that would be helpful?"

Fumi looked up at me and shook her head. "No," she said. "Is that all you needed?"

"For now," I said. "Is it all right to contact you if I have further questions?"

Her dark eyes narrowed a little in worry, and she shifted a little in her seat. "If you must," she said. "The theatre has my contact information. I would prefer if you went through them."

"Of course," I responded. "I anticipate no further questions."

"Thank you," she said uncomfortably, and stood. I stayed where I was, making notes in my memo book. Bowing a little, Fumi left the small office in which we had been talking, and made her way back out onto the rehearsal floor.

Marya Leonidovna had given me a list of the dancers and had informed me that she had drawn it up in the order that I was to see them, given their rank and rehearsal time in the company. I would start with the newest and lowest in precedence, and then move up. I was about halfway through the company now, and either they had no idea why or how Odell had gone missing, or they were convinced that Giselle had something to do with it. I looked out the window at the company practicing in the auditorium. Apparently opening night for the Nutcracker was in four days. They would put in an eight hour day of practice, break for two hours, and then practice some more.

In other words, I was conducting my interviews at the worst possible moment.

Not that most people saw my interviews as convenient, but it was difficult when every person in a fifty-two member company thought I was the ox in their mire of practice. At least I wasn't traversing new territory.

Rubbing my face tiredly, I looked at the next name on my list. Leonora Dovcick. Konstantin's fact checking had implied that she had been closest to Odell, aside from Giselle and Siegfried. Maybe she had more insight into what happened.

I pulled my phone out of my bag to check the time. 3:52pm. Practice was almost over. Then, directly beneath—

Forty-two texts.

I blinked.

Shifting my weight in the chair, I looked closer at the messages. Every single one of them was from Konstantin.

He'd been tracking down Rothbart. Konstantin was a caller, not a texter. If he had texted me once it would have meant something was wrong. Forty-two was nothing short of an unmitigated catastrophe.

The phone was locked, and only the sender was available in the preview. My heart pumped louder and louder in my ears as I attempted to punch in my password three separate times before I entered it correctly. I opened the first text.

*Im bord.*

What? I pulled in my chin, looking closer at the phone. What was that supposed to say? On board? Or...I'm bored? Wait. I looked down to the next message.

*Knstntn md me stay in th car.*

*It—*

*Smeone should report him.*

What?

*Thnk goodness for autorfcct.*

I stared at my phone, scrolling through the gibberish messages, mostly ramblings, with the odd crystal-clear statement. This could not possibly be what I thought it was. No way. Not in a million years. A new message pinged on the screen.

*Yu need to check your pin mr often.*

I stared down at the phone. And then typed my reply.

*Wednesday?*

A beat of silence. Then one short buzz.

*Yes?*

Blast it all.

I pinched my eyes shut and sighed. Just then, the door opened and a pleasant male face peeked into the door.

"Mr. Orris?" the man said.

"Hello. I was supposed receive Ms. Dovcick?" I said, frowning up at the man as I checked the list again.

He looked a little embarrassed. "Yes, sorry," he said apologetically. "She didn't realize she was next in line and went home for her break. I thought I might step into her place, given my schedule on Monday."

I shifted a little, letting a smile cross my face. "I'm game. Though, it might help to add your name to your testimony," I said. The handsome young man grinned, some small secret hidden behind it.

"My name is Siegfried Handel." The statement was simple. He looked different from his picture. His face was a little fuller, his hair just a touch darker. He continued. "And if I may be so bold, I believe you've heard of me."

He had intended to surprise me, and for a small moment it worked. Rather than letting myself visibly react, though, I let the moment rest, taking the time instead to study him. Despite his difference to the photograph, which, the longer I looked at him was not quite so pronounced as I had originally thought, he was the very image of a dancer: slim, muscled from head to toe, T-shirt paired with tights. A bright smile crossed from cheek to cheek.

"You are correct," I said, pulling up my notepad. "Please, take a seat." He did so with alacrity, alighting with an almost affected gracefulness. My phone buzzed beneath my notepad, and with an unconscious frown I looked down at the phone.

*Why? Wut r u doing?*

I sighed, shook my head, and stuffed the phone in my pocket.

"Bad news?" Siegfried asked. I looked up.

"No, it's my c—cousin's friend," I said, distracted. Had I seriously been about to say 'cat'? "She's discovered texting."

Siegfried smiled and nodded as though he understood. "Lots of messages?"

"Forty-four, at last count," I said, feeling the phone buzz in my pocket. "Forty-five."

Siegfried smiled. "My condolences. She's not, er, romantically pursuing you?" he asked. He surprised a laugh out of me.

"Oh, no. She's...*far* too young," I said. And furry. And feline. And Wednesday.

Another buzz from my pocket.

"And prolific," I added. Siegfried laughed. An easy smile crossed my face. Glancing down at my notes, I looked back up at the other man. "I suppose you know why I've called you in today?" I asked.

Siegfried's smile was back, calm and assured. "I think I have an inclination," he responded. "But if you don't mind running through it with me again, I can answer your questions a little more readily."

"Very well," I said. "Ms. Odell Richardson has gone missing. I've been told that you were one of the last people that she was seen with."

Siegfried's face drew together a little in concern. Shifting, he shrugged. "You're right, I suppose," he said thoughtfully. "The last time I saw her face was at the Old Mill near the State Park."

"Would you mind walking me through that evening?" I asked.

Siegfried shrugged again. "Sure. It was late August—sorry, I can't remember the exact day. We'd just finished up a production of Sleeping Beauty, and it was our wrap party. I came in a car with Giselle and Odell—Odell wasn't too excited about coming. She hadn't been feeling too well, and she'd wanted to rest up rather than come along, but Giselle and I promised that we'd come home early."

"That's interesting," I said. "None of the company members have mentioned that Odell felt ill that day."

Siegfried looked thoughtful, and then shrugged. "She's always played things close to the chest. I imagine that she didn't want to mention it in case Marya Leonidovna pulled her from practice for the next couple of days. She wanted to stay a soloist. It was in question."

I frowned. "Why?"

Siegfried shifted a little in his chair and sighed. "What do you know about hierarchy in ballet?" he asked.

I had to shake my head. "Not much. I have a friend that has tried to explain it on many occasions with...varied success," I admitted.

Siegfried smiled, a little ruefully. "Well, it's not pure competition, or pure merit. It's a combination of skill, presentation, and artistry. Odell, she's undoubtedly a good dancer, but her body was slowly wearing out. Giselle...was transcendent. She's part elf, you know?"

I shifted, trying to look surprised. "Oh really?" I asked.

Siegfried smiled and nodded. "Daughter of the great Stanislava Carabosse. Who was, of course, a well-deserved principal dancer in her own right, back in the day. Performed on all the premiere stages in Paris, London, Moscow. Knew Tchaikovsky. Giselle...she worked with the greats. Baryshnikov, Nureyev, Fonteyn..."

I resisted the urge to hold my breath. There was one fact that I hadn't been able to dig up on my own.

"Just how old is Giselle Carabosse?" I asked.

Siegfried smiled. "She looks excellent for a ninety-two year old, doesn't she?"

I turned to look through the window. There she stood. Shining brown hair, smooth skin, and as she turned around and around in the pirouettes, pink lips turned up into a smile under hazel eyes. She was beautiful. Yes, perhaps even transcendent. The picture of a confident, competent dancer in her prime.

"Yes," I said, transfixed for a moment. My pocket buzzed. Shaking myself, I turned back to Siegfried, trying to remember the thread of our conversation. "Was Odell in danger of losing her job?" I asked.

Siegfried shrugged again. He did that a lot. "Not as such. She'd most likely be simply demoted to the corps, which isn't bad, but you don't get paid as much. Her mom's not very well off, you know, and Odell tries to help as much as she can."

"I see," I said. "So there was a rivalry between the two?"

"Only professionally," Siegfried said. "And to my knowledge, no, it didn't carry over into their friendship. Of course, I can only speak to Giselle's opinion."

"Are you two...?" I asked.

Siegfried smiled happily. "We've been dating the last six months or so," he said. "Or at least as much as possible under her mother's watchful eye."

"I see," I said. Another bit of buzzing. This one lasted longer than usual. Pulling out my phone, I saw that it was a call. Konstantin.

If it was actually Konstantin, he would understand. Then again, he might be trying to let me know that he was actually here, in which case I needed to start wrapping up. If it was Wednesday, she was going to be on dry food for a week, hunger strike or no hunger strike.

"Do you need to take that?" Siegfried asked.

Konstantin *and* Wednesday could wait, I decided. "No," I said. "It's likely my ride back to the office. They'll leave a message." Siegfried nodded in understanding. I continued with my questions. "Do you think anyone is at fault for Odell's disappearance?" I asked.

He seemed to think for a moment. "I'm not sure," he said. "There would have to be a really good reason why someone would trouble themselves with Odell."

"Why is that?" I asked. "Was she into something dangerous?"

Siegfried's eyes lit up like they had before, like there was some sort of amusing secret that I didn't know. "Not *dangerous*," he said. "But she knew how to defend herself. She'd been studying magic the past few years." *Finally.*

"Really?" I asked. "Tell me about that." Siegfried shrugged. I didn't know why, but the small motion was starting to bother me.

"There's not much to tell. She was taking correspondence courses from the University of Maryland. She was supposed to sit the exams sometime during July to register in the American Association of

Sorcerers, but I don't know if she ever did. Maybe she sat and failed? That's unlike Odell, though. I've never seen anyone so determined."

"I see," I said. "So what *did* happen that night?"

Siegfried looked at me, something dark entering into in his laughing eyes. "We don't know," he said quietly.

I frowned. "Pardon?"

"Giselle and I...we've discussed it dozens of times. I replay the same thing time after time in my head. We three were walking around the Old Mill, around the back by the stream. Giselle and I were having a...well, heated discussion. Odell hung back a little. At one point, we looked back, and she was gone. We thought she had gone back to the party. Later that night, after a couple of carfuls of people had gone home, we looked for her, and when we couldn't find her, we thought that she had gone home with someone else. It wasn't until the following Sunday that we found out that she never came home."

"That must have been hard," I said quietly.

Siegfried shook his head slowly, as if trying to come to grips with the concept. "I don't know what to do," he said. He looked up at me, eyes unsure. "Do you know what happened to her?"

I shook my head. "Not yet. But I will do my best to find out."

Siegfried leaned forward, elbows on thighs, and nodded. "Please do, Mr. Orris," he said quietly. "I think we could all do with a little bit of closure."

# 15

## IN WHICH SEVERAL UGLY TRUTHS REAR THEIR HEADS

"Ninety-seven texts," I said sternly, holding the phone up to the white and tabby cat sitting in the passenger seat of the car as I opened the door. Wednesday looked at the phone, and then back at me, unimpressed.

*I was bored,* she said, before walking over into Konstantin's lap, and sitting down.

"Ninety-seven!" I repeated, climbing in and slamming the door shut after me. "Do you even know if Konstantin has unlimited texting?"

Wednesday blinked. *Is limited texting even an option anymore?*

I didn't actually know, but I frowned at her anyway. "It was very rude. I expect better of you on Monday."

*This is happening again Monday?* she said, sounding as though she would rather eat dog food for the rest of her unnatural life.

"I've got to interview the rest of the ballet company," I explained.

"I've got about half left, including Giselle, who is arguably the most important. Most of the company think that she's responsible."

*Is she?* Wednesday asked.

I shook my head. "I don't know yet. There must have been something going on between the two of them, though," I remarked thoughtfully. "Otherwise I don't think the company would know—or care—what was actually going on."

I looked over at Konstantin, who was gripping the steering wheel tightly and frowning.

Furrowing my eyebrows, I looked him up and down. "What's the matter with you?" I asked. Konstantin cast a glare over at me. "Whoa," I protested. "Please explain before you turn me to stone."

"I'm not a shade, Trillion," he grumbled. "I would simply like to know the proper reaction to a cat who has accurately hacked one's phone password."

*It's his birthday,* Wednesday said smugly. *It was my second guess.*

"How do you know his birthday?" I demanded.

"Why does your cat know how to text, Trillion?" he exclaimed in response.

"I don't know!" I said. "You're the one who said she was just a cat!"

*Maybe you should have Konstantin pull over before you cause an accident.* Wednesday's voice was a little more timid than normal as she slunk over to curl up on my lap.

"We're fine," I said, taking a deep breath, circling my arm around her. There was silence in the car as we drove to the office, and more silence as we trekked up into the old building. Konstantin handed the car keys to me, hoisting what I recognized as his overnight bag over his shoulder.

"Staying here tonight?" I asked.

"Running down the Rothbart trail," he explained. "I went there this morning. There's something I don't like about it, but I didn't want to leave Wednesday too long. I'll have to leave my stuff here, but I can make it on foot."

I smirked. "I'll keep her away from your phone."

He shook his head and sighed, letting his bag slump to the floor. "It's not that. Trillion, what if I was wrong? What if Wednesday's enchanted?" His voice dropped, and we both looked over at the fluffy cat, who was currently drinking from her water dish by dipping her paw in the water and licking it off.

I studied her as she moved on to grooming herself, washing her head and paws off until she caught us looking.

*Do you mind?* she demanded, affronted, before standing up and moving into the storage room. I looked over at Konstantin, hearing her begin to rustle around in one of the boxes almost immediately.

"I'm not convinced," I said.

"I think you might be deluding yourself," Konstantin said. "I mean, chat speak notwithstanding, your cat is literate."

I thought about that for a second, but the more I thought about it, the less I actually wanted to think about it. I could ask Wednesday how she knew how to read and write. She would respond that she learned at school. I would ask which school, she would say that she didn't remember. I would get frustrated, and then once again feel like this was all a waste of time.

And yet, there was that persistent little 'what if'...

The urge to call my father came on strongly.

I shoved it down, equally as strongly.

"What do I do if she is enchanted?" I asked turning to him.

"I don't understand," Konstantin said, frowning.

"If Wednesday is enchanted...how do I break the spell?" I sunk down onto the top of my desk, staring past him at the storage room where Wednesday was playing with one of the dust bunnies. "We don't know who did it—you couldn't even tell that she *has* a spell. If

I don't know who did it, I can't even begin to think how we could dismantle it. And that...enchantments are not my gift."

Konstantin was quiet for a moment, as if weighing what he would say next.

"We should call your dad," he said.

I glared up at him. "I'm willing to try out other avenues first," I said firmly.

Konstantin scoffed. "Trillion, come on. It's not like he's actually expecting for you to have caught Rothbart the next time you talk to him," he protested. "You were both angry. It was a tense time for everyone."

"He was the one who said it," I said quietly. "One does not gainsay King Auberon."

Konstantin sighed and shook his head. "You're his son, Trillion," he said softly.

I shook my head. "It didn't matter then."

"Your mother—"

"I'm not calling him. The matter is *closed*," I said, standing and walking away into the back room, looking for Wednesday. The room was full of boxes in various stages of emptiness from our recent move further into the city. After a few fruitless moments of calling her name, I found her curled up in a box on one of emergency blankets that we had.

*Are we going already?* she asked, blinking blearily as I picked her up.

"Yes," I said stiffly, tucking her in closely. "It's time to go."

*Put me down. I can walk.*

I did so without argument. Then, we left.

It was a little after six now, the sun long since dipping below the horizon, but the traffic was lighter than normal. Wednesday watched out the window quietly as we left the city, looking at the strings of lights in the windows, as well as the plentiful Christmas decorations. Every so often, I would catch her taking a surreptitious look back at me.

"What?" I finally asked. If it were possible, I could have sworn that she'd shrugged. Since it wasn't, I repeated myself. "What?"

*Nothing.*

"It doesn't look like nothing," I said. She pressed her nose up to the glass and didn't answer for a long time. Finally, as the lights of the city started to fade behind us, she turned and sat facing forward in the car, illuminated a faint blue by the lights and numbers on the dashboard.

*It's almost Christmas,* she said quietly.

I looked down. "Yes," I said. "A little over a week from now."

*Mother will wonder where I am,* she said, her voice somehow distant. *She will be lonely.* Wednesday looked up at me. *Do you remember your mother?* she asked.

I shifted in my seat, looking out at the dark woods that we were passing through. "Yes," I said. "She died a long time ago."

*How?* she asked.

I looked down at her. "Have you ever heard of the Black Death?" I asked.

*Of course. I thought elves were immune.*

"We are," I said, doing a small double take in her direction. "She would travel from city to city, helping people to recover, carrying out the dead so the living could stay that way."

*I don't understand.*

I sighed and shook my head a little. "Elves live a long time, Wednesday. People don't know what to do with us. And in times like those, when people are dying so regularly, and then you see someone like Mother—beautiful, helping, and so obviously not personally affected by what's going on... it turns people bitter. They don't know what to do, so they get angry and lash out."

*They killed her?*

"In Florence. The height of the plague there. 1348," I said. "From what I heard from my fath—from what I heard, there was a man who thought that she'd been spreading it from place to place, although now we know that we're not carriers. He killed her on her way back from a cemetery one night."

*Have you...visited her?*

I smiled. "Yes," I said. "My family put up a beautiful monument for her. I've been there many times over the years."

She waited for another moment before she spoke again.

*Did Rothbart kill her? Is that why you're hunting him?*

I looked down at her, my expression as blank as I could possibly make it. I could feel myself failing even as I struggled.

"No," I said. "No, Rothbart wasn't born until three hundred years afterward." I stared out at the dark night. Even in the lights of the passing cars, the stars were bright above us. Wednesday seemed entranced by them, chin tilted toward the sky. She sat quietly until we had almost reached the house. As we snaked around the long driveway and the house came into view, she spoke.

*You do not have Christmas lights on your house.*

"No, I don't," I said.

*Is it because you are unhappy?* she asked.

I looked down at her. Sure, I wasn't feeling great at the moment, but—wait. "What? No!" I said quickly. Come to think of it, why *didn't* I have Christmas lights up? It wasn't like I'd actually thought about it consciously, but there was definitely a reason. After a moment, I scrabbled onto the answer. "I'm not depressed, I'm just not usually here. There's not anyone in the neighborhood to see it. Not much of a point to put things up."

*If you put up Christmas lights, I would stay here,* she said, sounding surprisingly sincere as I pulled the car into the garage.

"That sounds suspiciously like an offer to bribe you," I said, opening the car door.

Walking across my legs, Wednesday jumped out, sauntering toward the door to the kitchen. *Take it how you will*, she said grandly. *In the meantime, I need sustenance.*

I smiled, and followed her into the house.

We ate, and then settled on the couch, Wednesday curled up against my chest, her head tucked underneath my chin. I turned on the weather channel, letting the weatherman Vito Klineman start the nine o'clock session.

*Do you ever watch anything other than the news?* Wednesday asked, a small burr emitting from her throat.

I scratched her head and smiled. "This is the weather channel," I said a little defensively. "What's wrong with that?"

*It's boring.*

"The weather changes all the time," I said.

*Don't you watch, like, movies or something? Maybe the History Channel?*

"I get enough drama in my real life, thanks."

*What about a ballet?* she asked.

I craned my neck to look down at her. "Where would I even find one?" I asked. She shifted under my chin, looking up at the television and blinking a little somnolently. I sat there for a minute, wondering why I kept on asking the feline how to do things.

*Channel 56*, she said quietly.

I stilled. "What?"

*Channel 56. I'm not even speaking audibly, how can you not hear me?* she demanded.

I picked her up and held her out, looking at her suspiciously.

*Don't pick me up*, she said flatly. Putting her down on my lap, I smoothed the fur on her head, but my expression didn't change. *Well?*

I changed the channel. Zito's voice flipped with a small warble into the smooth strains of an orchestra. Wednesday straightened up, immediately paying attention. Stepping onto my knee, her face was tilted up watching the television raptly.

"What is it?" I asked.

One of her ears twitched, but otherwise she remained completely still. *It is The Firebird*, she said absently. *It is by Stravinsky.* She lowered down, tucking her paws under her, and settling into an impossibly balanced position on my leg.

Reaching down to run my hand down the stripe on her back, I looked up at the screen. "What happens in it?"

*It is the story of Prince Ivan, and how he vanquishes Koschei the Immortal*, she said. *It is one of my favorite ballets.* I looked down at her. How did she know the ballet? Or the composer? Or the channel, for crying out loud? And now...

What did I do if Wednesday was enchanted? The concerns that I'd told Konstantin were all still real. I didn't know how to break spells. I was under a spell, or rather a curse, of my own—from birth— and in two thousand years I hadn't come close to breaking it.

Maybe Konstantin was right. My father was the oldest of the Faerie rulers. From his seat in Cumbria, he'd guided England since before the Romans had come to then-Britannia. He'd seen the rise and fall of civilization upon civilization, conversed with Alexander the Great on one of his rare visits to the Continent, and knew more about magic, and magical creatures, than anyone else that I had ever encountered in my own travels.

He'd been my greatest ally, my staunchest defender, my—

*Are you watching?*

I started, nearly knocking her off of my lap, eyes flying open.

"Sorry," I said apologetically, catching her as she started to slide off. "I must have dozed off." I wasn't entirely sure if that was the truth, but she didn't need to know that. "What's going on?"

*Prince Ivan has just caught the Firebird. She is begging for her life,*

Wednesday's voice hushed. I looked up at the television and watched the ballerina, dressed in fiery reds and oranges. Sitting on the ground, she reached one arm up at him, supplicating.

"What is a firebird?" I asked, entranced.

*Anything. Everything.* Wednesday responded, *She is able to grant any wish. Here, Prince Ivan is sparing her. In return she is giving Prince Ivan a feather. When he is in dire need, he can call on her and she will come to his aid.*

"But he nearly killed her," I pointed out, frowning.

*But he didn't.*

"But he was totally going to for a minute," I said. "And she's going to reward him for that?" Wednesday tail flicked up at my face. I batted it away.

*She looked at his final decision. Do you think that she shouldn't have? That she should have held him accountable for his first instinct?*

I looked down at her, and frowned. It was a good question. After a minute, I shook my head. "I don't know."

*You like being held accountable for your final result,* she pointed out. I nodded a little reluctantly. Then I looked back up at the ballet, and down at the enraptured cat.

On impulse, I shifted a little and asked, "Wednesday, if you were human, were you a ballerina?"

Wednesday's tail swished, and she didn't answer.

"Wednesday?" I prompted.

*I am* human, she said, her voice a little flat and oddly unemotional. Then, jumping off my lap, she trotted away. *You can turn the TV off. I am going to bed.*

Remembering the three inches of bed that I'd had that morning, I quickly followed, throwing on the T-shirt and sweatpants that I used for pajamas, and hopping into bed before Wednesday could get settled. Maybe if I staked my claim first, I'd have enough room in the morning.

It wasn't until I'd snuggled under the warm, fluffy duvet that I realized Wednesday hadn't actually answered the question.

# 16

## IN WHICH I ASSERT MY DOMINANCE AND MESS UP AN INTERVIEW

I wish I could say that I was able to rest the next day. I had always tried to preserve a day of rest once a week, the most convenient being Sunday, but given that I had been running around like a turkey with its tail on fire, the 'rest' portion of that particular phrase on that particular day was more principle than actual practice.

Actually, it was a barefaced lie.

First, Wednesday pushed me to the very edges of my bed all night. Then, I discovered that the thermostat had been turned down to sixty-five degrees. That was followed by the discovery of a large tree that had fallen across the road to the lake that needed to be removed, which had taken five hours with a chain saw. When I had finally gotten home, and discovered Wednesday drinking milk out of the cup that I had left out from lunch, I shook my head and headed off to shower before collapsing into bed.

Not that I actually slept well Sunday night either. Wednesday was awake all that night, sniffing around by the windows, and meowing exactly when I had managed to drift off into some semblance of slumber. It had gotten old after exactly once. It didn't help that there didn't even seem to be much meaning attached to her yowling. If only for a couple of seconds at a time, she seemed more like an animal than ever, sitting by the window in the early hours of the morning, staring up at the newly risen moon.

It was disconcerting, and when she had finally jumped up onto the bed and nestled in the exact center, it had filled my mind and I couldn't sleep.

"Whoa," Konstantin said, looking at me as I carried Wednesday through the door the next morning. "You look terrible."

I glared at him. "Thanks."

"It wasn't a compliment," he said, stunned. "Seriously, Trillion, did you sleep at all?"

I sighed, and looked up at him. "Why?"

"You're wearing grey. You never wear grey. You're like...not...grey."

I tried to think about it, and gave up. "What are you talking about?" I asked, fatigue rolling over my brain like a Highland fog.

Wednesday piped up. *He's saying that you never wear grey and it's freaking him out.*

"You never wear grey. It's freaking me out," Konstantin said.

I looked down at Wednesday, and then at Konstantin and shook my head, whatever brainpower I had shorting out. "I'm going home," I sighed, turning back toward the door.

"You can't," Konstantin said without moving. "I need the car, and you need to do the rest of your interviews and meet with Stanislava."

I couldn't think of anything I wanted to do less and yet needed to do more. Closing the door to the office, I turned back to Konstantin, thrusting the car keys at him with one hand.

"You drive," I said. "I sleep. Wednesday, you will be silent, or else I will muzzle you."

*You and what army?* she demanded.

I turned toward her and looked down, thunderous. "I will have you know that I have been a world-class mercenary since the first century A.D. I have fought in over a thousand campaigns on six continents over nineteen hundred years. I have hunted the unhuntable, I have killed the unkillable, and I can *muzzle* a *cat* if I want to!" I said, towering over her. She looked up at me silently for a moment, unaffected. Konstantin's eyebrows were raised so high they were in danger of disappearing into his hairline. I glared at them both, daring them to say something.

*If you say so,* she said finally, turning to walk into the back room, tail swishing through the air.

"Don't you walk away from me!" I demanded.

Konstantin caught my arm. "Maybe let's not argue with the cat, Trillion," he said. "If you get too worked up, you won't be able to sleep on the way to the theatre. Speaking of which, why don't you go catch a hour nap on the cot in the back room? They're not expecting you until ten." The hint wasn't subtle.

I sighed. "Wednesday's fur is all over it," I said petulantly.

Konstantin pursed his lips, then opened a desk drawer. He slapped a lint roller into my hand. "I've got five more," he said. At my shocked look, he shrugged. "I've got fur sometimes. Plus you shed like a Husky in the spring." He leaned forward. "Are you sure you're just tired?" I scowled at him, but made for the back room anyway. If nothing else, I could lay there and pretend I wasn't worrying.

*Why are you back here?* Wednesday asked suddenly as I stepped into the room. I jumped, glaring down at her as she sat at my feet, her large eyes blinking. She looked at the lint roller in my hand. *What are you planning on doing with that?* she asked suspiciously

"Cleaning off the bed," I said. I managed three swipes before I got impatient. I looked down at Wednesday, who was staring very pointedly at me, the tip of her tail twitching back and forth as it was circled demurely around her feet. "What?"

*Nothing*, she said finally, walking out into the main office. Shaking my head, I scrubbed the cot as hard as I could for another next three seconds before giving up. Cat hair didn't show up on grey suits, right?

I remembered staring up at the ceiling for a moment, grumbling to myself, feeling as though I was never going to fall asleep. And then I was gone.

I hated sleeping during the day. It always seemed to mess with my regular schedule, and besides that, I had really odd dreams. In this dream, I turned over to look into the room, my eyes half closed. Not two feet away, level with my head, there was a floating box. I opened my eyes wide, as the box lifted higher and higher until I saw Wednesday, sitting on the floor, looking up at the box, her eyes ever so slightly luminous.

"Wednesday?" I whispered. "Are you doing that?"

Her eyes dropped down to meet mine, the box never wavering. She tilted her head to the side. *Yes*, she whispered back gently. *Close your eyes.*

"I'm dreaming," I whispered at her, closing my eyes.

*Probably*, she said quietly, *but that doesn't mean this isn't real.*

"That doesn't make any sense," I whispered, turning onto my back. I heard a gentle tinkling sound that I couldn't identify for a moment. Then, as my sleep deepened, I realized that it was Wednesday.

She was laughing.

\*\*\*

I woke up with cottonmouth and breath that could have killed a goat. I turned my head away from where Wednesday's tail was flicking my nose, trying to protect the semi-innocent from the withering smell. There was something buzzing. My phone. I reached around Wednesday into my pocket, and then I pulled it out.

Konstantin.

Was calling me?

"Hello?" I said, my voice cracking.

"This is your wake-up call. It is now nine-thirty. Please be ready to go in five minutes," Konstantin's cheerful voice chirped through the phone. Sighing, but not feeling as nearly as combative as I had an hour earlier, I sat up slowly, allowing Wednesday time to wake up and crawl down into my lap.

*Time to go?* she asked. I blinked and nodded.

"Yes," I yawned.

*Fine.* She paused for a long moment, and then stretched. And stretched. And stretched. When she finally reached approximately twice her original body length, she yawned, condensed back into her original size, and hopped off of my lap as I stood.

Konstantin was already ready to go, backpack slung over one shoulder, a comb and a disposable toothbrush held out to me in his opposite hand. Grabbing my own satchel, I accepted the comb and toothbrush, put the harness on Wednesday, and headed out to the car.

I didn't fall asleep in the car like I thought I would. However how much sleep I hadn't gotten that night, the hour that I had just gotten had helped my mood make a complete reversal. It was frankly a relief. Not just to me, either, I was sure.

It was a stark confirmation that I needed eight hours of sleep to function.

Rather than speak, I pulled out my notepad, looking around Wednesday as I went over the basic questions I was going to ask and the remaining members of the company that I had left to interview. My phone buzzed. Marya Leonidovna, asking when I would be there.

*I am less than fifteen minutes away,* I texted back, sending it. Her next message had an attachment.

*Here is the new roll list,* the text said. *You may proceed directly to the office that we have set aside for you.*

"Stanislava?" Konstantin asked.

I looked up from my phone, where I'd pulled up the new roster. "No, Marya Leonidovna. It's the new list that I have for today."

"Huh, any notable differences?" he asked. I looked down at the list. To my surprise, there was one. There, first on the list, was Giselle Carabosse.

"One big one," I said. "Apparently our main person of interest just got bumped up to the head of the line."

"Giselle?"

"Yep," I said. Looking down at the list, I cocked my head to the side. "I wonder why?"

We pulled into the theatre what seemed like only a moment later. As I got out, Wednesday hopped out beside me, picking her way daintily across the wet parking lot.

"No, Wednesday, you're not coming with me," I said, before she got more than a few steps away.

She looked up at me from beside an enormous muddy puddle, green eyes bright, even in the dull weather. *I thought you said I wouldn't stay with Konstantin today,* she said, an accompanying meow escaping from her throat.

"No, I said you wouldn't use his cell phone," I said, lifting her up and placing her back into the car despite her noise of protest. "I can't take you into the theatre with me, Wednesday."

She seemed to wilt a little bit.

*Oh. All right,* she said quietly, sitting down on the seat.

I ran my hand over her head. "You're a good girl, you know that?" I said. She looked up at me. I fully expected her to say something like 'of course I am' or 'I am the best girl.'

But she didn't. She didn't say anything, not even as I closed the door, and walked into the theatre. She just looked at me from the window, a little forlorn, as I turned to walk away.

I tried not to feel guilty. It didn't work very well.

I didn't even know why I was feeling guilty. I just...did.

It was those ridiculously large eyes. It must have been.

I would have thought that most of the dancers would have already arrived by the time I got there—it was ten in the morning, after all—but as I walked toward the entrance, Siegfried Handel came around the side of the building, holding his dance bag. He looked a little surprised when he saw me, but not particularly disturbed.

"Mr. Orris, back again?"

"Just a couple more interviews," I said, opening the door to the theatre. Siegfried's smile seemed to turn a little sad, but he shrugged.

"Makes sense. Hey, I hope this doesn't sound weird, but was that your cat in the parking lot just now?" he said, pointing back into the parking lot with his thumb.

I smiled, as if Wednesday could belong to anyone. "No, she's not," I said. "How come?"

Siegfried smiled. "She's really pretty. I like cats. Always wished I was home enough to keep one." He looked up at the clock, and his expression changed, as though he hadn't realized what time it was. "Well, I've got to get to practice."

"Good luck!" I said, watching him speed up to enter the practice room.

Following him at a much slower pace, I walked through the swinging doors, nodding to Marya Leonidovna who was prowling between the dancers. Watching them carefully, she called out small bits of instruction to each of the dancers in turn, Tchaikovsky soaring through the background. As I settled down into the chair in the office, there was a small rap at the door. I didn't look up.

"Enter," I said, pulling my notepad out, and—just as a precaution—stuffing my cell phone into the slender pocket on the outside of my satchel. Then I looked up, just in time to see Giselle Carabosse walk through the door. If I thought she was beautiful before, the only way to modify that was to say that she was absolutely radiant.

I stood. "Ms. Carabosse, thank you for meeting with me." She smiled a little uneasily while she shook my hand and nodded, saying nothing, and seated herself gracefully in the chair in front of me. "May we begin?" I asked.

"Yes," she said. Her voice was light, even if her expression wasn't, and I nodded in return, looking down at my paperwork.

"I have here that you were one of the last people to see Odell before she disappeared," I said.

Giselle nodded once. "Yes," she said. "At the party at the Old Mill. You probably know all this. Siegfried told me he told you about it."

I looked up at her. "I would like to hear your side," I said.

She looked uncomfortable for a moment, but then shook her head. "I don't know what to tell you—she felt kind of sick earlier that day. She wouldn't tell us why. She might have just been tired from the final performance. It takes a lot out of you, you know?" Giselle looked up at me. "Siegfried and I promised that we would take her home early so she'd come—she usually outlasts all of us once she actually gets to the parties."

She took a moment, as if lost in her thoughts. Then, she shook herself. "I'm sorry, I don't actually remember a lot about the night itself—at the time it seemed like a completely normal party. We went for a walk around the building of the Old Mill. At some point she said that she was going to head back and join the others. Siegfried and I stayed a little longer, just talking... When we got back, she wasn't there. Some people had left, so we thought she'd already gone home. So we left. Then, well, everything seemed to spiral downward from there. The police investigation, people here in the company, you. There's a lot to deal with." Giselle looked around at the office interior miserably.

"Was there anything that Odell did or said that made you think that she would... wander off? Maybe get lost on purpose?" I asked.

Giselle looked up at me sharply. "Of course not," she scoffed. "If you've looked into anything about her past, you'd know that she's never had any sort of mental health issues."

"Things can develop quickly under some circumstances. I understand that she lost out to a promotion because of you," I said.

She looked a little uncomfortable. "I suppose that's true," Giselle murmured. She surveyed the room slowly, sighing. "I don't know, Mr. Orris. She talked to me about everything. She wasn't the type to let things fester. She would talk it out if she could, and try and come to some sort of understanding. If she had a real issue with my position in the company, I feel like she would have talked to me about it. And she didn't."

I studied her. This was a woman who wanted to be heard. A woman who, by all appearances, looked like she had something to prove.

If she wanted to be heard, I would listen.

"What do you think happened to Odell?" I asked softly.

She sighed so deeply, for a moment I was worried that I had asked the wrong question."I don't *know*," she said emphatically. "All I know is that most of the company thinks that I'm responsible somehow, but why in the world would I have done anything to her? She wasn't messing around with my boyfriend, *I* was the one that got the promotion... why in the world would *I* do something to *her*?"

Well, she had me there. By all accounts, that was exactly right. The only thing that really tied Giselle to the case was the fact that she was the last person to see Odell. There was no motive, though.

No reason for her to make anything happen to her coworker. Giselle was looking over my shoulder again.

"I've had so many nightmares about it. I think if her body had turned up, it might have been easier, you know?" she said, her eyes filling with tears. "But no, we just get to live with her emptiness. Not knowing what's happened to her. Not knowing where she is." Wiping at her eyes, she shook her head and looked down.

I let us sit in silence for a moment.

"I thank you for your time, Ms. Carabosse. I do have one final question for this interview, at least for now."

"Please ask it," she said, looking up at me with tear-filled hazel eyes. Those eyes. For the briefest moment, it felt like I couldn't look away. But then she blinked, and the spell seemed to break. I glanced back down at my notes.

"Did you know that Odell was studying magic?" I asked.

Giselle paused for a moment, and seemed to think hard. "I suppose. She had been for a while, but she never really...confided in me about it. She was setting up plans for after she retired. I don't think she liked talking about it very much."

"You said that Odell was the type of person to face challenges head on," I reminded her. She shrugged, reminding me suddenly of her boyfriend.

"She was taking care of her own problems, but I didn't have anything to do with her magic. Since that was the case, she didn't really need to talk to me about it." Giselle paused, and shook her head. "Sorry, that sounded a bit defensive. I didn't think it was any of my business. I was glad that she was working toward something other than ballet."

"Because you thought she needed to?"

Giselle shrugged. "Because she had to. Her knees were going—ballet dancers tear their bodies apart for the dance. Some bodies simply go sooner than later. She was thirty-three. Not too far off from the average retirement age."

"You don't seem sympathetic."

"We all get there some day," she said simply, but unrepentantly. "Like I said, some bodies simply go sooner than later."

"I understand you are of elvish descent," I said.

She looked up, a little taken aback. "Yes. Why?"

"And you are in your nineties?"

She shifted a little bit. "I see you have done your research on me. May I ask what the point is? It's not as if that would be particularly old to *you*."

I ignored the jibe. "How long have you been dancing with the company?"

"Twenty years," she said, her voice suddenly cautious.

"Is it... possible," I said quietly, "that Odell did not talk to you about her concerns about winning the principle dancer spot, because she found you less than sympathetic?"

Giselle's face twisted in incredulity. "You think I rubbed it in? Lorded it over her? Do you think I drove her away?"

I put my hands up placatingly. "No, that wasn't what I was saying."

"Then what *were* you saying?"

Yes, Trillion, what *were* you saying? I took a deep breath. "Nothing," I said. "Forgive me. That was all the questions that I had, Ms. Carabosse. I thank you for your time."

She stood, the motion jerky. "I'm not responsible for this," she said sharply.

I shook my head. "I never said you were."

She looked down at me, a pronounced frown on her face. "See that you remember that," she growled, and left the room.

I sat there, a little concerned. Not that I could have expected much of a different reaction, particularly for the type of questions that I had asked, and yet... I was a little surprised. The fact was, Giselle had no particular motive to get rid of Odell. Giselle's relationship with Siegfried was going strong. Giselle had been the one to win the principal dancer spot. But Giselle was the one still here, and everyone still seemed to think she did it.

# 17

# IN WHICH SOMEONE FINALLY WANTS TO TALK

Leonora Dovcick sat under my gaze a couple of hours later, shifting uncomfortably. Every interview since Giselle's had been equally unhelpful in one way or another, and now that I was at the end of them, I suspected I was just as ready to be done with this interview as she was.

"I'm Trillion Orris," I said, holding out my hand. She took it and shook it. A decent handshake, for what it was worth. Confident, firm, but not overbearing.

"Well, my name is on your call sheet right there, but I'm Leonora Dovcick," she said, smiling tentatively.

I returned the gesture. "Good to meet you, such as the circumstances are."

She nodded in return. "I've heard a lot about you," she said.

I raised my eyebrows. "Oh really?"

"You're a bit of legend in the magical world, you know. Especially around here," she said, blushing a little. At my confused expression, she smiled and waved her hand. "Don't worry about it. There just isn't a lot of—" she glanced up at me. "You know what, never mind. It's fine."

"You're all right," I said, still a little mystified. Looking down at my interview questions, and then back up at Leonora, I studied her for a moment. I had experienced pretty much everything over the course of the last two days. Indifference from most members of the corps, outright antagonism whether toward me or Giselle from others, and from a select few like Siegfried, welcome.

Leonora displayed none of these. In fact, I didn't quite know what was going through her head. Was it earnestness? No, that would have implied that she knew something that she wanted to tell me. Maybe she did? Or maybe she wanted to hear something from me?

I suddenly realized I hadn't talked in a very long time.

Thank goodness Wednesday wasn't here. I could almost hear her little voice whispering in the back of my head: *Say something. Look at her, she's practically dancing in her chair.*

*Shush*, I thought back to Imaginary Wednesday. I spent enough time being bossed around by her in person, I didn't need to do it to myself.

"I've heard from several people in the company that you were quite close to Odell," I said.

Leonora looked up, and nodded. "Yes," she said, "I knew her for almost ten years. We trained together at school."

"The University of Utah?"

"Yes."

"That's a good school," I remarked.

She nodded. "We both worked really hard to get there. And stay there," she added. "I worked a night job to put myself through."

"And Odell?" I asked.

"Scholarship," she said matter-of-factly. "I've never met someone with grades so high. As far as I know, she never paid for any of her schooling."

"A hard worker in general, then?" I said.

"At everything she did. Does. It's probably why she got hurt last year."

"I haven't heard about that," I said, frowning.

"As far as I know, it's not super relevant to your case," Leonora admitted. "She was up for principle dancer, and was practicing hard. Like ten and twelve hours a day. One night while she was practicing on her own, she tore the meniscus in her right knee and was out for two months. She fully recovered, and even danced a bit at the end of the season when she was back up to speed, but that sort of thing can damage your chances at being principle."

"They want people without injury?"

"Not necessarily," Leonora said. "But even after Odell said she recovered, when she was tired she walked with a little bit of a limp. And sometimes you could tell when she danced. I don't know whether she just pushed herself beyond what she should have, or it was psychosomatic, but it was there. Only when she got tired, though," she finished, a little defensively.

I smiled. "I believe you," I said. "You said you were close to Odell. Did she ever complain or worry about Giselle to you?"

Leonora looked a little uncomfortable. "Not... really."

"Oh?"

Leonora sighed. "Look, Giselle is—or, well, *was*—one of the nicest people alive before all of this. She's smart and witty, and I know that she never meant to hurt Odell or anything, but every once in a while, she could be a little callous. Not because she's mean spirited or anything. I just don't think she really understood. The woman is ninety years old, and she looks like she's in her thirties. Elvish blood, and all that. No offense to you, of course, Mr. Orris."

I nodded. "Of course not."

Leonora nodded and looked down. "Anyway it... well, I can only think of the one time, and I wasn't there for it personally, but after everything with Odell's knee, Giselle apparently said something that implied that Odell should have had another twenty years in her before she started experiencing injuries. Like Odell was somehow deficient because she wasn't of elvish descent. I highly doubt Giselle meant it that way, but Odell seemed to take it personally for a while. She's always been a little private about her personal struggles. Having it laid bare like that must have rubbed her the wrong way."

I frowned, letting it sink in. Something pricked in my memory. "You said that Giselle 'was' one of the nicest people alive? Did something change?"

Leonora frowned. "It—I'm sorry, it wasn't the best way I could have put it. Giselle has taken everything really hard. She's become really irritable in the last couple of months. That's probably why everyone thinks she did it."

"Do you?"

Leonora's silence was telling, but she shook her head. "I don't know. If I went off only the way she was acting now, yes, maybe. But...why would she do it? What in the world would she gain by bumping off someone she'd already beat in every aspect of her life?"

I shook my head. "I think if I had the answer to that, I would know where Odell was." There was another moment of silence between us. "Well, I don't want to keep you too long, but I do have one last question," I said.

"Of course," Leonora said.

"Did you know that Odell was studying magic?" I asked.

Leonora looked up in surprise. "How did *you* find out?" she blurted.

I'd take that as a yes.

"The police allowed me to go into Odell's apartment," I explained. "She had quite a few reference books."

WEDNESDAY'S BOOK · 141

Leonora looked a little concerned, but nodded. "Yeah, she was going to university."

"The University of Maryland?"

The ballet dancer nodded again. "Yeah, Odell was in her fourth year. She was supposed to sit the exam last month." Her voice was small and troubled.

Flipping my memo book back to Odell's page, I searched through the facts. "I had that she was supposed to sit in July," I said, a little confused.

Leonora's troubled expression turned downright worried. "It was originally July, but she put it off because she didn't feel like she was ready. Why, who did you hear that from?" she asked. Then, thinking for a moment, she squinted at me suspiciously. "Was it Siegfried?"

"Yes," I said, a little surprised, "how did you know?"

She smiled ruefully. "He was close to Odell. Not like, you know, dating her or anything, he's definitely attached to Giselle, but I've never seen her open up to anyone like that, particularly in the month before she disappeared. It was kind of a sudden thing, now that I think about it. I don't think they'd talked to each other much before he got sick in June."

"He was sick?" I asked.

Leonora nodded hummed in agreement. "For about three weeks, about six months ago? He had the flu, but apparently it went to his lungs. No one here will talk about it, but he's only really just come back to where he was before."

"Why won't anyone talk about it?"

Leonora looked a little subdued. "I guess it hits too close to home right now? I mean, Siegfried getting super sick, and then Odell disappearing? There's such a thing as too much loss—or even potential loss—for one group in less than a year."

"I wonder why Siegfried didn't mention it," I said. "He and Giselle starting dating right before he got sick?"

"Right after," Leonora corrected me. "I don't know many of the details—I'm not as close to either of them." I nodded, making a note. "Do you mind if I ask why that's relevant?" she asked.

"I'm not sure," I admitted. But it did seem relevant. It seemed very relevant, and I had no idea why. I didn't like it. Everywhere I turned, it was as though I was running into things that should have made sense, and I was just missing one obvious part of the puzzle.

To put it simply, it bugged me.

"Is there anything else that you need from me?" Leonora asked after a moment.

I looked up and shook my head. "Thank you, no. I think I have all I need for now." Pulling a business card out, I handed it to her. "Please let me know if you think of anything else that might be helpful," I said. She smiled, a little subdued, and nodded. We stood, and she held out her hand. I took it.

"For sure. Mr. Orris, I really hope you find her. She's...she's my friend," Leonora said.

I shook her hand. "I'll do everything I can, Ms. Dovcick," I said.

"Thank you," she said quietly. Then she slipped through the door. From there, I packed up all my things, checked my phone—no texts or calls—and left the office just as practice finished. The dancers left the barre and Leonora went straight to her bag, not really making eye contact with anyone. Giselle and Siegfried were off to one side, drinking from their water bottles and murmuring to each other. Neither looked very happy.

Marya Leonidovna saw me from across the room and approached, pausing briefly to make a comment to a couple of dancers along the wall as she passed them.

"So?" she said, her voice clipped.

"I have completed my interviews," I told her.

"And you will visit the Councilwoman now?" she asked. I noticed that her voice had changed a bit.

"That was Ms. Carabosse's request," I confirmed.

She seemed to think about that for a moment. "It is a good thing," she said finally. Looking across the practice floor, she looked at Giselle—the Councilwoman's daughter—her mouth pinched.

"Poor girl," she said, shaking her head.

I looked over at her strangely. "I was under the impression that Giselle is in her nineties," I said. Marya Leonidovna looked at me, neither amused nor offended, and motioned for me to walk with her. I followed.

"She is one of my dancers, Mr. Orris," she said. "That in and of itself places her under my care and concern." We walked out of the practice room, pausing by the ticket desks. One by one, the dancers started to filter past us and out the door into the dying light.

"You make it sound as though it's more than that," I said.

The producer shook her head a little sadly. "Unfortunately so. Giselle used to be very different," she said quietly, watching the dancers leave.

"How different?" I asked. Marya Leonidovna sighed.

"She used to be happy," she said simply. "And then Odell went missing. It all just seems to have gotten into her head. Even her dancing has suffered because of all of this. She's making more mistakes, and because of that she is hard on herself. Which makes her make more mistakes, and she's even harder on herself." Just then, the woman herself pushed through the swinging doors walking fast, her expression stormy. Siegfried followed Giselle at a slower pace, seemingly unconcerned. The older woman beside me shook her head.

"I do not mean to sound overly sentimental, Mr. Orris," she said. "I don't know whether Giselle is involved like so many in the company believe, but for Giselle's sake, not to mention the ballet itself, I hope you get to the bottom of this very, very soon."

"I will do my best," I promised. She straightened. I did as well, lifting my chin and squaring my shoulders instinctively. She was taller than me—probably six foot four, compared with my six foot two—and a part of me didn't quite know what to do about it.

"Good," she said regally, and swept back toward the offices.

In the next couple of moments, I had placed a call to Violente, Stanislava's assistant, who confirmed that I could speak to Stanislava if I was able to arrive within the hour. A couple of moments after that, I walked out of the theatre.

Konstantin was already there, idling in front of the entrance. I was surprised to see Siegfried leaning through the passenger side window. When I got a little closer, I saw he was reaching out to Wednesday, who was leaning so far away from Siegfried's hand without actually moving that she was in danger of falling over into the cup holder.

"Hey there," I said, approaching.

Siegfried looked back at me and flashed me a brilliant smile. "Hey. I just saw your friend and his cat here, and I couldn't help but say hello."

*Hello. Now he can leave.* Wednesday's voice was curt and uncomfortable, and despite the fact that Siegfried was only trying to pet her, I suddenly felt the need to step in.

"Yeah, Wednesday's not always too fond of strangers," I said, as apologetically as I could manage, stepping closer to the door. "She's usually a sweet little thing when she's had time to get used to you."

Wednesday made a noise in her throat at the man looking reaching through the window, one that I couldn't quite interpret.

Siegfried took the hint and moved back, allowing me to open the door.

"No worries," he said, smiling, glancing over at Wednesday. "I suppose you won't be coming around anymore?"

"Probably not," I said. "Not unless I have more questions."

Siegfried nodded easily. "Fair enough. Well, I hope you find lots of answers very soon, Trillion." He held out his hand. I took it, shook it, and then closed the door, rolling up the window. Konstantin looked a little troubled as he drove the car away.

"What is it?" I asked.

He didn't answer for a moment, as if he was thinking. Then he shrugged. "I think Siegfried kind of creeps me out."

I laughed. "What? Why?"

Konstantin shook his head as if mystified. "He's just so...perfect. He's exactly what you would expect a dancer to be. Not to mention the fact that he's weirdly obsessed with cats. He made a beeline to the car when he saw me out here, and immediately started asking questions about Wednesday. Where I found her, what her name was."

"Did you tell him?" I asked, unaccountably disturbed by the prospect.

Konstantin shook his head. "She's not really my cat, but I told him she was found, and her name was Wednesday. That's as far as we got before you arrived."

*I did not like him*, Wednesday grumbled, stepping into my lap, pressing into my chest. *He was... too keen.*

"You mean you've finally had enough attention?" I joked. She flicked her tail under my nose. Direct hit. I sneezed.

*I only accept affection from people of my choosing. It's the law of consent*, she said.

I looked down at her, raising my eyebrows. "You're a cat," I pointed out.

*Just because my physical form is currently a cat doesn't mean that I can't communicate*, she said sweetly, tightening her claws into my leg.

"Ow, ow, ow! Okay, point taken," I gasped. Releasing her claws, she stepped forward and bunted her head into one of my raised palms. Scratching her head with one hand, and rubbing my punctured leg with the other, I looked over at Konstantin.

"So what did you two do today?" I asked, trying not to wince at the residual pain.

*Developed my thumbs*, Wednesday said, a distinctively mischievous tone filtering through her words.

"Ha ha," I said, looking down at her. "What about you, Konstantin?"

He shrugged. "There wasn't too much for me to do on Odell's case, so I decided to work a little bit more on Rothbart's case, and looked into the area where we found the trail."

"Anything big?"

"I'm not sure. The more I looked into it, it looks like Rothbart's trail leads directly to the Old Mill building, like the other magical residue we found. In fact, it practically follows the other trail step by step."

A horrible coldness settled in my stomach. "There's no chance that Rothbart could change the scent of his magic, could he? And somehow be both?"

Konstantin paused before he shook his head. "No, magical scent is as separate as DNA." He paused. "I identified the other magical scent, though, Trillion," he said, his voice uncomfortable. "It's Odell's. I don't know what happened, but whatever it was, it was huge. If she's not dead, then she had to be pretty close when she left there."

I sat there, unable to think of a proper response. My next thought left me feeling like I'd been punched in the chest.

"Konstantin, that trail was *new*," I said. "When we found it two weeks ago, you said it was only about a week old."

He nodded uncomfortably. "It's more than that. Trillion, I've been thinking about it, and I'm not sure how to tell you this... but I think—oh, we're here." He pulled into the short road to the gatehouse. I stared at him, desperately wanting him to finish his sentence.

"Name?" the guard asked.

"Trillion Orris and Konstantin Vorkowitz," Konstantin said, displaying his Private Investigator badge. He glanced back at me, and the fluffy animal in my lap. "And cat."

Wednesday made a smug noise.

"Mr. Orris is expected. Mr. Vorkowitz, you will be required to wait. With your cat," the guard said.

I frowned, but Konstantin looked almost relieved. "Okay," he said, nodding.

The guard nodded in return, waving us through the gate. "Welcome to The Manor."

# 18

# IN WHICH I GAIN AN UNLIKELY PATRON AND MEET WITH A COMPLICATION

If there was one thing I consistently forgot, it was that Stanislava Carabosse was absolutely terrifying.

I had run into her several times over the last hundred and fifty years. The first time was watching her dance in Paris. The second was when she had emigrated to the United States shortly before the first World War. Since then we'd bumped into each other several times over the past fifty years as I had briefly dated Solange—admittedly for a case—and then at various political events as I had striven to get the police department to let me take on the magical investiga-

WEDNESDAY'S BOOK · 149

tive work. She had eventually taken my side, a commendation which had helped me win my point.

However, each and every time I met her in person it was as though I had walked into the room containing an empress. She was waiting for me in the parlor. Regal, with dark brown hair the same shade as her daughter's swept with grey, and eyes black as ebony. She sat majestically, radiating the feeling that she was doing one a favor by allowing them to meet with her.

It wasn't far from the truth.

I appreciated her as a councilwoman to the city. She was deeply involved with the politics and running of the city. Although she had never served as mayor, she was able to provide perspective at the best of times, and specific pointed warnings during the worst. And though phrased like warnings, everyone knew they were carefully veiled threats. Not toward the person themselves, but the fallout that they might cause. She was also the undisputed leader of the Domovoi chapter in the United States. In matters of magic, they answered to her, and if lines were crossed there were consequences.

Usually legal ones, which meant I became involved.

In a way, she was my most consistent employer.

"Councilwoman," I said.

Dark eyes met mine, and a soft smile crossed her face. She stood and held out her hand, clothed in a black glove. "Mr. Orris. It's been three years, hasn't it?" she said, her tone pleasant.

"Since the Gregorii case, yes," I confirmed.

She nodded deeply. "I appreciate your assistance in the case. I hope you have not been kept too busy since then?"

"Just my long-term cases," I said, trying to smile sincerely. "And then, as you know, Ms. Richardson's case."

"Yes," she said a little distantly. Then she blinked, and was once again present. "Violente said that you had finished your interviews.

As I said yesterday, I would like to hear your thoughts on the matter."

I nodded, thinking for a moment before I spoke. I had learned quickly over the years that she preferred silence to verbal brainstorming. I was more than happy to be silent for a moment to collect my thoughts rather than scrabble around, spewing about the weather until there was something meaningful to contribute.

"I find I am somewhat confused, Councilwoman," I said, looking over at her. Her head moved, the tiniest tip of her head to the side. Intrigue.

"Explain," she responded.

I took another moment to think. How was I supposed to tell her that I didn't have any evidence or motive, but I thought her daughter—her only child, and principle of her ballet company—was somehow involved or responsible?

For a moment, I wished Stanislava wasn't the type to wait for me. I wanted her to interrupt, start throwing out suppositions, to start asking questions of me that would keep me from dropping this frankly unpleasant bomb in her lap. But no. I was just going to have to man up and lay out my theory.

"So far, I do not have any particular evidence, but I have one primary suspect in mind. However, I am a little worried that you will be displeased with the result."

She sat back a little, chin raising a fraction of an inch. "I will withhold my opinion until the end of your case summary, Trillion," she said quietly. "Please share your theory."

"Well, going by the interviews that I have conducted, and looking at the facts of the case, I think it is unlikely that Odell disappeared on her own. There were enough inducements for her to stay—her job, which everyone said she loved, as well as the fact that she was in school, which she was almost finished with. Her mother lived here, and they had a good relationship. According to her criminal record, and a review of her financial records, she wasn't in abnormal debt, or owed anyone money, and she had good relationships with her friends and coworkers."

"That implies that there is no reason why she is gone."

"I can find no motive why she would disappear," I agreed.

Stanislava looked at me, dark eyes glittering in the light from the chandelier. "And?"

"And no reason why someone would take her, either," I said.

"So we have a missing girl, with no reason why she should be missing?" she summarized. I nodded in uncomfortable confirmation. She assessed me carefully. "You have said nothing that would make me unduly upset. Which makes me think you have a suspect that I could take issue with."

"Yes. Now, I already said I have no motive. I cannot prove anything yet, but—"

"But you think it is Giselle," Stanislava said softly.

Clenching my jaw, I nodded once. "Yes, I do," I said quietly.

Stanislava narrowed her eyes. "I agree."

...what?

I blinked, pretty sure that I had misheard her.

"Excuse me?" I said.

Her expression didn't change—a solemn, leveling look that pierced into my soul. "I agree with you," she repeated quietly. Rising to her feet, she walked toward the window, and looked out on her snowy grounds. I rose to my feet as well, but stayed where I was, simply watching her. As I watched, she seemed to collapse a little, her age pulling her down at the shoulders, bowing her frame. I didn't speak. It was my turn to wait until she explained. At length, she did.

"My daughter has changed, Trillion," she whispered, only audible because of my elvish hearing. "Ever since she was born, she has been like the sun. Bright, brilliant, not afraid to speak her mind, living with her arms wide open... Not anymore. Ever since Odell disappeared she has been irritable and withdrawn. Sharp. We've argued like we have never argued. It's possible that she is just... affected by Odell's disappearance, but..."

"But it seems as though it goes beyond that."

Stanislava sighed and turned back to me. "I believe that Giselle thinks that she is responsible. Whether or not that turns out to be the case is your purview." She looked me in the eye and straightened. In the blink of an eye, the years seemed to melt away, the glimmer of tears that I thought I saw turning into the rock solid self assurance.

I smiled.

"Is that why you had Odell's mother retain us?" I asked.

She didn't smile, but her eyes did, a deep satisfaction crossing her face. Her response was quiet. "How did you know?"

"Odell's mother doesn't have the financial resources," I explained. "My partner and I looked into both Odell and her mother's financial situation to rule the mother out. And then we found out that you knew each other. I knew you were the financial backer for certain when I started speaking to the ballet company. You're a major patron, you're involved with the ballet company on a regular basis and, most of all, until a few months ago, you and your daughter had a very good relationship. I think you're trying to preserve whatever you can of that. Hiring us yourself would have been as good as accusing Giselle yourself. That would be a disaster if she's innocent, so you reached out to Mrs. Richardson, who was just as invested as you were. Bottom line, you both want to save your daughters."

There was another moment of silence, and then a smile finally creeped up one cheek. "It seems like I have hired the right person. I trust that I can rely on your discretion?" she asked.

"You can rely on me," I said. I paused, thinking over my next question. "Stanislava, do you have any evidence of any guilt other than her altered mood?"

She shook her head. "If I did, I would have moved forward with the investigation myself," she said. "As much as I love my daughter, I am not afraid of her. Or her boyfriend, for that matter."

I frowned. "Is there something I should know about Siegfried?"

She sighed. "I would be lying if I said I liked the man. He's been with the company for about five years, and always seemed nice on the outside, but he has deteriorated on closer acquaintance. I will caveat that and say I'm not sure whether it's on his own merit or whether it's simply because he's dating my daughter, but I am quite sure he's not helping Giselle's mental state."

I shifted, thinking of how he leaned into the car after Wednesday as she leaned away. "Is he abusive?"

"I doubt that he would pay that much attention to her," she said simply. "Trillion, I'm not one to mince words. He puts in the lip service to try to convince me that he loves Giselle, but I've never seen anyone more concerned with what he wants and needs at the expense of others. If this was Giselle of six months ago, I do not believe she would put up with him. But Giselle, so affected now…" Her frown deepened. "Let me be clear—I don't think he is involved, but I think he has taken the situation from bad to worse."

"I understand," I said, nodding. She looked out the window again.

"Thank you for your investigation, Trillion," she said finally. "Please let me know if there is any way that I might assist you. Contact Violente, and she will get word to me."

It was a dismissal, but not an unkind one.

"I will," I said, inclining my head to her. "Please let me know if there is anything that I might further help with."

She looked up at me, dark eyes glistening. "All I ask is you find the truth."

I could feel the weight of the steady, but breathless, words. The possible repercussions behind them.

There was nothing that I could say, so instead of saying anything,

I inclined my head once more and turned to go. I made my way slowly through the house, following Maxwell the attendant at a reasonable but subdued pace.

The cold night wind hit me in a teeth-chattering blast, and I pulled my coat a little tighter around myself. I could see Wednesday in the passenger side window, watching for me. I smiled, wishing for the first time that I could keep her. My heart stopped a little as the thought cemented itself in my mind.

It wasn't a good idea. I couldn't keep her, and there were a thousand reasons why. I knew that.

Walking toward the car, I pulled the door open. Wednesday was already chattering a million miles a minute, short meows punctuating the air every couple of words.

*I missed you. Did you know it's a crescent moon tonight? We'll be able to see it in the in the morning if we get up early. It's supposed to be really big. I missed you. It was boring today at the office. I didn't like the guy who tried to touch me today. He smelled wrong.*

"Hello, Wednesday," I said, running my hand over her head fondly. She pressed into it, just a little, and I smiled.

"How did the interview go? You look a little...depressed," Konstantin asked, turning the car on. Picking up Wednesday, I slid into the car, pulling the door closed behind me. I sighed.

"Stanislava didn't take the news about Giselle well?" he guessed, pulling the car around the driveway and past the gate.

I shook my head. "No. She agrees."

"What?" Konstantin asked, turning fully to look at me as he stopped at the entrance to the road.

I frowned, looking over at him. "She agrees that Giselle is most likely responsible for Odell's disappearance," I repeated. "She's funding Mrs. Richardson's inquiry with us. She hopes to find Giselle's innocence, but will also to bring her to justice if necessary."

Konstantin's expression turned into one of absolute incredulity and confusion. "She did not."

"She did."

"Scary Stanislava?"

"Scary Stanislava," I confirmed. Wednesday chirped. Konstantin looked down at her, and then seemed to realize that he was still driving a car. Pulling out into the street, he shook his head in utter disbelief.

"The things you learn about people," he said. "Did you learn else anything that we didn't know?"

"Apparently Siegfried is a bit of a narcissist," I said. "Stanislava doesn't like him."

"Does she like anyone?" Konstantin asked under his breath. He shook his head. "I'm not surprised. He was a bit aggressive about petting Wednesday earlier, even though her body language was obviously not thrilled."

*I was going to bite him*, Wednesday confirmed seriously from my lap. *He smelled weird. I did not want him to touch me.*

There was something about her tone that unsettled me. I found myself frowning. "Good for you," I said sincerely, scratching her head. "You can bite him any time you like."

The rest of the car ride to the office was spent catching up on the interview. Konstantin was staying another night at the office, but Wednesday and I needed to head home sooner rather than later. The fatigue that I had felt earlier in the day was starting to drag on me, and I was going to be perfectly useless if we waited up much longer.

The parking lot was empty when we pulled up. It wasn't super surprising. The bookshop next to us closed at five thirty, and the Russian-Mexican fusion restaurant a couple doors down had closed that summer. After a habitual glance, my mind turned back to business. I didn't want to spend too long here—I was ready to get home.

Konstantin parked in his regular spot outside the front of the building. The boarded up windows of the vacant boutique underneath us reflected the light of the headlights back at us before Konstantin turned off the car, plunging the parking lot into darkness. I clipped Wednesday's leash to the back of her harness, looping the leash handle around my wrist.

"Come on," I said. "You might as well stretch your legs and relieve yourself while we're here, it's a little ways back to the house."

*Okay*, Wednesday said, hopping down from the car onto the wet asphalt. I was going to have little wet kitty prints all over my car later, but under the circumstances I was having a hard time caring.

Konstantin got out, clicking the lock button as I got to the door that led up to the agency. I patted my pockets for a moment before I remembered that Konstantin had my keys. Laughing at myself a little, and shaking my head, I turned back to Konstantin, who was making his way up the walkway.

"Do you have my—"

I never finished. In an incredibly bright flash, combined with a deafening blast that smashed me up against the door, my car exploded.

# 19

## IN WHICH A PROBLEMATIC INDIVIDUAL IS MORE PROBLEMATIC STILL

I wasn't sure which woke me—the ringing in my ears, or the million burning scratches on every exposed piece of skin. Magic crackled around me, from both within me as my body tried to heal itself, and without, as if it was in the very air. My gift had awakened—identifying the threat. Magic. Lots of it. It had destroyed my—I cracked open my eyes, squinting at the blazing fireball that used to be my car.

For a split second, I felt the keen sting as I mourned the vehicle. Then, as my hearing started to clear, the popping and swoosh of the flames becoming audible, I heard moaning fill the air.

Konstantin.

I jerked my head up, pushing away the pain as vehemently as I could manage, dragging myself to my feet, ignoring the buzz of magic about me. Was it the air? I saw the small bits of ash falling from the sky. No, it was from the explosion. My head swam and my ears began ringing again, but I stumbled down the steps, dodging bits of burning detritus, trying to get to my friend.

"Konstantin," I gasped, dropping to my knees beside him. He lay on his back, blood streaked across his face, breathing shallow and irregular. My heart clenched, and I did a once over. Like me, blood created a patchwork of wet and dry all over his body. Unlike me, however, he hadn't been even partially shielded by the distance or the overhang of the building.

Blood was spreading fast across his clothes. He was going to die if I didn't do something. I quickly stripped the grey jacket off my back and packed it against the largest wounds that I could see, avoiding as much shrapnel as I could.

My hands were shaking, but my training was starting to override my panic. I had spent the last two millennia with my face toward war, and I knew how to stare it down. I knew what to do. My hands worked quickly. Muscle memory was taking over, stilling the shaking as I moved.

"Stay with me, my friend," I said quietly, trying to be reassuring. I could see blood on the side of his face, trickling from his ear. His eardrum, at least the one on my side, had likely been ruptured. Could he even hear me? Sliding the cellphone from my pants pocket where it had miraculously survived both the blast and my fall, I pressed three numbers and held it up to my ear.

"911 Operator, my name is Mindy, what is the nature of your emergency?"

"Hello, this is Trillion Orris. My car exploded outside Orris Investigations. 527 Bohemian Avenue. My friend sustained multiple injuries. He's in bad shape."

WEDNESDAY'S BOOK - 159

"I have police and two ambulances on their way," she said. Her voice sounded muffled, as if there was something blocking her voice. Hearing damage of my own, I realized. As the woman on the phone kept on speaking, I looked down at Konstantin. His lips were moving. I couldn't hear anything. A pinprick of fear spread through my chest. Was my hearing getting worse?

But no, he was mouthing words.

"I can't hear you, Konstantin," I said taking the phone away from my ear. In the distance, I could hear sirens begin to wail. His lips moved again, and this time I could hear the rasp of air between his lips. Still no words.

"What?" I asked, leaning close to him. Leaning so his lips were right by my ear, I listened carefully over the crackling of the fire.

"Rothbart," he whispered laboriously. "Smell Rothbart."

He started to cough, the wet noise tearing at my soul.

"Okay, Rothbart was responsible," I said. "Don't talk anymore, Konstantin. The ambulance is coming." Minutely, he shook his head, grasping at my arm. There was something in his hands. Keys. Taking them gently from him, I leaned down almost involuntarily to hear.

"Wednesday," he whispered. I shot back up, looking around for the white and brown cat. She was nowhere to be found. I couldn't believe that I had forgotten her. I hadn't seen her—Konstantin grasped at my arm again.

"Trillion," he whispered. "Wednesday. Smell."

I drew back, shaking my head, completely lost. "What?" Konstantin's eyes were drifting closed. The sirens were almost present. I could hear the 911 dispatcher through the phone, but I ignored it. Konstantin's grip pulled me back one more time.

"Wrong. Help her."

Konstantin's body relaxed just as the first ambulance screamed into the parking lot, followed by two police cars and a fire truck. No, no, no! I ignored them, feeling for a pulse, my head light with shock and worry. The small thrum, thrum of his heart was still there. Weak, but still there.

There was only one thing left to do.

Every elf is creature of magic. We are born with it, and it grows with us as we age, honed and refined as our individual talents solidify. There are two sides to every gift.

Reaching within myself, placing my hand on top of Konstantin's head, I pulled a tendril of magic away from my core, tearing it away from where the magic was trying to heal me. As if trying to suction gel through a straw, I pulled it and pushed it, ripping it away from that center until it reached the palm of my hand that rested on Konstantin's forehead. It hurt. It hurt more than any other wound that I had, as it fought to heal me first, but I didn't hesitate. I forced it away, sending the jolt of magic into him.

Almost immediately his breathing began to ease, and as the ambulance worker ran up, the emergency worker took in the scene. He seemed to understand immediately.

"Can you heal him?" the EMT asked. I shook my head, shuddering as I broke contact.

"No," I gritted out. "Just keep him from dying."

The EMT's expression hardened in determination. "I can work with that," he said. "Don't you go dying on me either," he ordered as I slumped back to the side. Pain started to burn through every limb, and I gritted my jaw, shivering violently against the sudden cold.

"Jamie, get out here!" the EMT barked, examining Konstantin, shining a light in his eyes. A woman came running, kit in hand. The world was swimming. And then spinning.

Hands on my shoulders.

"Mr. Orris? Mr. Orris! Trillion!" My name brought my eyes open. The female EMT was looking down at me. The bright light shone in my eyes, causing me to blink and look away. As I did, I looked down across the parking lot. Flames flickered from the carcass of the car, smoke billowing from the glowing pyre.

The light burned an imprint into my eyes. I squeezed them shut, and fell into unconsciousness.

*"Trillion?"*

*I stared out at the forest, the green of the trees slowly giving way to oranges, yellows, and reds which glowed in the light of the dying sun. I looked back, looking at the tall man who had entered. The cold of the castle seemed to only be exacerbated by the refracted light that filtered through the uneven panes of glass. The man was not smiling, and I did not smile back at him.*

*"Father," I said, turning back to the twilight forest. King Auberon walked forward toward me, the jewels laid into the circlet on his brow winking in the subdued light.*

*"You are displeased with me." It was a statement, not a question.*

*"Not so much with you," I said. "Your decision."*

*"It was not my decision," he said softly. "The Lady wished it for herself."*

*"Luther will not understand," I said quietly. Father scoffed a little, and stepped up to stand beside me.*

*"Luther chooses not to understand," he corrected me. "The Lady has tried to speak with him about it. It seems that Luther is resistant to the idea entirely."*

*"The Lady is his mother, Father," I said. "It is not unreasonable for him to be against the idea of her dying."*

*Father didn't say anything to that, his expression hardening as he stared out at the forest. "I have tried everything," he said quietly. "Every argument, every plea I could think of. She is not convinced. She... believes that it is her time."*

*I frowned, but nodded. The Lady—a Bavarian baroness—was almost one hundred years old, an almost unspeakable age in this time. Father had met her just after her twentieth birthday, on a visit with her British uncle through the counties. Bright, intelligent, and spellbound by the elvish community, she had married him.*

*She loved us deeply, but had always been keenly aware and respectful of her own mortality. She had never expected or, it seemed, wanted to live past her allotment of days. It was something that none of the rest of us had apparently been quite willing to accept, especially the son of her body, Luther. My half-brother.*

*"I have kept her alive this long," my father said quietly, "but she has begun to decline. If she does not choose to transform now, she will be gone before winter begins."*

*Pain poured through my heart. Struggling to control my expression, I stared out at the dim landscape. Father noticed.*

*"You have not kept your distance as you ought," he said. His tone was worried. One more concern he had to address. I shouldn't have felt ashamed, not after seventeen centuries, and yet here I was.*

*"I have not become closer than was necessary," I disagreed.*

*"Trillion—"*

*"Father," I responded, almost as quickly. "I have survived this long. I have learnt my boundaries."*

*"Have you?" he responded. I cast a long look at him, and he fell silent. After a while, watching the last of the sunlight disappear, and the cold blue of night fall across the land, I spoke.*

*"I will speak to Luther," I said. Father looked up.*

*"Do you think he will listen to you?" he asked.*

*"I do not know. He has been willing before," I said, frowning.*

*More than once. The sixty-year-old man was still in his youth, even as a half-blood. We had grown close as brothers. He often looked to me for advice. Would he continue to do so?*

*Father looked a little pained.*

*"What are your thoughts, Father?" I asked. Father looked down and shook his head, the frown remaining firm on his face.*

*"I worry about your connection to him," he said. "I wonder—"*

"*I doubt that Æbba was referring to brotherly connections, Father,*" I said quietly. He turned sharply.

"*Do not dismiss curses out of hand, my son,*" he said, his voice a razor balanced on the edge. "*I will lose one of my loved ones this year. Do not subject me to two.*"

I tightened my jaw. "*I cannot remain aloof forever, Father,*" I said quietly. "*Do you not think I crave companionship as much as the next? That I do not wish for a family of my own?*"

"*The curse was clear, Trillion,*" my father said quietly. "*Care will kill you.*"

"*I am aware of my future,*" I said tightly.

"*Are you?*" he challenged. I looked up at him. Before I could answer, the door to the room opened wide. A young man with jet black hair strode in, clad in a fine black cloak. He was, it seemed, already in mourning for his mother.

"*Luther,*" Father said. The young man scowled.

"*How could you let her do this?*" he demanded. "*Father, it isn't fair!*" Father seemed to swallow. In that moment, I saw him retreat a little into himself. Was he afraid of Luther?

"*Your mother has chosen for herself,*" he said, a little stiffly. "*Nothing has been able to persuade her.*"

Luther looked a little taken aback at the admission, but no less fired up.

"*Well, try harder! There is no reason for her to die! She has lived in the Elven Hall all her adult life! Why should she choose to leave it so soon?*" Luther's voice broke a little. Father's expression went stony.

"*I do not know, my son. But she will not change her mind.*"

"*Try harder!*" The phrase was almost a shriek, born of childish desperation.

"*Luther!*" Father's chastisement cracked like thunder in the stone hall. The young man took a step back as the majesty of my father's station and *power became visible for a brief moment. I looked away quickly, but Luther froze, as if turned to stone.*

*Silence reigned as the young man's hard breaths turned to sobs, coming to himself, the imprint of King Auberon's power burned into his mind. Youthful face twisting in fury, he shook his head, limbs trembling from the magic's after effects.*

*"How could you?" he sobbed. Father simply watched him recover, expression thunderous, unspeaking. I could read the elf king's expression—what Luther's words had cost him, the pain and powerlessness that he undoubtedly felt. Did Luther know that? I stepped forward to explain, reaching out to him. Luther turned to me, and recoiled from my hand.*

*"Don't touch me!" he screamed. "None of you understand! None of you!" With that, he fled from the room.*

*I moved to follow. My father caught my arm. "Stay, my son."*

*I looked at him. "You did not explain your efforts. What you offered!"*

*"I do not think it would have assuaged his anger," he said sadly. "It is his anger that is born of the ages."*

*"I do not understand," I said. My father looked down at me; touching my shoulder, he shook his head.*

*"And I hope you never have to," he said quietly.*

# 20

# IN WHICH I AM ILL-DRESSED AND MAKE A RATHER IMPORTANT DISCOVERY

I awoke with a jolt. Quiet beeping surrounded me. Breathing hard, I stared up at the ceiling. White. Tiled. Sterile.

This was the hospital. It took me a moment to remember why I was here. The explosion. Konstantin.

He said that Rothbart had been behind it.

Wednesday.

My heartbeat sped up, each beat reflected by the heart monitor attached to my finger.

Stars above and earth beneath, she was somewhere out there. I looked up at the clock. Three a.m. I felt almost whole. At the very least, I was more well-rested than I had been in days. The hospital staff undoubtedly knew who and what I was by now. They would let me go. Reaching over, I pressed the call button. I only had to wait a couple moments before the nurse walked in.

"Yes?" the young woman asked. I was sitting already, and I motioned to the monitors attached to me.

"I would like help in taking these things off," I said. Blinking in disbelief, the nurse turned and raised the lights to get a better look at me. She blinked more.

"Aren't you the one that was caught in the car explosion?" she asked, a little stunned, reaching for my chart.

I nodded, pleased that she knew who I was. "Yes."

"You've only been here for eight hours," she said, looking me up and down.

I smiled tightly. "And here I am, healed. You've done a wonderful job. Now, if you don't mind, I would like to get a set of clothes, and then I have to go find my cat."

She stared. "Your—"

"Cat," I finished. "Yes. She was with me when the car blew up, and I'm quite invested in finding her as soon as possible."

"She's a cat. Surely she can take care of herself, at least for the night," the nurse said, crossing across the room, most likely to get me to lay back down.

"On the contrary," I said. "I find it very unlikely that she is going to be able to do well on her own. It's cold tonight."

"She's a cat, Mr. Orris. She has fur. I'm sure her survival instincts will kick in."

"She's a pampered house cat!" I protested. "She *has* no survival instincts!"

And yet, I had found her coming in from the outdoors.

Muddy, wet, and starving.

No...she definitely needed me.

"I need clothes," I repeated succinctly.

The nurse looked at me, unimpressed. "We don't have any for you. Yours were destroyed in the explosion, and we only have scrubs, aside from your personal effects."

I pressed my lips together. "Give me the scrubs. I'll run to the gift shop and—"

"Mr. Orris, it's below freezing outside. I am not letting you—"

"I am perfectly fine!" I interrupted her. Tearing off one of the bandages on my arm, I showed her the new, unmarked skin beneath. "See? I am healed."

She took a step back, as though she suddenly realized what I was.

"Good heavens, you're the elf," she said, sighing. Shaking her head, she turned to walk away. "I'll go get the release paperwork." As she left the room, she was muttering something under her breath. I thought I heard 'what's the use' and 'elves in the hospital.'

"Thank you," I called after her, sitting back, my thoughts racing. I had no idea how I was actually going to *find* Wednesday. I was going to have to think of that next.

At least I didn't have to worry about Konstantin. I wasn't able to give him much healing magic—not compared to if I hadn't been injured—but it was enough to keep him alive until his own innate healing abilities would be able to take over.

No, Wednesday was the one who needed my help.

I had to sign a waiver, of course, considering I had entered the hospital unconscious only hours before. I knew instinctively that I was whole, though. I had had far too many opportunities to heal over the years to be unfamiliar with the difference.

Regardless, I walked out of the hospital twenty minutes later dressed in baby-blue scrubs that were ever so slightly too tight across the chest, a cardigan in a rather odd shade of green, and a pair of white tennis shoes. Which I was wearing with black socks.

I'd never been so grateful that it was dark outside.

Walking out of the hospital, I pulled my phone out of the plastic bag that also held my now-useless car keys and wallet. I couldn't do anything about the car, but pulling the unfortunate cardigan around me, I headed to the nearest supermarket.

The fluorescent light nearly blinded me as I walked in, but ignoring the stares of the usually unflappable employees, I headed straight for the clothing section. Ten minutes later, I emerged from the store, once more dressed head to toe in black, grocery sack of supplies in one hand and a ten year supply of kitty treats in the other.

One way or another, I would find her.

\*\*\*

The streets by Orris Investigations were empty. In fact, aside from the police officer guarding the wreckage of the car, I couldn't see a single other sign of life—not an empty car, a light from the apartments across the street, or even a person loitering on a corner.

I made my way across the parking lot to the office door, standing where I'd stood when the car blew up, shivering a little as I looked at the pockmarked building behind me and the skeleton of the vehicle in front. The damage was tremendous. How either Konstantin or I had survived was a miracle.

I hope that miracle extended to Wednesday.

My breath created a cloud that wreathed my head as I looked around, trying to decide which avenue I should take first. Whichever one I chose, I was going to search until I became too cold. Then I would go back to the office, warm up, and then start again. I would find her. I was sure I would be able to sense her.

Somehow.

And so I began to wander. Feeling a little bit like a fool, but far too worried to stop doing what I was doing, I began to wander the streets, calling Wednesday's name, and shaking the bag of treats.

They were the best kind I could find.

Real chicken, even.

"Wednesday," I called. "Come out! I have treats for you!"

Nothing. The night wore on, the temperature dipping into the single digits, the thin crescent of the moon rising above the buildings. Eventually, despite my worry, I was driven back to the indoors as the sky was just beginning to lighten. I stumped, discouraged, back to Orris Investigations, unlocking the door to the stairwell and pulling it open. Shivering up the stairs, I entered the office and immediately plugged in the extra space heater that we had in the office. I frowned. Usually it was Konstantin who pulled the extra hours.

As I settled into my office chair, I leaned back, staring at the case board.

I knew I wasn't going to be able to sleep. Trying to sleep would remind me that I hadn't slept without Wednesday within three inches of me for the last two weeks. That would remind me of the fact that she was missing. Which would push me back outside. I looked at the clock. It was only six thirty in the morning. I'd go back outside as soon as I could feel my fingers again.

No, it was going to be another all-nighter for me. Well, half-nighter.

I continued staring at the case board for almost an hour, my eyes lingering over each individual person, trying to guess their secrets. The previous night Konstantin had weeded out all of the ballet dancers that we had already interviewed, leaving only our people of interest on the board.

Standing, I walked over to the whiteboard, studying the pictures. When I came to the picture of Giselle, her green eyes twinkling, I shifted, frowning at the picture. Something seemed a little bit off, but I couldn't put my finger on it.

Speaking of 'off,' Siegfried's face came into mind, that hopeful expression as he leaned into the car to try and touch my cat. I frowned deeper. Could either of them have been responsible for the bombing? Was one or both of them in bed with Rothbart? I examined my options. It didn't seem inherently likely. Giselle had left before Siegfried, and there was no way that she was going to blow up my car simply because Siegfried had paid attention to my cat.

Or was there?

*Wednesday. Wrong.* Konstantin's gasping words resounded through my head, and I walked back over to my chair, slumping into it. What in the world did that mean? That he was wrong about her? That I was wrong about her? That she was wrong about herself?

*I identified the other magical scent, Trillion. It's Odell's.*

It had only been a week old at that point.

Rothbart had been following it. He had to have been. He'd traced over it only a few weeks later.

*Wednesday. Wrong.*

*She smells like a cat, Trillion.*

*I've been thinking about it, and I'm not sure how to tell you this... but I think—*

I sat in my chair, stock still, thinking of a small muddy cat that had staggered through my door. With enough mud to have easily been out in the wild for about a week.

*The trail is about a week old.*

I exhaled sharply, rocketing to my feet.

*My mother will miss me.*

*I went to University.*

*I remember summer.*

I walked to the case board, transfixed by the picture on the board. The picture of a smiling ballerina, who may have in fact been turned into a cat.

My missing girl...was Wednesday.

And Wednesday was out there somewhere.

I rocketed to the door, grabbing my new coat off of the rack. I had to find her. Throwing the coat on, I barreled down the stairs, intending to run out without even zipping it up. I made it to the front door, throwing it open. I briefly saw someone walking across the parking lot, long, brunette hair obstructing their face as they hugged themselves and bowed their head against the cold, pausing to stare at the burnt-out car.

Suddenly, I realized I had forgotten the cat treats. Turning away, I let the door close, before realizing that I had somehow recognized the woman outside. Forgetting the treats, I turned on my heel again, yanking open the door.

And there she was.

# 21

# IN WHICH I GET A SURPRISING ANSWER AND AN EVEN MORE SURPRISING VISITOR

Tabby fur. White paws. Long fluffy tail.

"Wednesday!" I exclaimed, scooping her up into my arms, squeezing her uncomfortably tight in my arms.

*No lifting!* she gasped, reaching out piteously, as if trying to get away from me. I squeezed her a little tighter, and she meowed right in my ear.

*I will defend myself if you do not put me down right now,* Wednesday warned. I suddenly realized I was holding an enchanted sorceress in my arms against her will, and swiftly placed her on the ground.

"Sorry," I said, a little abashed, stepping out of the way, and gestured for her to enter the office. Swishing her tail with dignity, she trotted inside. Once in, she sat beside her water bowl, watching me put a couple of treats into the food dish.

*It is cold outside. And you did not come back here for a long while,* she said, a little tentatively. *I went out looking.*

"I was in the hospital," I explained. "The explosion did some damage."

*You are whole,* Wednesday observed, eyeing me up and down. *Those do not look like your clothes.*

I looked down at my cheap purchases. "What's wrong with them?"

*They do not smell like you,* she said seriously, *and the cut is not flattering. I like your clothes at home better.*

"Hey!" I said. "It was all the store had, and it was the only one open."

*Why did you not go home—oh.*

I glared at her. "Thanks for rubbing it in," I said sulkily. "I figured I'd go to a rental company once the businesses open, and we can go back home then." I rubbed at my eyes, the sandy grit bearing testament to the less-than-desirable night we'd both had.

*Have you slept at all?* Wednesday's voice was quietly concerned. I plopped down into my chair, and she jumped up onto my lap. Placing her front paws on my chest, she leaned close and sniffed my face.

*You haven't,* she said accusingly.

"I slept at the hospital," I said. "Besides, I wasn't going to be able to sleep until I found you."

*Why?* she asked. *I would have thought that it would have been a relief for me to disappear. You would not have to worry about me anymore. Or my...*

"Quirks?" I offered. She looked up at me disdainfully.

*I was going to say presence. Thank you.* Her tone was distinctly sarcastic.

"Anytime," I said. Then I remembered who she was, and winced.

Yes, Trillion, provoke the University-trained sorceress. I was impervious to most physical injury, but I could still be cursed.

Unfortunately, I knew that quite well.

Something licked my eyebrow. I blinked, not realizing that my eyes had drifted closed and pulled my head back. I blinked again, staring down at Wednesday disbelievingly.

"Did you just lick my face?" I asked, rubbing away the sandpaper feeling from my face.

*You fell asleep,* Wednesday said, sounding a little offended.

"I did—I did not," I said.

*You did!* she insisted. *I was talking,* she added sulkily.

"No, no, I was listening," I lied. She glared at me. The feline face perfectly accentuated the look of pure acid that she threw at me.

I sighed. "Okay, fine," I said, "I fell asleep. I'm sorry."

Her tail swished. *Apology accepted,* Wednesday said primly. I smiled a little. While her big green eyes and pink little nose stared back at me, I just couldn't think of her as Odell. *What now?* she asked.

That was an excellent question. One that I didn't have the answer to. Should I question her now? Would she even remember anything?

One thing was for sure, I couldn't have this conversation while she was sitting on my lap. Holding her close while I leaned over, I pulled Konstantin's chair toward me, ignoring the screeching wheels. It looked like he'd been sitting in it while he'd been in dog form, and Wednesday made a noise of distaste as I set her down in it.

*Why am I in Konstantin's dog-chair?* she demanded. *You are warm. It is cold outside. This chair has fur that is not mine.*

"I'll talk to Konstantin," I half-promised. "But first, I'd like to ask you some questions."

*Oh?*

"About when you were human," I said.

If she had had eyebrows, I imagined that one would have been raised at this moment. *And you believe me now?* she asked, her voice unconvinced.

Discomfort wiggled through me. "I believe so, yes."

*You believe so? How stalwart of you,* she said, her voice unsympathetic.

"Wednesday, I'm trying to work with you here," I sighed, pinching the bridge of my nose.

*No, you are trying to fit me into your view of how life should be.*

"Wednesday, were you a ballet dancer?" I burst out. Through the fog of my tired mind, it was the only thing that I could piece together, and she sat there for a moment, absolutely, unbelievably still.

*What?* Her voice was breathless, and when I looked up at her, her back stiff and hair raised, I saw how tense she was.

"Were you a ballet dancer?" I asked, almost desperate, holding out my hands to her. She reached out one paw and placed it in my palm. I looked into her eyes.

*Yes,* she whispered. I blinked. My tired brain shorted out, and in the haze of that simple confirmation, I marveled in the fact that she actually had given me a straight answer for once. I wanted to ask her something else. Anything else. Everything else.

"Wednesday—"

There was a knock at the door.

Wednesday retracted her paw, hopped off of Konstantin's chair and fled to the back room before I could blink. Wondering what just happened, I stood in a daze and made my way over to the door.

It would likely be one of our building-mates, asking why there was a burnt-out car and police in the parking lot. Or Odell's mother. I frowned uncertainly. Could I tell her that her daughter was currently in my back room in the form of a fluffy tabby cat?

That was probably a conversation that would go better over a cup of coffee. Or perhaps ice cream. Or just...well, was it possible that Wednesday could tell her herself?

There was also the fact that I had absolutely no idea how to change Wednesday back again. Did I mention that first, or wait until Mrs. Richardson got over the shock of having a feline as a daughter? I got to the door, bracing myself for the motherly ire that I was about to plunge myself into. Reaching for the door knob, I suddenly and irrationally wished that I could be facing the Ottomans in Constantinople again. We'd lost, badly, but I felt like I'd made off far better than I was going to.

Another knock, more tentative. The glass wasn't thick. Whoever it was could probably see me on the other side of glass.

I needed more sleep.

Like, lots more.

Then I pulled open the door.

I was still sleeping. I was. There was no rhyme or reason for Giselle Carabosse to be standing on the doorstep to Orris Investigations.

If it had an actual doorstep.

"Oh! It's you!" Giselle's voice was deeply shocked. I paused, contemplating whether or not I should snap the door closed. Before I had a chance to decide, however, she pushed on the door, coming halfway in.

"I'm sorry," she said. "I heard that you had been in an accident. I didn't—I mean, you're okay! I'm... glad!" She didn't sound like it. She sounded more like she'd been caught with her hand the cookie jar. Despite that, or perhaps because she didn't know what to do any more than I did, she pushed her way past me into the office. Bemused, I watched her walk in, closing the door behind her.

"Thank you," I said cautiously, watching her as she crossed the room, and turned back around to face me, her back to the desks. Her hair gleamed in the fluorescent light, and I wondered just how in the world I could admire her hair when she had almost certainly blown up my car the night before.

She must have expected me to say more than I actually did, because she waited uncomfortably for a few moments, before barreling on.

"I'm sorry for coming. I just...I couldn't help but worry, after the way that I treated you in the interview yesterday, and then your car—Mr. Orris, I just—"

"You just wanted to make sure I was okay?" I offered quietly, my cold words almost foreign to my own ears. She opened her mouth, and then closed it.

"Well, yes. I-I had heard you'd been discharged from the hospital from Mother. I figured that you would be here. I...wanted to be sure. I felt...responsible."

Normally I would have been moved, especially from someone who was as beautiful—or uncomfortable—as she was. Her tone was surprisingly sincere, and her expression was exactly what I would have expected from someone in her position.

Thankfully, an explosion and a near death experience for me and my closest friend anchored me. Not to mention that she had quite possibly enchanted her best friend, who was currently a cat in my back room. Predominantly, however, was the fact that she had been there, walking toward the door this morning, just before Wednesday had shown up. She'd been wearing party clothes—completely different from the ensemble she wore now.

No, perspective was a grand thing.

"Ms. Carabosse," I said quietly, taking a step forward. She pressed her lips together and looked up at me, hugging her purse to her chest over her winter coat. I stopped where I was, but didn't attempt to reassure her any further.

"Yes, Mr. Orris?" she asked quietly.

"Do you know who blew up my car?" I asked, deathly calm. She blinked. If she did, she knew it was Rothbart. And if she knew enough about me from her mother to know that I had been released from the hospital, she would know what my relationship was with Rothbart.

"No," she said, not meeting my eyes.

It was a lie. My magical abilities didn't extend to being able to sense the truth, but over seventeen hundred years in military service more than made up the difference.

"I think you are not telling me the truth," I said, very quietly, and very deliberately.

She looked up at me, her eyes wide but determined. "I don't know," she insisted. "If I knew, why would I keep that from you?"

"Because I believe that you were in on it," I said quietly. She scoffed. I glowered, and she took a step back.

"Why on earth would—"

"Because," I said quietly. "I keep on finding you in every corner of this investigation. She was your friend. You dance in the same company. You were one of the last people to see her. You knew about her magic, you knew about her struggles, you were vying for the same position. If you are not here because you were involved, you either know who is responsible, or you *are* responsible. Now which is it?" My words were sharp and clipped by the end of the sentence, and she winced at the forcefulness of them.

Then, swallowing hard, "It was Rothbart," she said tearfully, looking down at the bag in her arms. The world seemed to spin a little, and I took in a deep breath to right it.

"Tell me more," I growled.

"What?"

"Tell me *more*," I repeated. "Where did you meet him?" I demanded. "Where is he now?"

"I don't know where he is now," she said quietly, "But I—I met him outside the theatre a couple of months ago."

"And?"

"And nothing else!" Giselle exclaimed. "Who else would it be? I haven't seen his face since then. But this...I've read my mother's files on him. After you as good as told me you thought I was responsible for...for—I couldn't let you think I'd done this, too!"

I narrowed my eyes.

"So this visit is just a guilty conscience?"

Giselle looked at me, expression caught between definite discomfort and definite guilt. "I knew this was a mistake," she breathed. "Siegfried told me this would be a bad idea."

"It wasn't your best," I agreed darkly.

Giselle looked up, the fire that I had seen the day before reigniting behind her eyes. "Well," she growled in return, pushing me aside as she made her way to the door, "forgive me for trying to show some human decency."

A laugh burst from me. Wednesday's face flashed in my mind, and I shook my head, turning around. "I know more than you think I do, Ms. Carabosse," I warned. Giselle yanked the door open, and glared up at me.

"You have no idea what you're talking about," she spat. I narrowed my eyes. Leaning closer, I tipped my head to the side.

"How are your mother's transfiguration studies going, I wonder?" I asked cooly.

Baring her teeth for the briefest moment, she sneered back at me. "You don't have the faintest idea of what you're talking about," Giselle repeated vehemently, and whipped out the door. I watched her leave the building, stepping outside the office to watch her stalk down the stairs, and push violently out the door. I took a deep, calming breath, purposefully unclenching my fists.

It felt odd to be so wound up. Was it just fatigue? I was definitely tired enough. But no. I'd made it through my interviews yesterday without blowing up. What was it?

Konstantin's face blasted through my mind, prone and motionless on the ground. And then, Wednesday's sweet face, looking up at me expectantly. Pain ripped through my chest. If anything happened to either of them, I'd—

I stopped, my heart freezing in between beats.

Panic gripped me with an unexpected, tight handed fist.

*Care will kill him.*

What had I done?

That one admission. My best friend. This ridiculous, endearing—or was it ridiculously endearing?—cat... I shook my head. The cat who wasn't even a cat.

I couldn't let myself get any more attached than I was. I couldn't. I hadn't put myself at risk for more than three hundred years. Father—I pinched my eyes shut.

*Trillion?* Wednesday's voice came from just inside the door. I looked over, breathing heavily. Upon seeing my face, she took a few more dainty steps outside of the door. Pressing her forehead into my leg, she whispered to me. *Trillion, come inside.*

"I—" My words strangled for a moment before I nodded. She let me go in front of her, and once I had closed the doors and sunk into my chair, she hopped up into my lap, pressing the top of her head into the underside of my chin.

*Tell me what's wrong,* she said quietly. I blinked and shook my head. One claw punctured my synthetic slacks and I jumped. *Tell me.*

I shook my head. "Not here, Wednesday," I whispered, running a hand down her soft, striped head. Somehow sensing that I wasn't going to budge, Wednesday curled up in my lap, and rested her head on my forearm. The weight of her there was comforting, despite everything in my brain screaming at me to kick her off before I got even more attached.

I leaned back, closing my eyes against the panic.

It was too late, though. It was far too late for that.

# 22

# IN WHICH I FIND OUT
# I AM WRONG

I couldn't move. The ten percent battery notification popped up on my phone, and I looked down at Wednesday, mutely perplexed. She was on her back on my lap, front paws over her head, tummy moving slowly up and down as she lay there, sound asleep.

I couldn't move her.

Well, *physically* I could have. She was only about seven pounds. It wouldn't have taken anything to pick her up, move her to the chair, and leave her for the twenty minutes that it would take to go get the rental car.

Emotionally, it felt somewhere between grand theft and murder. I just...couldn't.

She was so cute, too.

Those little foot pads. They were like...toe beans. Pink little toe beans.

*Get a hold of yourself, Trillion*, I told myself. *You're not that tired.*

*Besides, she's a reclusive sorceress who has been turned into a cat. By all accounts, you should hope that she doesn't think* you *did it.*

It might have been more convincing if every once in a while a paw hadn't twitched as Wednesday dreamed. Or her tail. Or her nose.

I smiled despite myself. Then, purposefully, wiped it off of my face.

Stars above, this was hard.

After the short nap that I'd managed to capture in the armchair, I had texted Konstantin. He had awoken sometime in the last hour, and had just barely answered. Shapeshifters weren't elves, but being part of the larger subspecies of faerie had its advantages. Normally he'd heal at almost the same rate that I would have, perhaps a little slower. He had taken almost twice the time that I had to heal, even with the jolt of magic that I'd been able to give him. It was disturbing to think how close I had come to losing him.

*How are you feeling?* I asked.

*Ready to go, can you come pick me up?*

I opened my mouth, and then closed it. Looking down at the snoozing kitty in my lap, I wrote in response.

*About that...*

*What, are you okay?* he asked. I sat there.

*Yes,* I wrote. *Wednesday is sleeping.*

*...I don't follow.*

*She's in my lap,* I typed. He'd understand, right?

*You're not taking her "no lifting" thing seriously, are you?* Konstantin asked. I could practically see his eyes roll. *Trillion, she's what, seven pounds?*

*I don't think you understand,* I said, and sent a picture.

A couple seconds later Konstantin replied. *You're right, I don't,* he texted back. *Fine. I'll call a ride share. If you're not up and around by the time I get back, expect me to roll my eyes at you.*

*What, no tongue lashing?* I asked. The dots indicating Konstantin's text blinked on and off. I blinked in return.

*Wait a minute,* I wrote. *Konstantin, why are you texting?*

The dots cleared for a moment, and then reappeared.

*I'll explain later,* he said. *I'll be by in about twenty minutes. Get out of the chair, will you?*

I smiled, but didn't reply. Looking down at the sleeping cat, I still felt a little bad. Still, she had been sleeping for two hours. She wouldn't be mad, right?

No.

Then I had a moment of clarity.

Yes, she would. She was tempestuous even when she was in a good mood. What in the world was I thinking? She would yell at me. She would claw my laundry. She would sleep on my neck tonight.

I blinked.

Was it appropriate for her to be sleeping on the same bed as me? I mean, she was an enchantress. But on the other hand, she was so thoroughly a cat in her current form...

*Did you say something?* Wednesday's voice paused as she twitched hard, her eyes peeking open. I looking down at her, and touched one of her velvet paws.

"Not out loud," I said quietly. She sighed a little, and then tipped onto her side. She yawned, sharp, white canines pronounced as she did. Then, she hopped down. Once she had accordioned to twice her length and condensed into Wednesday once more, she trotted off to her food bowl.

*I hope you got some sleep,* she said, crunching down the cat food. *You don't look quite so drawn out as earlier.*

"I got some," I confirmed, rubbing my eyes and standing up. One of my feet was asleep. Of course it was. Hopping on my other foot for a moment, I made my way to the back room for the lint roller.

*I didn't shed that bad,* Wednesday called after me.

"I'm wearing all black, Wednesday. It doesn't matter how much you shed, I'll always come out of it looking like I've been tearing out tufts of your fur."

There was an audible pause. *I don't like that imagery.*

I thought about it. "Sorry, me neither."

*Have you heard from Konstantin?* Wednesday asked from the doorway. I looked up where I'd been swiping at my clothes.

"Um, yeah. He's on his way here."

*Then he is all right?* she asked. *He had the smell of death on him last night.* I frowned, turning to look at her.

"You were there? I thought you'd run away by then."

*I was there. Watching. I thought you saw me,* she said quietly. I searched my memory. I didn't remember seeing the cat after the initial explosion. I shook my head.

"I'm sorry, I didn't see you."

Her tail swished, but she didn't bat an eye. *It is all right. I ran away very fast. It was hard to fight the cat instinct to run away.*

I frowned down at her.

*Did you contact the rental company?* she asked, standing at my feet. I tried to stifle a smile. *What?*

"Oh, nothing," I said. "I'm just being asked by my cat if I remembered to rent a car."

She sniffed. *Well, as much as I love the office or playing homeless, I prefer sleeping on an actual bed.*

"Fair enough," I responded. Smiling, I pulled my notes together and we waited for Konstantin. It took longer than I expected for him to arrive. When he did, hauling himself up the stairs tiredly, dressed in hospital scrubs in the same fit and color that mine had been, he looked between Wednesday and I.

"You let her wake up on her own, didn't you?" he whispered voice raspy.

I frowned. "Why are you whispering?" I asked.

He sighed. "Apparently—" his raspy voice broke, and a vehement look of annoyance crossed his face. Fishing his phone out of his pocket. After a moment of texting, he looked up at me, and my phone beeped. Fishing my own phone out of my pocket, I read his message out loud.

"Apparently my voice isn't considered a 'vital system.'" I looked up. "Oh." Konstantin typed something.

Ding! *Yeah, oh.*

I watched him in concern for a full minute.

"Do you want me to take you home?" I asked. After a moment of mute frustration, the shapeshifter sighed and then nodded.

"Well, I was about to go get the rental car. Do you want to stay here with Wednesday?" I asked. He nodded, slumping into his chair, looking perfectly healthy but vastly dissatisfied. I ordered the ride share and then looked back at other man.

"You realize I'd feel more sympathetic if you hadn't spent the last two weeks ribbing me about—" Almost as soon as I'd started talking, Konstantin had grabbed his phone, typing a furious text.

*Just go*, he texted. I smirked. Bowing slightly, I left.

The rental car was the exact same model as my old car, but even as I sat behind the identical dashboard, it just wasn't the same.

*You're mourning an inanimate object*, Wednesday said blandly as Konstantin stalked back to his house. *Also, what is wrong with him?*

"Konstantin resents anything that limits or circumvents him, even when its his own body," I said, pulling out of the driveway onto the highway.

*Oh, like you?* Wednesday's voice was far too innocent, and I looked over and glared at her. She noticed. *Eyes on the road.*

"I'll glare at you if I want," I said.

*Do you really want to wreck two cars in two days? Your insurance rate would be terrible.* She paused. *Do elves need insurance?*

"I'm not going to wreck, and yes, I do have insurance. It's the law."

*Oh. How many cars have you wrecked?*

"I'm not going to answer that."

*You probably started with the Model T and have just been working up through the last hundred years or so of automobiles,* she said thoughtfully. Then she looked over. *Did you ever wreck a stagecoach?*

I sighed. "I'm not answering that."

Her feline smirk broadened. *You totally did.*

"Wednesday!" I exclaimed exasperatedly.

*Trillion!* she said, much more happily than I had. *Lighten up. Did I ever tell you that I am very happy that you're okay?*

I paused before I shot something sarcastic back, caught off guard by the comment. I remained silent I turned up the long driveway. As I passed the fence that marked the edge of the property, I stiffened.

*What was that?* Wednesday asked. I looked down at her.

"You felt that?" I asked.

*It felt like an electric shock,* she said, looking up at me, eyes large. I furrowed my eyebrows

"That was the wards," I said. "Someone's been here."

Wednesday's silence was uncomfortable. *A friendly UPS man?* she offered hopefully.

"Probably not," I said grimly.

*Are they still here?* she asked quietly, slinking down in her seat.

I looked down at her. "I don't know yet. There are separate wards around the house," I told her. "I'll know more when we get there."

*What if those are broken?* she asked. She seemed incredibly nervous about something. I supposed I couldn't blame her. I was nervous, for goodness' sake. I scanned the stark white fields around the house, thankful that I'd had the good sense to not have any trees within a half mile from the house. No one was overtly lurking in the non-existent shadows.

Thank goodness it was noon. I wasn't scared of much, but after the day I'd had, if I'd crossed the threshold after dark I would have turned around and spent another night at the office.

*Trillion?* The fear in her voice sparked something in me, and I frowned in determination. Nothing was allowed to frighten Wednesday like that.

"Then I will deal with it," I said firmly, a sharpness to my tone that was more than just my words. She blinked slowly as she looked up at me, appraising, but seemed to relax.

*You're different when you say stuff like that,* she noted.

I blinked a little, and relaxed my grip on the steering wheel. "I don't take well to threats. And I don't like seeing you scared. You have enough to worry about," I explained.

*Me?* she said, a little bemused.

"Aren't you trying to figure out how to turn back into a human?" I asked.

She looked up at me. *Oh. Well, yes, I suppose,* she said, a little shocked.

"Aren't you?" I repeated, my tone a little more insistent.

*Of course I am,* she snapped. *I'm just shocked that you're the one spitting stuff out like that now.*

"Okay," I said, a little worriedly. Was she not focused on her human side anymore? What had changed? Subdued, we rolled up to the house, the garage door opening as we came close. I drove us right in.

Wednesday sat in the passenger seat, watching me. *Well?*

Finding that pit of magic within myself, I reached out to the house wards.

"No one's been in here."

Wednesday sighed audibly, which made me blink and turn, expecting to see Odell sitting in the seat beside me. But no, Wednesday, cat-like as she ever was, sat on the seat, furry head a little bowed.

I fought down the feeling of relief. My goal was to find Odell, not find the only cat in the world that I wanted to keep.

"You can head in," I said. "I'll check the grounds."

*Are you sure you don't want me to come with you?* Wednesday asked, standing up on the seat as I opened the door.

"Why?" I asked, smiling. "Would you claw the eyes out of any intruder?"

She straightened up. *Maybe. Or give them a severe tongue lashing.*

"I would have to translate," I pointed out. She walked over my lap.

*Perhaps you could do a literal interpretation of my message,* she said primly, jumping down out of the car. I smiled and followed her into the house. I put out a can of cat food for her, and then I went to my room to change.

I stood in my closet for a moment, just a touch amused at the fact that I was so happy to be standing among my old clothes.

Then I remembered the green sweater.

No, I was completely justified in feeling this happy.

Donning all black, carefully tying back my hair and noting that I needed to shower when I returned, I grabbed a long, thick coat and strode out into the front room. Wednesday was walking across the room when I came out, but when she saw me, she stopped, dropping into a sitting position, her the tip of her tail dancing as it wrapped around her.

"What?" I asked, pausing when I saw her staring at me. She didn't reply for a second, but looked up at me inscrutably.

*Nothing.*

"You're staring at me," I pointed out.

*You're inherently entertaining,* she said, as though it was obvious. *And I take back what I said the other day—black looks very good on you.*

"Did something happen while I was changing?" I asked suspiciously, glancing into the kitchen just to make sure the refrigerator was still closed. She met my eyes, and then started to walk away.

*No.*

Not sure whether that was the cat or the enchantress talking, I decided to take a step back from that metaphorical edge. Shaking my head, I left the house.

The day was bright and cold. Much like the day before, the sky was clear and blue. Now that I was out of the city I could enjoy the clear air. In fact, it was one of my very favorite types of days—it was a pity that there was potentially a mass murderer on my property.

It wasn't as though I could prove it was Rothbart if I couldn't find him, but I knew better than to think that it was a coincidence that someone was at my house the night I wasn't there. I went around the perimeter of the wards. The one con of having wards was the fact that even if I could tell there was a breach, I couldn't automatically tell which border had been burnt out.

It took me a little before I found it on the south east corner of the property, precisely where the path led straight to the Old Mill. The path that, if Wednesday were Odell, the cat had taken to reach my house. I surveyed the clearing. I knew Rothbart wasn't anywhere around the house—I had just searched it. But he was nothing if not clever. If he was still hiding here, then I wanted to know.

There were a couple ways I could do that. One of them involved shaking a lot of trees—less than effective in a forest. No, there was a better way. One that I had not employed in a very long time. This gift did not work in the city, and it had been a long time since I had hunted men in the woods.

Closing my eyes, I knelt down on one knee. Placing the palm of my ungloved hand through the snow and onto the frozen ground, I calmed my mind, letting it focus on the swirling pit of magic within myself. Reaching into that tempestuous mass, I breathed in deep, and then exhaled, letting the magic spread through the ground.

It sped away from me, and then came back to me in waves, golden images filling my mind as the magic fanned out around me in a complete circle. It rushed over the house to the north, and deep into the forest to the south, spreading across the fields to the east and west. I saw every rabbit, every hibernating chipmunk in the trees. Reaching out to the land, the land spoke to me, whispering her secrets.

The forest was teeming with life. But no humans.

Whoever it was, they had left.

Reluctantly, I lifted my hand from the frozen ground. There was nothing like being so connected to the Earth. She was so willing to speak. To communicate, even after all of this time.

Satisfied, I made my way back to the house. I didn't immediately see Wednesday as I walked in, and as a result, yawning, I decided to throw caution to the wind and take a nap. Entering into my room, I saw her stretched out on the white comforter on top of my bed in a patch of sunshine. It looked so inviting that, kicking off my boots and dropping my coat onto the floor, I sank into the pool of sun and fell asleep as well.

I awoke with a jolt fifteen hours later.

I blinked furiously awake in the pitch-black room. Hunger twisted in my stomach as I lay there, trying to get some sort of sense of what time it was and what had awakened me. After a moment of reflection—and a subtle reach out to the wards, which were blessedly whole—I shook my head and pulled myself out of bed.

Wednesday had left already. I pulled the door to my room open. And then paused, looking at the door, which had been closed. Looking into the kitchen, one of the lights was on. I hadn't turned it on. It had barely been two in the afternoon when I'd fallen asleep. Now, according to my phone, it was five-thirty in the morning. Feeling well-rested but remarkably confused, I walked into the kitchen and saw six glass cups sitting on the edge of the counter.

I looked around, catching my breath. Could it be that—

No. Wednesday jumped up onto the counter, fluffy tail held high. The warm yellow light radiated down from the lights above, and she stopped beside the glasses, the bar lights acting like a spotlight.

"Wednesday?" I gestured to the cups on the counter. "What's going on? What's all this?"

*I've been thinking.*

Uh oh.

*We need to have a talk,* she said, her tail flicking back and forth. All six glasses were precariously balanced on the edge of the counter. I was confused. If it was only Wednesday here, and she was still a cat, who had put up the glasses?

Unless—

"Wednesday," I asked, my voice a little strangled. "Can you move stuff with your mind?"

She looked at me, unresponsive for a moment, and then a sigh floated through my head.

*Finally.*

"'Finally?'" I demanded. "What do you mean 'finally?'"

*I was waiting for you to notice,* she complained. *You took ages. I thought you knew it for sure when I left the kitchen a mess. And that you were just toying with me when you woke up yesterday and saw me practicing with the boxes. Incidentally, you're out of frozen chicken in the freezer.*

"You were in my freezer?" I demanded.

She shrugged. *It's lower to the ground. It was easier to access last week.*

"It—but—" I said looking around.

*You look like you need a chair,* she said. One of the kitchen chairs skidded across the room, hovering just above the floor before stopping right behind me. Absolutely staggered, I sank into it. Wednesday continued.

*Admittedly, I'm not perfect at it. Still, it's come in handy, particularly when I need to reach something that's a bit too high.*

"Do you have this talent as a human?" I asked, breathless.

Wednesday paused. *I used to,* she said, *before I was transformed. But we're getting sidetracked. Look here, Trillion.* She walked along the counter, brushing up against the glasses in such a way that it looked like they were going to fall. I tried to jump up to catch them, but an invisible hand clapped down on my shoulder, holding me in place. Sighing frustratedly, I didn't try to get up again. Wednesday didn't look at me, but continued to pace back and forth.

*We need to talk about yesterday.*

I thought about all the things I had done that day and frowned.

"What part?" My voice was a little more desperate than I would have ever admitted to, feeling completely out to sea. Was she talking about the car? The hospital? The green sweater—No, she hadn't seen that. On purpose.

Wednesday turned her head, green eyes pinioning me to the chair. *The part where I came into the stairwell and you were crying.*

"I wasn't—"

*I'm talking.*

I clamped my mouth closed.

Wednesday walked by the glasses again, dangerously close. *I've always wanted to try this,* she said quietly before looking up at me. *Here's the deal, Trillion. I will ask you a question. When you answer, I will answer one of your questions. For every questions you don't answer, I will knock a glass off of the counter.*

"You will no—"

*This is not a negotiation,* Wednesday said flatly. *You're ridiculously bad at listening, let alone answering questions, and this is important. I've had enough of your dithering.*

"Yes, but why *now*?" I demanded.

She looked at me evenly. *Because things have changed. First question: Who is Rothbart?*

I gaped. "He's...well, he's a mass murder with a penchant for violent insanity," I stammered.

*I know that already. Who is he to you?*

"What?" I gasped, watching her paw get dangerously near one of the glasses. "Okay, okay, stop! He's my half brother."

*You've said that. That does not explain why you are hunting him. Or why you are actually* not *hunting him.*

I stared at her. Gritting my teeth, my stare turned into a scowl. "Run that by me again?"

*You and Konstantin have been tracking him, but going by the fact that you've been working consistently at Orris Investigations for the better part of the last fifty years, you have not made a preemptive move against him for quite some time. Why is that?*

"How do you even know that?" I demanded.

Her tail swished. *I am literate.*

I stared at her, frowning furiously. "This is extortion," I growled.

*Of course it is,* she said matter-of-factly. *But seeing how you're not much amenable to answering anything that's not immediately important to you, I took the opportunity to create such a scenario. You have to admit you brought it on yourself.*

"You never asked about any of this before!" I moved to stand up again, but the invisible hand pressed down again firmly.

*How would you know?* she asked flatly, almost coldly.

I didn't want to admit that she was right. In fact, right at that moment, I'd rather—

*Well, if you're not going to answer,* she said, and knocked the glass off the counter.

"Wait!" I said. Miraculously, the glass caught itself in the air, slowly revolving in the air a couple of inches off of the ground, and she looked up at me, an ear twitching.

194 - REBEKAH ISERT

*What?*

"He..." I stopped. I stared at Wednesday, opening and closing my mouth. I knew I couldn't go dancing around the situation forever. But actually saying—

*Too slow.* Raising the glass, Wednesday sent it hurling hard to the ground, harder than it should have, shattering.

"He killed one of my brothers!" I gritted out. She paused by the next glass, head turning toward me. I folded my arms, glaring at her. "My brother. Rothbart's half brother. Rothbart's been going around for the last three hundred years, killing anyone or anything magical that crosses his path. The only thing that has been keeping him at bay has been me."

*So why are you here?* she asked quietly.

I looked up at her. "What do you mean?" I asked.

*If you are trying to defeat him, why did you settle here? How are you keeping him at bay if you won't confront him?* Wednesday asked, green eyes vivid despite the light hanging over her head.

"I haven't—" I spluttered. "I have *not* settled."

*You have been working Orris Investigations for the last fifty years. Even I had heard of you before I was transformed. You would take leave to hunt for Rothbart, but always return here. Work the magical cases. Why?*

I glared at her. How did she have the power to lay me bare like that? Why did I let her?

"Because you matter to me," I whispered, bowing my head. Shaking my head, I corrected myself. "I mean, the city. The magical beings, and people who have run into magic that just plain can't help themselves."

*And stopping Rothbart isn't important?*

Of course it was. I could see my father, holding my brother Kaldinion in his arms as the younger man writhed in his death throes. King Auberon had stared up at the unrepentant face of Luther von Rothbart. I could see the sword, dripping with blood, clenched tightly in Luther's rage-trembling hands. I had stood there in shock.

Father screamed at me.

Grab him. Defeat him.

Kill him.

Do not return without doing so.

"He is still my brother," I said. "I will kill him. I know it is what must be done."

*But?*

Care will kill him.

"But it will kill me." I finished quickly, looking up at the cat. She looked down at me. There was a different feeling about her now. Her irritation had slackened, and she now looked almost remorseful, as far as that feline face of hers could carry the emotion. But I had started now, and I could not stop without finishing.

"The truth of the matter is that he is unpredictable. Yes, I have almost twenty centuries of experience. I have tracked, and I have killed. I have destroyed things so thoroughly that their only trace on this earth is my remembrance. I remember every face that I have ever fought. Everyone that I have ever killed. I have trained so hard and so long to become a killer. But *never—*" I looked up at her "—have I killed a brother. I find... I do not know how."

Wednesday looked down at me from the counter. I could feel waves of worry permeate off of her. When had we gotten that close? I stumbled on.

"He's always escaped my grasp because I've chosen to help the wounded rather than chase after him. To make sure they live rather than to ensure he dies. I'm still not sure that has been the right decision, but I have made it, and I stand by it. One day I will not have to make that choice, and then I will be able to return to my father."

It was an explanation. I didn't know if it was good enough. It didn't feel like it. We sat in silence for a long time, staring at each other.

*You have told me enough*, she said quietly. I looked away, down at the floor, and felt the invisible hand lift off of my shoulder. Hopping down from the counter with a light thud, she reached up, her paws on my knee. I reached down and smoothed back the striped fur on top of her head.

"There is more," I said quietly. She looked up at me.

*I know there is. But there is something that you must understand. I know who Rothbart is. I have met him.*

I frowned. "What?"

*And you have, too*, she said quietly.

I frowned. "I don't understand."

*Follow me. It is just about time*, she said softly, setting her front feet back onto the floor. She trotted toward the front of the house. I followed her, mystified, practically tripping over my feet as I rounded the corner to the front of the house.

The front door opened wide as Wednesday jogged to it. Outside, a crescent moon was rising into a blue and purple sky, huge and luminescent above the trees. The early morning sky silhouetted the cat as she paused on the threshold, as though deciding whether to step over.

"Wednesday?" My voice was shaking. "What are you doing?"

Wednesday looked back at me.

*It is time*, she said, and stepped over the threshold.

She immediately began to grow, her form hunched over as it expanded and stretched. Paws turned into long, willowy limbs, fur retracted from her arms as long hair tumbled down her back. She twisted, and a long hollow gasp split the air as her form changed, from cat to human.

And then she stood there, back to me. She was still dressed in the clothing from the August party, shivering slightly against the

December morning. I stared at her, completely dumbfounded as she turned back to me.

"Trillion," she whispered, green eyes glittering back at me in the faint light from within the house. She was silhouetted, but I could make out her features. The lithe ballerina body. The long, gorgeous brown hair.

"Giselle," I whispered back.

# 23

## IN WHICH MY BRAIN CEASES TO FUNCTION, AND I RESIST THROWING CAUTION TO THE WIND. SORT OF.

"I——" I could barely remember how to speak, let alone know what to say next. Giselle stared back at me, shivering in the cold glow of the moon behind her. I opened my mouth, and let whatever was going to tumble out tumble out. "I'm going to make pizza," I croaked.

"What?"

What?

"You... you said you wanted pizza." I stumbled over my words, trying to find where in my brain I'd found *that* particular gem. I blinked. When had we even talked about that, anyway? "You should come inside. You look cold."

"I... am," Giselle agreed hesitantly, as if feeling every word in her mouth. She stepped inside, and closed the door behind her. And then she stared at me. I stared right back.

She was beautiful. The vivid green eyes—which had carried through even in her cat form—were offset by rich brown hair that framed her face and tumbled down her back. I would have been lying if I'd said my brain didn't grind to a complete stop in that moment, simply taking her in.

It was ridiculous.

Trillion, I reminded myself sternly, she was your cat five minutes ago. Don't be creepy. Think of something else.

"What sort of pizza do you want? We have Hawaiian and pepperoni." My voice sounded strangled, and words tumbled over each other as they left my mouth.

For heaven's sake, Trillion, move on from the pizza! Giselle looked at me, as if she was trying to remember what pizza was. Then, blinking, she shrugged.

"Pepperoni, I guess," she said. I nodded, patting down my pockets for my phone. It was in my bag. I turned away, trying to pull myself together, realizing that I didn't need it. Right. It was morning. Pizza places weren't open. That didn't matter. Taking a deep breath, I pulled open the freezer, pulling out a frozen pepperoni pizza. Not bothering to preheat the oven, I forced shaking fingers to press the right temperature, added five minutes onto the timer, and plopped myself down on the coach, staring blankly at the dark TV screen.

Stars above and Earth beneath, what was I going to do with all of this?

"Trillion?" The sofa shifted slightly as Giselle sank down onto the sofa beside me, placing a small hand on my knee. I jerked a little bit, and she frowned. "Trillion, I don't think you're coping well."

"I—"

"Don't argue with me," Giselle said, Wednesday peeking through. It made my heart ache a little.

"I wasn't going to," I said, leaning forward, burying my head in my hands.

"Liar," she said, and as I had my eyes closed, I could practically hear Wednesday rolling her eyes. I straightened, scowling at her. She smiled back at me, the smugness reflecting the feeling I had gotten from her cat self for the last two weeks to perfection.

"I—" I shook my head and looked down, sighing.

"Is it because I am human, or is it because I am Giselle?" she asked quietly. When I didn't answer, she settled a little deeper into the couch, resting her shoulder against mine.

"I could lay in your laundry basket, if you want," she said quietly. All of a sudden, the world righted itself in an instant. I snorted despite myself, and lay my head back against the back of the couch, a smile on my face. Looking down at her, I noticed her holding her light summer jacket to herself, bare legs curled up underneath her for warmth.

"You're cold."

"I don't have a fur coat anymore," she responded dryly. "Turns out sixty-five degrees *is* too cold for most humans."

I frowned. "So you *did* play with the thermostat?"

"On the plus side," she said simply, "I probably helped you save on your electricity bill."

"The house is solar powered, Wednesday, I don't have an electricity bill," I said. She looked up at me, the soul of innocence. It was about as convincing as when she was a cat.

"Rude!"

"Did I say that out loud?" I said, frowning.

"You know, sometimes I wonder how you actually were able to be a mercenary."

"Well, apparently warriors and soldiers are easier to predict than animals and...women," I said.

She snorted and sat up. "I told you you have a problem," she said.

"I do not!"

"Do, too!"

"Do—" I cut myself off, a new thought popping into my head. "Wednesday, when are you going to turn back into a cat?"

She blinked. "Are you that tired of me—"

"That was you this morning, right? In the parking lot?" I said. It made sense now. Giselle in the last light of the moon before the sun rose, looking over at the wreckage as she passed it. Standing somewhere where she really had no reason to be.

"Yes."

"And you turned back into a cat?"

"Yes," she said quietly. "When the moon sets, or sunrise, whichever comes first."

I nodded. "Where did you go last night?" I asked. "If you were human—"

"I went to the hospital. Before I was human," she said, frowning. "By the time I got there, you were already checked out. I snuck in before they noticed, and I left when I knew that Konstantin was going to be all right." She exhaled, as though that had been a memory she wasn't sure she wanted to remember.

"Did you turn into a human on the curb?" I asked.

"Yeah, there was a drunk on the corner who has possibly given up drinking," Giselle said in response. She blinked, a smile blossoming across her face. "You called me Wednesday."

"Did I?" I said. "I'm sorry, it must be hab—"

"No, no." Her hand was reassuring on my arm. "It's fine. In fact,

202 · REBEKAH ISERT

it might be more convenient since apparently there are two of me running around right now."

I grimaced. "Our missing friend Odell."

"I think so," Wednesday agreed, her smile dimming.

It made sense. An infuriating amount of sense, in fact. Odell, who had no reason to be missing, swapped with Giselle, who had *every* reason to be missing made a lot more sense. Odell as an almost-graduated enchantress could have carried off something as complicated as transfiguring a human. The enormous readout at the Old Mill was one thing, but—

"*That's* why Konstantin couldn't tell you were a human!" I exclaimed. "If Odell was the one who enchanted you, you wouldn't have smelled any different from the house!" I frowned. "Right?"

"I think so," Wednesday said, a little quietly. I frowned. She saw it, and shrugged. "It's slow coming back. I wasn't lying about everything, Trillion. I didn't remember my name until last night when I turned back into a human. It was only the second time since I was transformed in...well, whenever I was transformed. I think I actually wondered if I was Odell, for a bit."

I let that sink in.

"August," I finally said. "You went missing in August."

She nodded. "A week before I found you, the night I escaped from the Mill, I turned back into a human. I didn't know where I was. I...had to turn back into a cat again. I wouldn't have lived through the night."

I hummed in agreement. It had been below freezing that night, even though the snow hadn't blown in yet. Wednesday looked at the fireplace absently, lips pursed in thought. I watched her out of the corner of my eye, not entirely sure what to do. Or ask. Or say. No matter what form Wednesday took, the one thing in common was her ability to absolutely catch me off guard.

"Trillion?" she said, her hand on my arm. "You okay?"

"I was just getting used to you as a cat!" I said, burying my head in my hands. Again. The hand on my arm paused for a second.

"One sec," she said, standing. I heard her walk to the kitchen, open a drawer and rifle through it. What the— I looked up over the counter. Wednesday faced away from me, holding up...a spoon?

"There we go," she said, and turned around. A permanent marker was clutched in her other hand, and six black marks were on her face.

Whiskers.

"Oh dear—"

"Maybe this will help with the transition," Wednesday said cheerfully, cutting my exasperated exclamation off, walking around the counter again. "What might also help is if I could get a different set of clothes? I've been wearing these for three months. This is a record I would like to forget I ever broke."

I blinked, and stood automatically. "Um, yes? You are...smaller than me. I'm not sure I have anything that could fit you."

"Some things never change," she said, sighing. "Good thing I have no one to impress."

"I don't know what you'd—"

"How about sweatpants and a hoodie? I know you've got a pair of them hidden in your closet."

"How do you—"

Wednesday looked up at me, and I shut my mouth. She smiled, sharpie whiskers crinkling. "Because I slept on them for most of the past two weeks while you left me at home."

I frowned. "How did you get into my closet?"

"I opened the door," she said, grinning.

"How?!"

"With my mind!" Her gleeful proclamation gave way to muffled footsteps as she kicked off her party shoes and ran toward my room. Halfway there, she paused, looking around. "Huh."

"What?"

"Your house seems so much smaller now," she said. She paused. Before I could answer, she barreled on. "Clothes first, then we need to talk about Rothbart."

"Wednesday," I protested, following after her. Right as I got to the door, it slammed shut, and I heard the lock click. "Wednesday, do not go through my closet!"

"Like I haven't been through it before. Knock when the pizza is done!" she said, voice muffled. I heard her footsteps retreat from the door, and I breathed out, a familiar, almost comforting frustration spreading through my chest.

I sighed. "Fine!" I exclaimed, stalking away from the door back toward the kitchen. When I got there, I saw the shattered remains of the glass that Wednesday had hurled down at the floor, and I rolled my eyes.

Cats.

"Are you sure you weren't half cat *before* you got cursed, Wednesday?" I muttered under my breath, grabbing the broom and dustpan from the pantry. I cleaned up the mess, and then sat on the couch, staring at the dark TV screen.

So, Odell was pretending to be Giselle. Giselle was Wednesday. Who was Rothbart? I frowned, breathing deeply, trying to relax my mind. It was more difficult than I was accustomed to, and I frowned again. Realizing that that was moving my progress backward, I accepted the frustration, allowing the muscles in my face, and then neck, and then shoulders to relax.

Odell was still a student. She obviously knew a lot, but there were only so many things that she could study without coming under suspicion. Even without having Wednesday around, if she had overtly studied transformation it would have come up somewhere in the discussions with her friends. Then again, even with the know-how of being able to turn someone into a cat, having practical experience was vital to the success of any magical project. Someone like Rothbart, who went through a turn-your-enemy-into-a-swan phase a couple hundred years ago.

So who was around Odell, who currently looked like Giselle, who knew about Odell using magic, who could be Rothbart? The real Giselle—Wednesday—did, for sure, but she was currently going through my closet. Leonora?

No, she was too upfront. Too genuine in her concern. Too...nice.

Was she, though?

A phrase entered my head then. Said quietly at the end of an interview, deep sincerity running through it. *We could all do with a bit of closure.*

*I know who Rothbart is,* Wednesday had said. A vivid image of Siegfried leaning through the window of the car, mouth moving in a wordless beckon to Wednesday, who was nearly in Konstantin's lap. He had gripped the door handle, even when he didn't need to.

"That son of a—" I broke off, shooting to my feet. "He blew up my car!"

Of course, it made sense. I'd spent the last three hundred years chasing after him, but he'd tried to kill me just as many times. Even so, blowing up my car, especially since I wasn't even inside, seemed excessive.

Not that Rothbart had *ever* been an example of restraint, but—

"You are an adult, Trillion," I said, taking in a deep breath. "He is your kid brother that simply has a propensity toward murder and violence. You already knew this, it's nothing to get upset over.

Nothing to get upset over.

Breathe.

I was gonna—

"Trillion?" I whipped around to see Wednesday, practically swaddled in sweater material, hair wet, drawn-on whiskers slightly blurred. My heart stuttered a little. She was...adorable.

That thought was also completely inappropriate. Those words would never leave my lips. Say something else. *Anything* else.

"Rothbart is Siegfried. And he blew up my car," I huffed. Well...at least it was *more* normal.

Maybe Wednesday was right. I saw the smile a second before she wiped it off her face.

"I'm—I'm so sorry."

"No, you're not," I said flatly.

She shuffled, for once a little uncomfortable. "Well, I can tell it matters to you," she said after a second. "And for that, I am sorry."

I frowned. "Thanks." I thought about it for a moment. "He's also a wretched clod, and I want to belt him for making you uncomfortable in the car that day." I paused again. "And also for possibly turning you into a cat."

Her expression brightened into something that couldn't quite seem to decide between embarrassed and incredibly pleased. "Thank you," she said, her voice rather delighted.

The buzzer on the oven rang. I smiled. "That'll be the pizza."

"So, you've put me through the third degree on what kind I wanted and how I wanted it. Are you going to ask me how I want to eat it? Plates? Napkins? The floor?" Wednesday asked, following me as we made our way into the kitchen.

I rolled my eyes. "Do you need me to?"

"I feel like I can manage without additional instruction," she said, stepping lightly after me in her bare feet.

"I don't know, I feel like you'll just lick it or something," I said, pulling the oven door open. The transition from pizza slab to stovetop was handled seamlessly, and after a moment, I turned back to Wednesday, pizza piece on plate. Her eyes were big and excited, and she practically jumped forward. I held it up.

"If you throw up on my rug later because you still have a cat stomach, we will have words," I told her.

She smirked. "If I can resist throwing up salmon cat food, I'm sure I can resist throwing up pizza."

I wrinkled my nose. "Was it that bad?"

"Considering I don't actually like seafood, it tasted like an abomination had thrown up, and I had to eat the abomination vomit," Wednesday said, taking the plate from me. "And no, that is not an exaggeration."

"Baby," I said, following her into the kitchen.

"This from the man who—for the entire two weeks I have been here—has not stepped within fifteen feet of a vegetable?" she said, sliding the pizza onto the counter and hopping onto one of the barstools.

"Irrelevant," I said, serving myself a pizza slice.

"If you say so," she said under her breath, leaning in close to the pizza and inhaling deeply. She looked up at me, placed a hand over her heart, black marker whiskers creasing and green eyes twinkling.

"Thank you," she said quietly. It seemed to carry more weight than one pepperoni pizza. Stepping close, I pulled her into my side, running my hand over the top of her head.

I said, "Of course."

What I meant was "Always."

# 24

# IN WHICH ROUTINE
# PLAYS AN INTEGRAL
# PART

"So tell me about this curse," I said, stuffing another slice of pizza into my mouth. I had retreated to a respectable distance, and then a little bit more, just to be safe. As much as my emotions—or, more likely, hormones—didn't seem to care about the curse that I carried, I actually didn't want to die any time soon, and so I kept my distance. Wednesday looked up, eyebrows raised at my words—and possibly my distance—and shrugged.

"I... turned into a cat. And I can only turn into a human when the moon is out and I'm outside," she said.

"What about breaking it?" I asked. She looked over at me, confused. I frowned. "What, you're planning on staying a cat?"

She blinked. "I—Well, I knew I *would* break it someday. I just haven't given it thought in a while. Since...well, since shortly after I was turned."

"Why?"

"It was depressing," she said succinctly. "*You* try getting locked in a barn—"

"Mill."

"—Mill for three months. You end up focusing on what helps you keep going. I found I didn't know nearly enough about my curse to make any useful deductions. It was better to learn how to hunt, and jump, and stay alive than try and puzzle something out that I was never going to solve."

"Hunt—Didn't they feed you?" I asked.

Wednesday thought for a moment, taking another bite of pizza. "Every couple of days? I remember seeing Odell more than Siegfried—sorry, Rothbart, it's still kind of spotty—and she'd leave me a couple of days of food. At first I'd fight the rats to get it. Soon I learned to use it as bait."

I looked over at her, pity pulling at me plaintively. She stared across the kitchen for a moment, a frown pulling at her lips.

"I'm sorry you went through that," I said quietly. She blinked from her trance, looking at me, and shrugged, sighing.

"It's not your fau—" She broke off, a sudden look of contemplation on her face.

"What?" I asked, disturbed. "Was it—"

"Never mind," Wednesday said, waving a hand dismissively. "I had a thought, but now it's gone. Don't worry about it."

"I might if you think I'm responsible," I said.

She scoffed. "Trillion, you have the most severe hero complex I've ever seen. Of *course* you'll think it's your fault. But think about it: what could you have possibly done to inspire Rothbart and Odell turn me into a cat?"

Even though I wanted to, I couldn't think of a good reason.

"Fine," I said. "But if Rothbart's motives—"

"If they have anything to do with you, I will give you a hearty apology." Her voice was reassuring. "If you'd like, I could even promise to kick you in the shins."

"I think I'll pass," I grumbled, looking away. Flashing me a brilliant smile, she finished off her slice of pizza and took another from the pan, apparently thoroughly enjoying herself. I smiled, realized I was smiling, and wiped the smile off my face. Maybe Wednesday wouldn't notice. She stood up, heading over to the sink. Looking at me over the bar counter, her eyebrows together.

"Are you okay?"

Blast.

"I'm fine," I responded.

"You look like you're trying to express like five different emotions and doing them all poorly."

"Thank you, Wednesday, for that vote of confidence."

"I figured you'd like to know."

"You know, I used to think that I was actually a competent adult. Now I wonder how I lived to one hundred with how well you read my expressions."

"I'm a ballerina, Trillion," she said, sipping from her glass of water, "I'm a master of subtlety."

"Says the woman who, as a cat, started smashing glasses so I would answer her questions," I said.

She looked up at me, smug. "Well, I said *I* was a master of subtlety. I had to communicate on your level." Her face shifted into a smile, eyelids half lowered in a self-satisfied smirk.

"Ouch!" I said.

"Don't ask questions you don't want answers to," she said simply, shrugging.

"It wasn't a question!" I exclaimed.

She looked up thoughtfully. "I suppose you're right."

"Aw, thanks."

"You're welcome."

"That was sarcasm, Wednesday." I rolled my eyes.

"Why? You were right," she responded innocently. I rolled my eyes harder. "If you go blind in a year from eye strain, don't blame me," Wednesday said evenly. I almost rolled my eyes again, but instead took a deep breath, wondering why I was so fond of this woman.

"So how are we going to solve this?" I said. "I can't guarantee that we can get a useful answer out of Rothbart."

"Why not?" Wednesday asked.

I cleared my throat. "Because when I meet him, I imagine there will be violence involved," I said dryly. "I don't know how you turned into a cat, but I imagine that there wasn't much talking involved."

She thought about it. "Fair point, I guess. Although, I'm pretty sure it was Odell..." she trailed off, chewing contemplatively on her mouthful of pizza.

"Just pretty sure?"

"It's fuzzy still, but slowly coming back. I remember seeing her face after, but to be perfectly honest both times I was cursed, my back was turned," she said.

I frowned. "Wait—both times?"

"Yeah. The big one, at the party. But...now that I have the benefit of knowing what it feels like, it could have happened before that? Once?"

"When?" I demanded. "And where?"

She seemed to think for a moment. "At home?"

"Your mother's house?" No one in their right mind would transfigure Wednesday on her mother's turf. Stanislava was the forefront practitioner of transfiguration in the United States, if not the entire Western Hemisphere. If she didn't notice the magic outright, then she would have been able to sense the remnants shortly thereafter.

She blinked, and her frown deepened. "No, mine. My apartment uptown. I can't remember when. Before the party. There's a big blank that—"

"You said you're having a hard time remembering beforehand. How can you be sure your big blank isn't just another... gap?"

"Because it's... different?" she offered tersely. "Don't interrupt me."

I still felt dubious that it was actually different, but since our reading minds thing only apparently went one way, I had no choice but to trust her. Then again, did I really have any reason to doubt her?

No. No, I didn't.

Something tickled in the back of my brain. "Wait a minute, you live on the same floor as a couple of your ballet company people?"

"Yes."

Glancing at the clock, and realizing it was almost seven in the morning, I reached into my pocket, pulled out my cell phone, and called Konstantin. It rang a couple of times, and then cut off, requesting me to leave a message. I frowned, pulling the phone away from my ear, staring at the illuminated screen before disconnecting the call.

"Did Konstantin not answer you?" Wednesday asked, forehead creased.

I nodded. "It went to voicemail," I explained. A moment later, the phone buzzed, a new text message popping up.

Wednesday read it aloud over my shoulder. "'*Sorry, Trillion, my voice is still gone. What did you need?* Is that normal? I was under the impression that most of the Faerie races healed completely given enough time."

"They do," I agreed. "Plus, Konstantin hates texting enough that he would most likely still try and talk to me until we both got frustrated."

"Any chance he's grown as a person?" Wednesday asked.

"About as much chance as I have," I admitted. Wednesday blinked at me. "What?"

"It's no fun if you make it easy for me," she grumbled, still looking over my shoulder at the phone. We both sat contemplatively for a minute. Worry permeated the air between us. Finally, Wednesday said, "Want to go and check out his house?"

There was a brief pause.

"Yeah."


It was a little odd, Wednesday sitting in the passenger seat as we sped down the driveway. She was still dressed in the too-big sweatpants and hoodie, feet now smothered in socks and hiking boots that were also way too big. She looked a little pensively outside the window.

"What is it?" I asked.

She lifted her chin to the east. "The sun's about to rise," Wednesday said quietly. Sadly.

"Is it hard?" I reached out and grabbed her hand.

She looked from the hand to my face and didn't pull away. "To change?"

"Yeah," I said. She looked away to where the horizon, hidden as it was between the trees, brightened with every passing minute.

"Not really," she said. "In some ways it feels as natural as breathing. In others... it feels like it takes a piece of my soul."

"We're going to find a way to stop it, Wednesday," I said, squeezing her hand. She squeezed back.

"Thank you, Trillion," Wednesday said. Then she turned, her hand slipping from mine, and a second later a small tabby sat in the passenger seat, blinking as her brain caught up with the transformation. She didn't look over at me, but instead stared out the window, as if mourning the moment.

I let her, urging the rental car a little faster down the road. I'd meant to call the dealership to see what they had by way of reliable transportation yesterday, but I had fallen asleep and then slept longer than I had in several hundred years. I'd have to do it today. Hopefully, if all went well, I could walk away later tonight with a car that was properly mine.

Wednesday had said it jokingly, but she was actually right—it was easier on my insurance if I actually owned the cars that I was wrecking. Not that I would ever—*ever*—tell her, but I was actually getting better at having them last a couple years before completely obliterating them. What's more, this particular incident wasn't even my fault.

I turned into Konstantin's gravel driveway. Bee, Konstantin's sister, was supposed to be home, but I couldn't see her car in the driveway. Some of the curtains were drawn but even so, I could tell that the lights weren't on.

"It's too dark in there."

*If he is in dog form, he would not need to turn on the lights. It is getting light,* Wednesday said, one of her ears flicking. *We should knock. Then we will know.*

"What if someone else is there?" I asked.

She looked up at me. *Then I will run away, and you will punch them,* she said succinctly. She turned to the door, as if she was going to open it up, and turned back to me. *If you could get the door...*

Opening my own door, I let her walk across my lap and climb out. She jumped and landed on the snowy gravel gracefully, trotting toward the door of the house.

"Wait for me!" I said.

She looked back. *Hurry up!*

"You've got twice the amount of legs that I do, don't you think that's a bit unfair?"

*Well, you're approximately twenty-eight times my size, and you don't hear me complaining, do you?* she demanded in return.

"You *always* complain about me," I pointed out.

*But always in an overarching, pleasant, joking way.*

I thought about that. "No, you don't," I said.

*Of course I do.*

"No, you don't," I repeated, looking down at her as we stepped up onto the doorstep.

*You should knock.* Rolling my eyes, I lifted my hand and knocked at the door. Konstantin had responded to the text, so he would be awake, right? That was another thing that niggled at the back of my brain. Konstantin wasn't one to be up early. Up late, for sure, but even about seven for Konstantin was that grey hour that he was rarely conscious unless previously agreed upon.

*He is not answering.*

"No," I agreed, pulling my cell phone from my pocket again.

*He will not answer the phone.*

"I know," I said, pulling up the contacts list and finding a name. I almost hesitated, but pressed it anyway. If I called, she was liable to come bounding down here, but Konstantin was in trouble, and I needed to get to the bottom of this. It was a risk I was going to have to take.

"Trillion?" Bee's voice was a low murmur in my ear.

"Hi, Bee," I said. "Sorry for calling so early. I was just wondering if you'd seen Konstantin today?"

"No, I've been in Virginia since Sunday. Why?" she asked. Almost immediately, her voice dropped into a growl. "Has something happened?"

*Aside from her brother being almost blown up and possibly kidnapped?*

"I'm not sure," I said turning from the house. "Konstantin is only texting me when I call him and—"

"He's in trouble," Bee broke in, her low voice suddenly urgent. "Konstantin would rather die than text. You know that better than anyone."

I did. I had also been just a touch distracted by a certain cat-turned-woman-turned-cat.

"Yeah."

"Well, do you know who would have taken him?" Bee demanded.

Boy, did I.

"Yes," I said, "I think I do. Bee, do I have permission to search your house? I have the spare key that Konstantin gave me."

"If you don't, I'm strangling you once I get back," she said gruffly. "You do what you have to to get Konstantin back, do you hear me?"

"Yes, ma'am," I said, and hung up the phone. When I looked down at Wednesday, she was looking up at me, and the emotion of awe seemed to radiate toward me. "What?"

*H-how did she do that?* she said, her voice almost breathy. *She just told you to do something, and-and you* agreed.

"Yes, well, I wanted to do it anyway. And she may or may not make me just a little nervous," I grumbled, pulling the keys from my pocket. Sorting out Konstantin's key from the rest, I pushed the key into the lock and twisted. It moved easily, and I swung the door open.

Furniture, papers, and objects lay strewn across the room in almost impressive disarray. Glass cracked under my feet as I stepped inside, and I leaned down to scoop up Wednesday. She must have heard it, because for once she didn't protest as I gathered her into my arms.

We made our way into the middle of the room. The damage was more severe the further that we went in—cushions ripped apart, curtains on the windows facing the back of the house torn from their rods. And then, in the middle of the room, something dark in a circle that was simply too wide. Leaning down, tucking Wednesday under my arm, I touched the center, moving my fingers toward the outside.

Wet.

I looked at the residue on my fingers.

Red.

*Trillion?* Wednesday's voice quavered in my head.

I rubbed my fingers together. "It's a few hours old," I explained. "Dried around the edges."

*Is he dead?* Wednesday whispered. I looked around, taking in every overturned chair, every scratched piece of furniture. Now that I looked closer, I could see blood spatter on almost everything, as though whoever had left the puddle had continued to fight.

"Not yet," I said quietly. They'd regret it if they left him to recover too long.

*Where did they take him?*

"I don't know."

*What do we do now?* Wednesday asked, her voice small.

I looked around the room once more. "We'll have a look around and see what we can find. If it's Rothbart's doing, he won't leave a trace once he's left the house."

*What if we don't find anything?* Wednesday asked.

I frowned. "Rothbart will have taken Konstantin for a purpose. Most likely ransom or exchange. We wait."

*But what if they—*

"If Rothbart wanted to warn me, he would have left Konstantin here, dead. He will be in contact."

*I hope so*, Wednesday said quietly, unconvinced.

I hoped so, too.

# 25

## IN WHICH THERE IS FAR TOO MUCH TECHNOLOGICAL LITERACY

There was no trace, of course. Even after spending a full two hours looking for any physical evidence left in the house, all I had was a single footprint that seemed to belong to Odell. Despite an on-the-fly tracker spell, it led nowhere, hidden by Rothbart's shielding spell. If Konstantin had been with me, her location wouldn't have been nearly as untraceable, but he wasn't, and here we were.

I wasn't particularly surprised, but it was still disheartening. The feeling was contagious, and the drive back to the house, and then on to the office was quiet and subdued. I turned my phone off silent, keeping it within arm's reach as we made our way up to the office.

I surveyed the empty office, my frown deepening, along with my disappointment. I didn't know why I had hoped that he was here—maybe I'd hoped that he'd escaped, or that it was all a misunderstanding, but no.

We would have to wait.

I sat at my desk, ruminating furiously for a good five minutes. This was exactly why I had always taken Father's advice to never get attached to anyone. Not only the curse, but the leverage that Rothbart was able to have over me right now. I hated it. I hated it, I hated it, I hated it.

It was worse than knowing that one of those relationships was going to kill me.

I stared at the door furiously, my stare blistering into the wood, trying to think of something—anything—that I could do in the meantime, before my eyes locked on Wednesday. She noticed right away, freezing, and looking up at me.

*What?*

"You're still cursed."

*Clearly.*

"Odell's spell books are here," I said. "Do you think the spell that she used would be in them?"

*Do you seriously think I know the answer to that question?* Her tail swished as she walked toward me.

I pursed my lips and shook my head. "No," I said. "But a quick look won't hurt."

I had forgotten how many boxes we'd brought in.

*Are you going to start with* Spells through the Ages, *or do you think you'll jump straight to* Intermediate Transfiguration? Wednesday asked innocently as I shuffled through the books.

"Both," I said, putting them in a pile. Not all of her book were spellbooks. Some were Latin texts, or magical theory, but there was also a substantial amount of magical history, and even a couple of potion books. I put those aside, and carried on through. By the end, I had seventeen enormous textbooks stacked beside me teetering over Wednesday.

*If those fall on me, I'm sleeping on your face tonight*, she said grumpily, stalking out into the main office. Dividing the one enormous stack into two, I brought them out one at a time, setting each one on my desk. Then, checking my phone every two minutes to make sure it was still on, I went to studying.

Four hours crawled by. I was skimming for the most part, skipping anything that didn't have to do with animals or people, which included the majority of the spells. Every once in a while I paused to read a spell in detail, but nothing seemed to stand out. Finally, at almost two, Wednesday pawed at my knee.

*You need to eat.*

"I'm not hungry."

*You didn't eat breakfast.*

"I had pizza, and I'm reading."

*That was before. If you don't keep—*

"Wednesday—"

*Look, if you don't get something to eat, I'm stealing your phone and ordering as many dishes from as many places as I can until you catch me or I max out your credit card.*

I looked down at Wednesday.

"I seriously doubt you'll be able to." I said. The small cat glared up at me.

*Yeah, Konstantin said the same thing about his password. I had it in two tries.*

"Yeah ri—"

*Two.*

"Wednesday—"

*His birthday is March 2, 1937. Yours is January twenty-fourth.*

My mouth dropped open.

"How did you—"

*I bet they wouldn't allow you to put the year 57 BC on your birth certificate, because of the four-digit year requirement, so it's probably something from the first millennia. On a six-digit password, though, I can see you doing the day and the year. You're not a zero sort of person, though, so you'd choose the year 1157 for your official birth year. My educated guess is your phone password is two-four-one-one-five-seven.*

I gaped at her. She looked up at me, smugness radiating off of her.

*Tell me I'm wrong.*

I couldn't. And it made me angry. I scowled.

"It doesn't matter. I'm not hungry."

*Doesn't matter. I'm making an executive decision.*

"You can't make executive decisions, you're a c—"

*If you say cat, you will never leave this room,* she warned.

"Client." I raised my hands. "I was going to say client."

She stared at me warningly before swishing her tail in annoyance.

*If I'm a client, then you're my staff. I can and will feed you anytime and anything I please,* she finally said. *Now, give me your phone.*

"I'm not giving you my phone." I picked up the book that I had placed on the table in my dismay, and started flicking through it. Wednesday sat on the floor beside me for a moment before stalking away.

*Fine.*

I didn't think anything of it until twenty-five minutes later, when I heard knocking on the door. Frowning, I made my way to the door. A young man, probably not more than seventeen years old stood there. He only came up to about my chest, and his eyes widened as his view panned up to my grim face.

"Um, you ordered some pizza." His voice shook a little, changing his statement into a question. I stared at him and then turned into the room.

"Wednesday!" I growled.

The young man gulped. "Um, yes, it is."

I turned back to him.

"I wasn't talking to you," I snapped.

Wednesday didn't respond. After another moment scowling into the room, not seeing the fluffy cat, I dug into my pocket, fishing out a tip. The boy, shaken out of his intimidated gaze, thanked me, and handed me the pizza. Closing the door with a definitive click, I turned on my heel to see Wednesday sitting by my desk, tail wrapped demurely around her feet.

*Well,* she said sweetly, *eat up. The Thai food will be here in twenty minutes.*

"You didn't!" I protested, patting down my pockets.

*I left your phone on your desk,* she said simply, turning to walk into the back room. Then she paused. *And, for the record, yes. Yes, I did.*

I swiped my phone from the desk and opened it up. I had left it on the desk—just out of my eyeline—to force myself to stop checking for notifications every two minutes. Clearly this had been a mistake.

Twelve Notifications. I clicked them open.

*Your order from Pizza King is completed. Please rate us!*

*Your order from Bamboo Thai is on its way!*

*Your order from Wu Qing's Buffet is on it's way!*

*Your order from the Apple and Aubergine is on its way!*

*Your order from—*

"Wednesday!" I shouted.

I heard a snicker from the back room. Sighing, I flipped the pizza box open and took a slice.

It would have been nice if food had made everything better. It

didn't, but my mood, as terrible as it was, moved from actively an-
tagonistic to merely depressed. I made it through the last book as
my phone read seven, and leaned back into the chair, frown settling firmly on my face. Wednesday, who had been dozing on my
lap, looked up, blinking sleepily.

*What did you find?* she asked. Reaching over, I grabbed a cream
cheese rangoon from one of the packages that Wednesday had ordered and stuffed it in my mouth.

"Nothing," I said around it, glaring at the door. I hadn't meant it
to come out so sulkily. Wednesday looked up at me, one of her ears
twitching.

*We should call my mom.*

I looked down at her, frown between my eyebrows deepening.
"What?"

*We should call my mom,* she repeated. *She's one of the most accom-
plished transfigurists in the country.*

"She's also the scariest transfigurist in the country, and I need to
keep my phone line free in case Rothbart calls."

*So give her a video call,* she suggested, as if it solved all my problems. *Most people are just scary because you can't guess what they're thinking.*

"Turning on a video call won't help me with that. I never know
what your mother is thinking," I grumbled.

Wednesday blinked. *Well then, it's a good thing that I'm here, isn't
it?* she said evenly. *Mother won't be able to get mad at me for letting you
know what she's actually thinking.*

"How am I supposed to even make said video call?"

*Leave that to me.*

"How? You don't have thumbs," I pointed out. Wednesday looked
up at me, catching my gaze. Then, slowly, she looked over at the
enormous of mountain of food that sat off to the side. I pressed my
lips together. "Fine," I said, and pushed the phone to her. Using an

oddly purposeful paw, she unlocked my phone, and opened up the video chat app, carefully pawing numbers onto the touchscreen.

It rang.

*Pick it up, pick it up!* she said, swiping it toward me. Licking a bit of sweet and sour sauce off of my thumb and wiping my mouth with my napkin, I picked up the phone, swallowing nervously.

Stanislava's face, large and close to the camera, filled the screen. She looked incredibly confused for a moment.

"Trillion?" she asked. "How did you get this number?"

"Um." I stared at the phone, and then looked down at Wednesday, who was just out of shot. She blinked expectantly. "I will explain. And it will be...a good explanation." I turned the phone away from myself and made a face at the cat. Wednesday blinked again, unfazed.

"This is a private number," Stanislava's tone didn't change, and neither did her expression. She looked like she was going to hang up. I looked over at Wednesday, and then back at Stanislava.

*Go on,* Wednesday urged.

"I—" I looked down at the fluffy cat. She put a paw on my hand, as if she was trying to comfort me and I sighed.

"I got this number from your daughter," I said hesitantly. Stanislava's eyebrows furrowed and it was abundantly clear she didn't understand.

"Why would Giselle give you my number? Particularly my private number? I was under the impression she was gone for the weekend. And, interestingly, that she didn't like you."

I fought the urge to blanch, and shook my head.

"There's a very good reason for that," I said, pressing my lips together.

"So you've said," Stanislava said, the camera a little too close to her face. "Explain."

*She's interested,* Wednesday said, *tell her.*

"Um, well, she's here with me," I said. Stanislava started to make a noise of protest when I turned the camera on to Wednesday. Wednesday mewed a little, pawing at the camera.

*Hello, Mother,* she said quietly, paw slowly moving over the screen.

"Trillion, is this a prank call? Who is that cat?" Stanislava's voice demanded. I turned the screen back onto myself. Silently suffering, I talked.

"That's... Giselle," I said. I paused for a good long while, trying to think of the best way to put it. Wednesday prompted me, and I repeated the words that she said. "She was turned into a cat by Odell and Siegfried, who's really Rothbart. They've abducted Konstantin, my partner, and we're not sure how to break the curse." I frowned a little as Wednesday bunted against my shoulder with her head, as if to tell me I'd done a good job. "I...we wanted to know if you had any insight. I've looked through all of Odell's spell books. I haven't found anything helpful."

Stanislava looked from me, to Wednesday, and then back again. And then did it again. And again.

"That cat...is my daughter?"

*Ah, I should have known she would get stuck on that part,* Wednesday said sagely. *That's unfortunate.*

I turned my head. Wednesday's ear twitched.

*She's about to be super helpful, or blow up.*

"Which one?" I whispered at her.

*I don't want to guess. I don't have the best track record at being accurate about that.*

I fought the urge to bury my head in my hands.

"How did my daughter get turned into a cat? How long has she been a cat? Where is Odell? Why did she turn my daughter into a cat? Rothbart is Siegfried? I'll kill him! He dated my daughter and turned her into a quadruped! I—"

She continued to rant, voice so loud it made the sound quality on the video a little fuzzy.

*You should cut in now,* Wednesday said, *She's going to work herself up into a tizzy, and she's not going to be useful to anyone.*

"I—"

"Get over here," Stanislava ordered, and I nearly straightened and saluted at the imperious tone. I'd only ever heard that from generals and drill sergeants who meant business, and I wasn't about to disobey.

"I—" I started tell her that I would be right over. Stanislava misinterpreted my tone.

"Now!" The word was a stern bark. I nodded.

"Yes, ma'am."

The video went blank. Wednesday and I both sat there, blinking down at the dark screen.

*Well,* Wednesday said, voice slightly taken aback, *that went better than I thought it would.*

# 26

# IN WHICH
# WEDNESDAY GETS A
# MOMENT OF
# COMEUPPANCE, AND I
# COME TO A
# REALIZATION

The car ride went too quickly. By the time we pulled up to the Manor, I had to wipe the sweat off of my hands onto my trousers. Even Wednesday seemed a little uneasy, pacing back and forth across the seat as we drove through the city. I paused after I turned off the car, looking over at her.

"Are you okay?" I asked, reaching my hand out to her.

Wednesday looked up at it, and then back up at me. *Are you?* she retorted.

"I'm going to take that as a 'no'," I said, opening the door. Wednesday walked across my lap, claws carefully pokey, and hopped down onto the wet pavement. I also exited the car and, following her, made my way rather slowly to the door. Wednesday was waiting at the door for me. As I raised my hand to knock, the door swung open to reveal Stanislava.

"What took you so long? Did you choose to actually follow the speed limit for once in your life?" she demanded.

"I didn't realized you were monitoring me," I said, trying to sound nonchalant. Stanislava glared at me.

"Get in here," she said, throwing the door open wide. Wednesday trotted in front of me, looking up at the older woman. She chirped a little.

*Hello, Mother*, she said.

Stanislava didn't understand. A little hesitantly, I shuffled indoors, and gestured down to the cat.

"Wedne—er, Giselle, says hello."

"Does she?" she said, looking down severely down at the cat. Dressed in black from head to toe, it seemed very reminiscent of an enormous looming dragon. Wednesday sat at her feet, almost kitten sized, her only movement the very tip of her tail dancing from side to side. Her ears were forward, paying complete attention to her mother.

I watched with bated breath, half expecting Stanislava to evict us both on the spot. Then slowly, gracefully Stanislava lowered into a crouch, reaching out one hand. Wednesday leaned forward into that hand, the tension in her feline shoulders relaxing. Stanislava closed her eyes briefly, and in that moment, I knew she could feel the enchantment.

"When did you find out?" Stanislava asked, her voice deep and husky.

"This morning. I thought she was Odell, until she changed back into her human form briefly before sunrise," I said quietly. "I've spent most of the day trying to figure out if Odell's spell books had the answer in them."

Stanislava scooped Wednesday up into her arms. Wednesday tucked her head up against Stanislava's neck, and Stanislava stroked her soft fur.

"I would be surprised if it were," she murmured. She looked up at me, queenly demeanor restored, despite the presence of the fluffy cat in her arms. "Follow me."

"Where are we going?" I asked, pulled into motion at her words.

"My workshop." The heels of Stanislava's shoes clicked purposefully as she marched away from the staircase that I had ascended the previous time I had entered the house. We continued down one of the long marble halls, lit by fake flickering candle light. I frowned at the inconsistent light, but followed swiftly. I half-expected her workshop to be something out of Shelley's Frankenstein with ye olde torches and a rack or two, but when we finally entered, it was bright and cool, and the room was full of clean white surfaces. If nothing else, it looked like a modern medical laboratory.

She noticed my surprised expression, and looked down her nose at me.

"Just because I do not study traditional human sciences does not negate the need for the scientific method. Nor cleanliness," she said.

I looked around. "Forgive me." I bowed slightly. "My expression is one of admiration. Many do not go to such lengths."

Stanislava placed Wednesday on one of the tables. Wednesday made to wander off, but Stanislava put a hand on her back. "Stay there, Giselle," she said. "I have some tests that I would like to run on you."

Wednesday looked up at her mother, and then at me, and I nodded. So she sat, looking distinctly uncomfortable as her mother rushed around her lab for a couple moments, pulling out two pairs of what looked like very old spectacles, scissors, a metal circumference gauge, and a tongue depressor.

Wednesday looked at the instruments, then up at me.

*If this turns out like the vet, I'm never speaking to you again.*

I reached out, running my hand over her head, and whispered to her under my breath. "I'm sure it'll be fine."

*Our relationship is on the line if it isn't.*

"Something wrong?" Stanislava asked, walking up with a glass dome. Wednesday looked at it, and then furiously up at me.

*Get an explanation.*

"Giselle seems to be worried that these tests are going to be fairly invasive," I explained, motioning to the instruments around us. "We had an... incident at the vet's a couple of weeks ago."

Stanislava's eyebrows rose, and then she looked down at the small cat, something curved and pleasant hovering around her lips. Wednesday sat there, the tip of her tail twitching, daring her mother to make a comment.

"Oh really?" Stanislava asked mildly. She looked down at the small cat. "You deserve it."

"What?" I lifted my head, caught off guard.

*Mother!* Wednesday's voice was scandalized, short shocked chirp erupting from her.

Stanislava waved her hand at Wednesday. "Not being turned into a cat, my love. But you've been a force of nature ever since you were born. You deserve a little inconvenience every now and again. It's good for you. Don't let her treat you like a doormat, Trillion. I'm not surprised that of all the animals on earth, she was turned into a cat."

*But—it—Mother!* Wednesday was practically speechless, and I couldn't help but grinning. She noticed. *You wipe that smile off of your*

*face, Trillion! There is nothing entertaining about this situation, and you
tell her that!*

"Heavens, no," I said, turning and walking toward something interesting—I wasn't sure what yet—on the other end of the room. "I
am not getting in the middle of this."

*Trillion! You get back here and translate!*

"I find I'll probably live longer if I don't," I said.

Wednesday glowered and growled deep in her throat. *We'll see
about that.*

"Sweetheart, don't threaten our guests," Stanislava said, running
her hand down Wednesday's back. "Besides, if you'd done as I asked
and came to observe my work every once in a while, you would
know what I was doing."

*Yes, well, I didn't know I would be enchanted seventy years later!*
Wednesday protested, yowling, and Stanislava smirked, not able to
understand the words, but obviously recognizing the reaction.

"Yes, yes," she said placatingly, taking the first pair of glasses, and
slipping them onto her face. Almost immediately, the look of concern dropped back over her face, and I watched, my own stomach
dropping as Stanislava's expression grew darker and darker.

None of us spoke, instead choosing to watch as Stanislava made
a couple of marks on a paper, switching to the other pair of glasses.
Then she had Wednesday open her mouth for her, measured something above Wednesday's head and clipped a bit of hair off of
Wednesday's belly. Finally, placing the glass dome over the severed
fur, she ran one finger down the glass.

The fur burst into flame, first burning a hot blue, then green, and
then smoldering into an ugly grayish black, billows of acrid-looking
smoke filling the dome.

Stanislava's expression turned black, looking from the glass
dome, to Wednesday, to myself. "I certainly hope you are looking for
the individual responsible?" she said, grabbing me by the elbow and

pulling me away from where Wednesday still sat on the counter, her voice low and dangerous again.

I nodded. "Yes, Councilwoman."

"You say it was Siegfried?"

"Rothbart, disguised as Siegfried. You mean to say that Odell was not the one that cast the spell?"

"On the contrary, I can definitely confirm her as the spell caster." Stanislava paused. "I know of Rothbart by reputation. Knowing Odell as well, I wonder if she is the leader or the follower in this situation."

"Odell is the one with motive against Wednesday," I pointed out.

Stanislava hummed in agreement, but then looked back toward Wednesday. "But she is not a murderer," Stanislava said quietly.

It took me a moment to realize what she was saying, and I glanced back to Wednesday in alarm. "You mean—" My voice broke, just a tad, and I turned back away from Wednesday to look back at Stanislava. Stanislava's expression cracked, just a little bit.

"This was not a transfiguration spell," she explained. "This was a soul harvesting spell. Black magic. The caster of this spell receives the soul of the cursed individual, allowing them to take over their appearance and know every aspect of the victim's lives. The transfiguration is a by-product that is a house for the... life that is left over. A receptacle where that remaining life is put safely to die."

I stared at her in disbelief for a moment before fury, hot and colorful, burst into life in my chest.

"Wednesday is going to die?" I whispered. Stanislava looked back at her daughter, sitting patiently on the table, looking up at the lights, apparently unaware of our conversation. For a moment I wondered why she hadn't followed. Perhaps her mother had enough private conversations that she was not in the habit of interrupting.

Then Wednesday looked up at me. I looked away quickly.

"Unless we can somehow break the spell, yes," Stanislava said, her voice tight and soft.

My face darkened into a frown. "So how do we do that?" I demanded, not taking my eyes off of Wednesday. The tip of her tail was twitching again.

"I'm not sure," Stanislava said quietly.

"If her soul was sucked out of her, how on earth did she turn back into a human?"

Stanislava looked down and away. "I'm not sure about that either. It's a reach that I even know about this spell."

I stared at her, feeling as though I'd been punched in the stomach, realizing that she didn't know any more of what to do than I did. "Then what do I do?" I asked anyway.

She sighed, and ran her hand over her hair, eyes dark and serious. "There is one person who would know for certain what to do," she said slowly, carefully. I knew in a moment exactly who she was talking about, but I didn't say anything. A buzzing sound filled my ears, and I turned from her.

"Don't say it," I said quietly, gripping the edge of a nearby table-top.

"King Auberon would know." Her voice was careful, but confident. I knew she was right. There was very little about magic that he didn't know. But was it worth it to go against his edict for something like this?

For...Wednesday?

"Yes," I whispered, "he would."

"Will you...ask him for me? For Giselle?" Stanislava asked quietly, carefully. Pleadingly. It was easy to forget that Wednesday was her daughter. The reason why I was investigating Odell's case in the first place.

I looked at Wednesday again, and she looked up at me, green eyes bright and luminous. What would the world be like without those eyes? The brightness. The intelligence.

*Trillion?* she asked. I looked up at Stanislava.

"Of course I will."

*You and Mother looked very serious,* Wednesday said on the way home. She stood with her front paws on the passenger side door, watching the cars as they passed by in the street. It was a little warmer today, and a wet sheen reflected the headlights and traffic lights as we passed by.

I was surprised that Stanislava had allowed me to take Wednesday back with me. I wasn't so sure why I had felt so insistent about it, either. There was a part of me that didn't like having Wednesday where I couldn't see her. Stanislava must have sensed that, even without my added explanation that I would be in a better position to protect her against Rothbart when the time came.

It didn't mean that she liked it.

"She didn't like that you were coming home with me," I said, turning onto the highway out of the city. "I explained that I would be able to protect you better from Rothbart this way."

*Oh,* she said, her voice flat.

"You disagree?" I asked.

*No,* she said. *What else did she say? After the dome with the smoke?*

I looked over. For the barest of moments I thought that I could keep the secret from her. There were a lot of different reasons to keep it from her. I didn't want to scare her, and there was a possibility that we could keep her from dying.

But then I thought how I would feel if someone kept something of this magnitude from me, and I sighed to the depths of my soul.

"It's not a transformation curse." My voice was subdued. All of me was subdued, and my heart hurt as I pressed on. "Your mother was able to find out that it was black magic, with the purpose of stealing your soul and giving it to the spell caster."

*So why am I a cat, then?* Wednesday asked. I frowned. Everything in me didn't want to tell her, and I my grip on the steering wheel tightened.

"To give you a form that could die," I gritted out, my jaw clenched. And she would have. If I hadn't taken her in. If I had done what I had to every other person and animal that I had ever saved—given acute care and then passed them on to a shelter.

*Trillion?* She turned toward me,

"I would have let you die!" I exclaimed, and she sat back on her haunches, shocked into silence. "And I would never have known! How many people have died once they left my care? How many animals could I have helped even more if I kept them with me? I was taught never to care about anyone or anything to save myself, to lengthen my life, but what has that gotten me? What if there's just a trail of broken people, animals, and things left in my wake simply because I wanted to live a little longer? What's the use of that? What's the use of living longer if it's at the cost of other peoples' lives? Their hearts? Their dreams? All I can see is the lost chances to help—*really* help. Not just acute care. Not just making sure that their bodies live. And now I see the very real possibility of losing you. I hate it. *I hate it.*"

I struck the top of the steering wheel. All that did was make my hand hurt, and I stared out of the windshield at the dark road, ignoring an unfamiliar, prickling feeling at the back of my eyes.

Wednesday didn't say anything for a long time, simply looking at me in the lights of the oncoming cars. I stared forward furiously, refusing to look at her.

*So what will you do now?*

"I don't know," I said harshly.

*Yes, you do.*

"No, I don't!" I exclaimed. "I don't know how to save you! I don't know how to save Konstantin! I don't know how to kill Rothbart, I—" I broke off, clearing my throat furiously. Taking a deep breath, I slowed the car and turned into the driveway. She had a point. What *was* I going to do?

What was the point of railing at the universe if I wasn't going to change anything?

We pulled into the garage and I shut off the car, sitting in the darkness for a moment, weighing my options and then my words.

"I'm going to call my father," I said quietly. "Your mother's right. He'll know what to do." I reached over, and ran my hand over her soft head. She leaned into my palm, and I smiled despite myself. "I'm not going to abandon you, Wednesday. Please count on that."

She opened her eyes, but kept leaning into my hand. *I know*, she whispered.

We sat there for a long moment in the dark car.

"Are you okay?" I finally asked. She seemed to sigh and stepped forward into my lap and curled up there.

*Not really. You?*

I smiled, and huffed out a humorless laugh.

"No."

# 27

## IN WHICH I CALL HOME

I couldn't call my father right away. England was five hours ahead of Maryland. As I already felt like I was taking a chance calling him, I didn't want to wake him up at three in the morning.

So I called the police instead. Sergeant Barlow wasn't particularly happy to hear my voice under regular circumstances, but his excitement level dropped to an all-time low as he listened to my explanation of why I was calling.

"You want me to ping your partner's phone? Isn't that what 'Find my Phone' is for?"

"He's got an off-brand smart phone," I explained. "Besides, what else are you going to be doing at this time of night?"

"Trillion, I can't just ping his phone. That's super illegal. Besides, to get a warrant, I would have to have good cause, and no judge in the world is going to sign off on something like that."

"Oh really? What about if Luther von Rothbart has it in his possession?" I asked flatly.

Sergeant Barlow paused. "You can't be serious."

"As a heart attack," I said solemnly.

"How do you know?" he demanded.

"Why would I ask you to spy on my own partner?" I demanded. "If he wasn't in danger, at his house, or even answering his phone calls, why would I bother ruining both our days by talking to you?"

I grimaced as soon as it was out of my mouth. I was trying to preserve whatever tenuous relationship that I had with the police station, and telling them what I *actually* thought of their treatment of the faerie species and magic in general would definitely not help, even if it would make me feel better.

So I waited for a flat refusal, and the probability that not only would I have to call my father tomorrow, but also make reparations with the police station.

I'd also have to buy a car.

I needed to make a list.

"Fine. I'll get the request written up and sent to the judge. I'll even put an urgent mark on it, since you think Konstantin's in trouble," Sergeant Barlow said, grumbling a little. "They won't get to it until tomorrow at the earliest, though. Don't hold your breath."

I almost said 'what?' in disbelief, but I thought that might have been pushing my chances a little. "Fine," I said instead. It wasn't much, but it was the best I could do for now. It was enough. As soon as I hung up, leaning back against the couch cushions, Wednesday trotted over from her food bowl.

*We should sleep*, she said.

I looked over. "What?"

*We should sleep. Your father is in England. We cannot call until four in the morning. If we to go sleep now, it'll be easier on us in the morning.*

I leaned forward and rubbed my head.

"I don't know, Wednesday," I said, sighing. "I'm not sure with everything going on that I'm going to be able to lay down for any length of time, let alone sleep."

She jumped up onto my lap, making me lean back against the cushions again, leaning back even further when she put her paws up onto my chest and brought her face in close. *You*, she said, *are a menace when you are tired. Go lay down. I bet sleep will come easier than you think.*

I was about to reply with a recalcitrant 'I don't want to go to bed' but I didn't think that it would convince her that I was any less of a menace. Why that actually mattered to me, I had no idea. But it did, so I dragged myself to my feet, stumbling toward my bedroom door.

To my credit, I actually changed into pajamas and brushed my teeth before I collapsed into bed, noting that Wednesday hadn't taken the whole thing over quite yet. Situating myself in the exact center of my bed, and noting how much I had missed having a firm border of mattress around myself, I made sure my phone alarm was set for four in the morning. Then, mentally grumbling at the futility of it all, I shut my eyes.

The next thing I knew, a bright happy ding from my phone woke me up, announcing the time. I blinked blearily at it, suddenly aware of Wednesday's comforting weight on my shoulder as I lay on my side. "Sorry, Wednesday," I whispered, slowly reaching out and disturbing her position as I swiped the my phone off the bedside table to turn off the alarm. Wednesday stirred and climbed off of me, stretching as she walked toward the edge of the bed.

There was a strange exhilaration as I grabbed my phone and shuffled out into the front room to sit on the couch. Not that I would fall asleep now that I was awake and faced with what I needed to do. I sat down cross-legged on the couch, pulling the flannel throw over my legs against the chill of the morning. Wednesday, who had woken herself up by crunching on a few pieces of kibble left in her dish from the night before, trotted over to me and nestled into my lap.

I held the phone for a moment, staring down at the bright screen, wondering if I was actually brave enough to make this call.

How would Father react? When last we spoke, telephones hadn't even been invented yet. I'd received a post card every once in a while, letting me know his current number, but other than that, nothing. I had honored his last wish to the letter. Would he be angry that I'd broken my silence now? Particularly when, all things considered, it was less about how to take down Rothbart, and more on how to save someone that I cared for. Cared for very deeply, when it came down to it.

But what other options did I have? Even if there were other transfiguration experts in the world, I didn't have access to any of them, and doubly didn't have the time to track them down. No, I needed help from him. If he wasn't willing to help, I would find someone who would. If that were possible.

*Are you awake, Trillion?* Wednesday asked, yawning deeply as she settled into my lap.

"Yes," I said, "Just trying to think of what I'm going to say."

*Just tell him you need help*, she suggested. *You can get into other stuff later.*

It seemed like it should have been more nuanced than that, but it was a sound suggestion, and before I knew it, I had pressed the number listed under the name 'Auberon'.

It rang. I frowned worriedly, and ran my hand over Wednesday's back, trying to distract myself from the nerves that seemed to be running relay races up and down my body. It rang again. And again. And again.

I suddenly realized that my father did not have my phone number. I could have been anyone calling from the United States. I knew that he had a Global Access phone, but that didn't vouch for the fact that I was me.

I was going to hang up. I could contact my brother Fevarion, and maybe he could get a message to—

"Hello?"

His voice was deeper than I remembered. The word moved smoothly through the air between us, like butter in caramel, the word relaxed, and somehow welcoming.

My hands went numb. Gripping the phone tighter to make sure I didn't lose my grip on it, I forced out a word.

"Father?"

There was a sharp intake of breath, and a stab of panic shocked through my chest. He was going to hang up.

"Trillion?" Father's voice was disbelieving, but not angry or disgusted. He—what was that emotion? What did I hear in his voice?

"Yes," I said—the only thing I could think of. It didn't seem like enough, but it was the only thing that I could say that didn't threaten to strangle me. Silence sat between us, stretching the entire three thousand miles inch by inch while neither of us spoke. I found my words first.

"I need help," I said, rubbing Wednesday's head a little more vigorously than before. Apparently it was too much, as she reached up and batted my hand off her head. I gripped the blanket that lay over my lap instead.

"Name it," Father responded.

That was it? No recrimination for not calling? No recrimination for calling? No demands for reparation? No request for Rothbart's head?

"I—it's not related to Rothbart. Well, not really," I admitted. Maybe hearing Rothbart's name would help shock my Father into awareness. Help him realize what was actually going on.

"I understand," Father said. "What do you need help with?"

"I need to know how to break a curse that Rothbart—or, well, one of his friends—put on..." I looked down at Wednesday, "someone close to me."

There was a pause on the other end, and a small voice in the back of my mind idly wondered if I was going to try to press *all* of my father's tender spots in the space of what would probably be—at least at this rate— a two-minute phone call.

"Describe the curse," he said finally. I stared at the phone in disbelief. I stared at it longer than was probably necessary, as after a minute I heard Father say distantly, "Hello?"

"Er, yes, sorry," I said. "According to Stanislava Carabosse, it's a black magic soul stealing spell. It had the side effects of physical transformation into a cat."

"What else?"

"I can hear her in my mind, and she can turn back into a human with direct light from the moon at night."

I heard my Father shift. I pictured him in his study. Surely it wouldn't look the same as it did three hundred years ago, but I could see him in his old leather-upholstered chair, behind the enormous cherrywood desk. I couldn't picture him with a mobile phone.

"Is she aware of her surroundings? Can she communicate in human terms?"

Boy, could she.

"Yes to both. She can also move things with her mind, but from what she tells me, she had that ability before her transformation."

Father was quiet for a long time. "Is she there with you?" he asked.

"Yes."

"I am not sure either of you will like my answer."

My heart stuttered for a moment, and then sank just a little. "Oh."

"There is a chance that we can save her," Father said quietly, "But

I must warn you that the possibility of your friend dying is much, much greater. What is the name of your friend?"

*Giselle Carabosse*, Wednesday said, meowing a little into the receiver, as if she forgot that I was the only one that could understand her.

"Well, hello, Giselle," Father said, and I blinked in surprise. Then I shook my head. Of course my father could talk to animals. He had always been able to. I just had no idea that he could understand them over the phone.

In my defense, they hadn't had phones back in the eighteenth century, and it wasn't like I could have tested it out between Konstantin and Wednesday.

Well, I could have, if I'd had a moment to breathe over the last two weeks.

Had it only been two weeks?

Wednesday was speaking. *—would this kill me? If it's just a curse, then shouldn't there be some method of lifting it? It's not engrained, is it?* Her voice was pragmatic, and it seemed just a touch ironic to me that she should be so straightforward about it when I was a bit of a mess.

"An excellent question," Father said, his voice quiet and gentle. "Unfortunately, in cases like this—like most instances involving black magic—the curse has usually interwoven itself into your soul. Removal is almost impossible."

*Then why didn't I die months ago?* Wednesday asked, chirping into the phone.

"If you are related to Councilwoman Stanislava Carabosse, which I'm presuming you are, then you have quite an impressive elvish pedigree."

*But I'm not an elf. Nor was my mother*, Wednesday pointed out.

"No, but certain genetic traits can have unexpected, and in this case welcome, results even several generations later—such as resistance against curses and other forms of magical manipulations. In your case, it is very possible that it was your elven heritage which enabled you to come back your humanity. It will not hold out forever, but it has kept you with us for this long."

*You mean if I wasn't part elf I wouldn't have...woken back up?*

Father's voice was matter-of-fact, but if I didn't know any better, I could have sworn that he sounded slightly uncomfortable. "Correct."

"So what do we do?" I asked.

Father took his time to answer that one, sounding thoughtful, and... hesitant? No, that wasn't exactly it. "With your permission, my son, I will be of the best use in person."

I blinked, looking down at Wednesday, who looked back at me, eyes curious. "You mean you would come here? To help me?"

"I could be on a plane tonight," he confirmed. "There's a direct flight from Heathrow."

*Say yes*, Wednesday's small voice came without an accompanying meow, protecting it from the ears of my father. Her small paw was on the hand in my lap, and I looked at her in the dim glow from the lights over the counter.

*Please, Trillion.*

How could I say no?

"Please," I said, something lodged firmly in my throat. I swallowed hard, but it stayed exactly where it was. "Please come."

I heard a sigh. Had my father been holding his breath? Had he been hoping that I would claim independence, and refuse his help? But no. I heard clicks from the other end of the line. Mouse clicks? Father had a computer?

"My plane lands at at seven o'clock tonight, your time," Father said.

"I'll be there," I confirmed. Then I paused. "Isn't that... expensive?"

"My son," Father said, with the barest hints of a smile in his voice, "do you think one can afford to live to be millennia old without a retirement plan?"

"That's some retirement plan," I said, impressed. Not that I was particularly poorly off myself, but... still. I could almost see him smile. He didn't say anything more for a minute, and I wondered if he would say goodbye. Wednesday jumped off of the couch, wandering toward her food bowl, but I stayed there, unable to hang up.

"This isn't just about Giselle, it sounds like," Father finally said.

I settled back into the couch, running my hand over my face. "Yes."

"Another friend of yours?" he asked.

"Yes, a shapeshifter named Konstantin."

"From our neck of the woods?"

"From Poland, I think. Mid twentieth century."

"Are you close?"

"He's been my business partner for fifty—"

"Trillion." Father's voice was not unkind, but there was a quiet plea in there.

"He's my best friend," I said, the lump in my throat coming back. "Roth—Luther has him." I cleared my throat, and looked out the window at the back of the house. The darkness to the west seemed to shimmer. I frowned and swiped at my eyes.

Hold it together.

"My son," Father seemed to sense the pain in my voice. "I am sure you are more than aware of the...dangers that these attachments could cause you. Is this...worth it to you?"

I pinched my eyes shut, but not from irritation. He was right to ask. Even with the gap of the last few hundred years, he had known me longer than anyone else on Earth. I looked over at Wednesday, and then thought of Konstantin.

"Yes." I had never meant a word more. "Father?"

"Yes, Trillion?"

I didn't know what I wanted to say. Was it possible to catch up on three hundred years of history in a half-hour conversation? I was willing to give it a try. But...I couldn't do that to my father. He had a lot to do. Despite the fantastical nature of the job, King of the Faeries was not without its responsibilities.

"Nothing," I finally said, my voice a little thick. "You'll have a lot to do—"

"Trillion." My father's voice was firm.

I winced in anticipation. "Yes?"

"I'm sorry for...the last time I saw you," he said. His voice was quiet, but slightly throaty, as if he was was having a hard time expressing himself, but couldn't quite stop himself. "I have written so many letters, almost called so many times. I didn't want to—" He cut himself off, and then sighed deeply. "I'm sorry, my son."

"I'm sorry for not calling you," I responded, my voice tight. "I'm sorry for not...being able to explain. I'm sorry for Kaldinion. I'm—" I broke off, my breath shaky. Burying the heel of my hand into my eyes, I bowed my head, breathing carefully.

"I am, too," Father's voice was gentle. Understanding.

We let the silence hang between us. Finally, though, Father broke the silence.

"I must prepare for my trip, my son, but before I go, I have one more question."

"Please," I said, thinking of zero and also a million questions that he could ask me.

"Is Giselle there?"

I looked over. Wednesday had wandered off somewhere. I couldn't see her. It was almost five, she'd probably gone back to bed.

"No, she's wandered off," I said, turning back toward the front of the house. "Did you want to ask her something?"

"No," Father said, "this question is for you. Humor an old man, would you?"

I fought the urge to smile. "You could outpace men fifty times younger, Father."

"Nevertheless," he said, "considering I have no right to receive the answer, your honesty is most appreciated."

"Ask your question," I said, game to at least hear him out.

"Do you love Giselle?" Father asked baldly. "You mention that she is currently a cat, but you speak of her fondly. Like a friend. Like more. So I must ask: Do you love her?"

I stared at the empty fireplace, feeling both utterly mystified and exposed. As if a private part of myself that I didn't know existed had been ripped bare, open to interpretation. Open to injury.

But did I love Wednesday?

"I don't know," I admitted. It was as close to the truth as I knew myself. Was it even appropriate to go there? Safe? For her or myself?

"It is all right, my son," Father said after a moment more of my stunned silence. "I suspect I know the answer."

"Why do you ask?"

"No reason, particularly," Father said, and I felt no lie in his words. "I hope that should never change."

"What does that mean?" I asked, disgruntled. Father laughed, and I couldn't help but smile at the sound. I guess in some ways my father was exactly the same.

"Only time will tell, my son," he said. "Only time will tell."

# 28

# IN WHICH I STRESS BAKE AND MAKE A PROMISE

I didn't go back to bed. I probably should have, but my mind was buzzing, and my heart was equal parts light and confused, so instead I made a pizza.

I had no idea how I magically had all the ingredients for one—and hoped sincerely that there wasn't anything microscopic or otherwise living in the flour or sugar—but I pulled up a recipe online and started mixing things in a bowl.

Wednesday had appeared from somewhere and had switched on the TV. I was surprised when it didn't turn on to the weather channel. Instead an almost sinister sound of an orchestra started up. I looked up in confusion. I wasn't one to listen to classical music. How did I recognize this one? It clicked.

"Is this The Firebird again?" I asked.

Wednesday, sitting enraptured on the couch looked up at me and brightened as a man in a heavily bejeweled costume came onto the screen. *Yes, isn't it wonderful?* she said blissfully, sinking into a little loaf on the couch. I kept mixing the dough, and glanced at the clock. It was five forty-five. The moon would rise over the horizon in less than an hour. I relayed the message.

*Will the pizza be done by then?* she asked.

I smirked. "I see where your priorities lay."

One of her ears twitched and she looked back at me. *I'm not the one stress baking.*

"I am not."

*Are, too.*

"Am not! Stress baking isn't even a thing!" I said.

Wednesday turned back to me, and if she had currently had eyebrows, I had the feeling that she would have raised them. *You're kidding yourself, Trillion. Speaking of as a...well, a part-time woman, I can most assuredly tell you that stress baking is a thing, and just because you don't want to acknowledge it doesn't make it not real.*

I pursed my lips and tried to glare. It didn't really work. Despite everything that was going on, I was in a surprisingly good mood.

*Careful, your angry face is slipping*, she said.

"Hush, you," I muttered under my breath, furrowing my eyebrows to keep myself from smiling. Leaving the dough to rise, I turned to the sauce and toppings, listening to the swelling of the orchestra.

"You're going to have to tell me what's going on if you expect me to know anything," I said.

There was a slight tinkle of laughter from the couch. *It's pretty easy to follow. The Firebird and Prince Ivan are dancing together. Soon he will find a princess.*

I frowned. "Wait, Prince Ivan and the Firebird aren't the couple?"

*She's a bird, Trillion.* Wednesday's head twisted around and she seemed to give me an odd look. *Of course he finds a princess. It's a ballet. There's always royalty involved somehow.*

"Huh," I said, slicing vegetables, frowning.

*Why?*

"Why what?" I asked.

*Why does that bother you?*

Yes, Trillion, why does that bother you?

My father's voice trickled into the back of my mind. *Do you love her?* I cleared my throat. "No reason."

*Liar.*

"Fine, why do you think it bothers me?" I asked, leaning forward over the counter. Wednesday stared at me for a second, and then flicked one of her ears and turned her head back to the television. "Well?"

*Hush, you.*

I nearly dropped my knife. "Did I just win an argument?"

*Well, not now,* she said stiffly. I smirked. *Stop it.*

"No," I grinned. "I've been waiting my whole life for this moment."

*You haven't known me your whole life,* she said flatly.

"No, but unlikely victories have been a consistent goal." I waved the pizza sauce spoon at her.

*You didn't help Napoleon march on Russia, did you?* she asked, deadpan.

I snorted. "I have never been that desperate."

*Are you sure about that?*

"When have you seen me desperate?" I asked, my voice still light. I felt like laughing for some reason, and was in far too much of a good mood to actually fight with her. I could practically hear her thinking, ignoring the TV screen behind her where a flock of women in white danced on the stage.

*You seemed pretty desperate when you were trying to pass me off to a shelter.*

"Yes, well, what would have been your initial response when you met a talking cat?" I asked defensively.

She twitched an eyebrow. *Take it to my mother.*

"I got there eventually," I pointed out.

*Under duress. And I literally had to dial the phone for you.*

"I didn't know your mother's personal line! That would be weird! It was only not weird because you were there with me!" I protested.

*Be that as it may, you still didn't do anything for like, a week.*

"Because I didn't think you were human!"

*I told you I was human!* she said.

I rolled my eyes. "Wednesday, if there is one thing that has been consistent with cats through the ages, it is their complete certainty that they are human." I smiled brightly at her and she flicked her ears back at me again, not responding. "What, no retort?"

*Quiet, I'm watching the ballet.* But her voice wasn't angry.

"I'm right, aren't I?"

*I'm watching the ballet,* she repeated, but I heard the laugh in her voice. Smiling, I finished constructing the pizza, popping it into the oven. I hadn't baked in quite a while, and it felt oddly soothing.

Maybe I was stress baking.

A couple minutes after I put the pizza into the oven, I checked the clock.

"Wednesday, it's almost time," I said. She looked up at me. She flicked an ear in understanding, but she didn't move immediately.

"What is it?" I asked, studying her carefully. It wasn't as though I thought she was turning cat, again, but apparently Wednesday thought I did, because she hopped off the couch.

*Don't worry about it,* she said, *I'm not going feline.*

"What is it, then?" I asked. I followed her, watching her walk slowly toward the door. It swung open under Wednesday's direction, and the brightening sky illuminated her as she stepped down onto the front porch. The moon rose above the trees, a thin strip of white in the sky. Wednesday turned to me and, stepping forward, she stretched from cat to human, brown hair tumbling down her back.

She looked up and smiled at me. She still wore the oversized grey hoodie and sweatpants, hiking boots on her feet.

"Nothing," she whispered, her voice ever so slightly raspy. I didn't believe her, but I didn't quite know what to say to help her speak her mind.

"Will you tell me when there is something?" I asked. She blinked, as if she wasn't expecting the question, and her eyebrows drew together. She looked at me for a long time before she shivered.

"Let's go inside," I said, drawing one arm across her shoulders. She leaned against me, letting me guide her into the house. As we stepped in out of the cold, I could smell the pizza and smiled a little. There was still fifteen minutes left on the pizza, and the Firebird seemed to be drawing to a close.

I sat myself down on the sofa and Wednesday sunk down next to me, leaning her head on my shoulder.

"Wednesday, why do you like the Firebird so much?" I asked. She didn't answer right away, staring at the dancing figures on the screen. I didn't know whether she just didn't hear me, was thinking about her answer, or simply didn't want to answer the question. She didn't seem to have as much snap as before, and it worried me a little bit.

"Wednesday?" I asked. She was looking at her hands, rubbing her fingers together. I took one of her hands in mine. She looked up at me, and quickly looked away, expression serious.

"Why do I like The Firebird?" she said, looking back up at the ballet. There was a goblin thing standing opposite on the stage from the woman in red playing the titular character. She sighed. "I like it because it shows that kindness and mercy are the true power in this world. The Firebird could have cursed Ivan for capturing her, but instead she gives him a feather to be able to call her if he needs help. Because of that, they are able to defeat Koschei, something neither of them would have been able to do without the other. She does it without needing to marry the prince at the end." She was quiet for a moment. "I don't think I could do what she did. I'm not the Firebird."

"You are kind," I said, squeezing her hand. "And you're... mostly merciful."

She snorted. "Like I said, not the Firebird."

"You're doing better than you think you are," I insisted.

She shook her head. "I've been selfish most of my life," Wednesday whispered as the Firebird started taking her final bows. "My whole life, I thought that all I wanted was to dance. But the more that I watch you, the more time I spend doing stuff outside of what I thought I was supposed to be doing with my life... I never thought that something else could possibly be just as fulfilling. And it is. Ironically, I don't think I've ever been as happy as the last two weeks with you."

I thought about that for a second. "You did just come off a three-month stint as a cat trapped in a mill, Wednesday. Maybe you shouldn't think so highly of us."

"Yes, and before that I spent seventy years in the world of ballet," she said evenly. "You're a diva, but you're not that much of a diva."

The oven timer dinged, and I stood. "I'm not a diva," I said cheerfully, making my way over to the oven. Pulling the circular pan out of the oven, I breathed in the aroma of bubbly cheese and tomato sauce. I cut two slices, and made my way over to the couch again, sitting down. She took the pizza from me and placed the plate on her lap. I looked down at her.

"You're not really hungry, are you?" I asked. Looking regretful, Wednesday shook her head.

"I'm sorry," she said, tears filling her eyes. For the barest of moments, I felt panic rising in my chest, wondering what I was supposed to do. And then I put my arm around her and pulled her close into my side. She turned into me, wrapping her arms around my waist.

"There's nothing to apologize for," I whispered, running a hand over her hair.

She sniffed, and pulled closer. "I just never thought I would find out so much about life when I'm dying." Her voice broke, and she buried her face into my shoulder. Tightening my embrace, I ran one hand over her hair, smoothing it back as she sobbed, rocking her from side to side slowly. I didn't shush her. I couldn't think of any soothing words, so I just held her, hoping that would be enough.

My father's voice, while it had been my joy, had been her death sentence. My relief at his forgiveness, and his desire to identify what was wrong with Wednesday had become her anxiety and her fear with the possibility that she might never be whole again. My heart ached, and when Wednesday's tears had slowed—her human tears, down her human face—I pulled back slightly, looking into her red rimmed eyes.

"We're going to find a way out of this," I breathed, voice tremulous. "I promise you."

Her face crumpled, and she bowed her head. I buried my face into her hair, feeling the pain radiating off of her. I pressed a gentle kiss to the top of her head.

"I promise," I said again, feeling it from the depths of my soul. And then, because nothing else would come, I whispered it once more.

"I promise."

# 29

## IN WHICH I GET A CALL FROM MY INSURANCE AGENT

I fell asleep on the couch with my feet up on the ottoman and Wednesday secure in my arms. She breathed in and out slowly, already asleep and utterly spent, a piece of chestnut hair fluttering with each breath in front of her red, blotchy face. She was beautiful.

My strong, courageous Wednesday.

*Do you love her?* My father's words swept through my head as my own eyelids drooped.

Did I?

I still didn't know the answer. I didn't know the answer as I fell asleep. I didn't know the answer when I briefly woke up when Wednesday transformed back into a cat, and I didn't know when I woke up for real at three in the afternoon to a buzzing from my pocket, Wednesday having stretched most of the way across the couch.

"Hello?" I said groggily into the phone receiver.

"Hello, this is Melissa from Complete Coverage Insurance. We wanted to let you know that your claim was approved, and that your deposit should end up in your account later this afternoon. Changes in your rates will be reflected in the yearly review."

"Thank you, Melissa. Um, I'm sorry, I don't remember filing the claim." I frowned, a little confused. There was a pause that I could have easily interpreted as a smirk, and she continued in her most reassuring voice.

"This is not a scam call, Mr. Orris," she said kindly. "I'd be happy to give you my extension so you can call the main line and get back in touch with me."

"No, no, Melissa, I remember you from our previous conversations," I said, rubbing the back of my neck. Beside me, Wednesday stirred from my lap and looked up at me, half asleep, and half suspicious.

*Who is Melissa?*

"My insurance broker," I whispered, holding my hand over the bottom half of the phone. That was the problem with all this new technology—I wasn't actually sure where the receiver was. Wednesday stared at me for a moment, as if trying to decide whether or not I was telling the truth, and then laid her head back down on my leg. I turned my attention back to Melissa. "I was just wondering where the claim came from."

"Let me see," Melissa said, and I heard the click-clack of her keyboard as she typed. "Well, it looked like it was from your authorized contact, Konstantin Vorkowitz, in the afternoon three days ago, on Tuesday? He called in."

I nodded before I remembered that she couldn't see me.

"All right," I said. Something clicked in my brain. "He called in? When did that happen?"

"About three?" Melissa said. I could hear the mouse click furiously on the other end. "According to my phone note, he said he was at the hospital, and did the paperwork over the phone. It took us until about three-thirty."

"And he was *talking* to you?" I asked.

"Yes?" Melissa sounded very confused.

"And he didn't sound raspy or anything?"

"A little?" Her voice was almost hesitant, like she could tell it was important, but had no idea why. "Not really, though." I pressed back into the sofa, gripping the phone a little tighter than necessary. If that was true, it meant that either Konstantin had been abducted on his way from the hospital to the office, or—if the destroyed house was anything to go by—he had made it home and Rothbart and Odell had ambushed him there.

I had two options. Either Rothbart had taken the time to impersonate Konstantin and chosen to take a half an hour out of his life to fill out my insurance forms, or Konstantin's last act before he was abducted was to file the claim.

My determination to find him before something happened to him redoubled. I would not let Konstantin's last act be bureaucratic twaddle.

"Thank you," I said. "I'll watch for the deposit."

Melissa told me to have a good day and clicked the phone off. Blinking around the bright room, I frowned.

*What do we do now?* Wednesday asked. I looked down at her. I wondered whether it had been Konstantin who had come into the office. And yet... It couldn't have been Rothbart. He wouldn't have known that Konstantin never texted, but no one filled out insurance forms when they didn't have to—even for an alibi.

"We have a timeline," I said grimly. "I think."

*What did he do to Konstantin?* Wednesday asked. *Would he have done to him what Odell did to me?* Her voice was uncomfortable, and I reached out instinctively to pet her head. I shook my head.

"It's harder to curse magical beings, particularly shapeshifters. The animal part of them is kind of like a built-in defense mechanism," I explained. "It's more likely that they've got Konstantin held somewhere."

Or they had killed him outright. I frowned. No, even if they had killed Konstantin so Rothbart could steal his face—as he had undoubtedly stolen Siegfried's—Rothbart, or rather Siegfried's, body would have been found.

Wouldn't it?

"Fancy a walk?" I said, pulling my phone out again. Her tail twitched.

*Why?*

I pursed my lips. I could hardly tell her I wanted to tell her I wanted to go outside to look for a body. "I need fresh air. You may turn into a human at the light of the moon, but I need sunshine to be happy."

*I'm pretty sure that's never helped before*, Wednesday grumbled and I rolled my eyes. It should have made me angry, and I was already thinking of the appropriate snark to fire back at her, but it was frankly relieving to hear something that even resembled normalcy from her. I knew better than to think everything was okay now, but it—

*Are you thinking, or did your millennia year old brain finally kick the bucket?* Wednesday asked, her voice tired.

Then again...

"There's one thing that Rothbart can do that makes me afraid for Konstantin," I said before I could talk myself out of it.

Wednesday tipped her head to one side. *What is that?*

"I—" I didn't have any—

*Stop censoring everything you're telling me,* Wednesday growled. *I'm older than most peoples' grandmothers. If your father can tell me I'm dying, then you can tell me what your theories are without making them 'appropriate for young ladies' ears.'*

"But—"

*Trillion?*

"What?"

She glared at me instead of answering and I sighed.

"More black magic. Rothbart could have stolen Konstantin's face." I leaned back against the couch, and stared down at her. She blinked a couple times without saying a word. Finally, sitting down, and wrapping her tail around her feet, she looked up at me.

*I don't exactly regret asking you to tell me, but...what?*

"Basically, it's how Rothbart took over Siegfried's body. He killed the part of Siegfried that makes Siegfried 'Siegfried' with magic and then stole his body. If Rothbart did... do this, he would have taken over Konstantin's body, but... well, we'd need to look for Siegfried's body, because that would be our proof."

*So you just casually asked me if I want to go on a walk? To go body hunting? Ew!*

I grimaced. "I... would have told you on the way."

*You lie.*

"I would have!"

*When? Once you'd spotted his body in the woods? I can just see you now. You'd turn to me, and say, 'Now, Wednesday, there's this thing you need to know about Black Magic. There's face stealing! Look—a prime example!'* She stood and stalked toward the edge of the couch. Jumping off the couch, she walked purposefully toward the window, and sat with her back to me, clearly disgusted.

"I wouldn't have said it like that!" I protested. She didn't respond. "Do you actually think this is convincing me to tell you more?"

She turned back to me at that. There was a pause, and she sighed. *I guess not*, she said begrudgingly. *Please continue.*

"I don't think it's likely," I said. "And I don't have to go wandering out in the woods. I can usually sense dead bodies—"

*Ew.*

"Not like that!" I sighed. "I mean... well, kind of like that. It's part of my tracking abilities. How I can kill effectively. I can sense live creatures... and dead ones."

*So...why weren't you able to find Rothbart before now?* She blinked. *If you tell me he's neither one, I'm leaving and taking my chances as a cat.*

I doubted that, but responded anyway. "No, it just doesn't work as well in cities. Trying to tell one biped from another—well, in a city this size, needle in a haystack doesn't even begin to cover it."

*I guess that makes sense.*

"You guess?"

*It makes sense*, Wednesday amended. *But it's still kind of weird.*

I rolled my eyes. "I'll keep that in mind."

*Good. I don't think Konstantin is dead.*

"What?" I shifted, leaning forward onto my knees. "Why? Rothbart has a vendetta against almost all magical beings. If he's not using him for leverage, it's definitely a possibility, and we haven't heard back from him."

*Because Rothbart is a killer, but Odell isn't.*

"She cursed you in a bad way," I reminded her.

Wednesday seemed to think about that. *Yes*, she said slowly, *but she isn't the type to leave a body in the woods.* She thought about it for a moment longer. *Some members of my dance company would. Mother probably would. But not Odell.*

My first thought was to scoff, but she had a point. Wednesday knew Odell far better than I did. She was also right about Stanislava, but I'd rather cut my tongue out and eat it than agree with her out loud.

"Do you think she would keep him from killing Konstantin at all?"

*That I don't know. But if she's involved she would more likely keep him as leverage. She is definitely not accustomed to murder.*

I looked past Wednesday out the window, and frowned. She knew Odell, but I knew Rothbart. As much as Odell probably wasn't 'accustomed to murder,' Rothbart definitely was. He was also far more persuasive than people generally gave him credit for.

"Okay," I said, "but I'd still like to go out before we have to head to the airport to pick up Father."

And then there was a buzzing in my hand. I jumped, forgetting that I'd pulled out my phone a moment earlier, and stared down at the screen. Auberon. "Speak of the devil," I said pressing the green button and putting the phone up to my ear. "Father? Is everything all right? I thought your plane would have been halfway here by now?"

"Everything is fine." Father's voice was a little staticky, but his voice was calm. "My flight has been canceled for tonight. There was a storm that rolled in. It was originally forecast to blow right over and just delay my flight, in which case I was going to call you when I left, but it decided to sit here over London until the early hours of the morning. They've rebooked me on tomorrow's flight."

By all accounts, I shouldn't have felt so disappointed. I had only known that he wasn't angry with me for a couple of hours, and yet it was if I had been anticipating his coming for years.

Maybe I had.

"Oh," I said.

Father's voice was regretful. "I'm still coming. I promise you, it's just—"

"Oh!" I exclaimed, realizing what he was trying to say. "No, I didn't think you were backing out. Just...excited to see you, I suppose. Don't worry about me, Father. I'll see you tomorrow, then. Do you have a place to stay tonight?"

"Yes," Father's rumbling voice said. "The airport has me set up at a hotel tonight. The plane leaves at four tomorrow afternoon."

"Are you—"

"I'm still coming, Trillion," he said quickly.

I smiled a little. "That wasn't what I was going to ask." I looked across the room where Wednesday was looking at me in interest. "I was wondering, are you familiar with face swapping?"

"Moderately." His voice was cautious. "Why? Has Luther—" He broke off. "Would you mind waiting for two minutes before I answer? I'm in the hotel lobby," he paused, "such as it is. While London is a rather liberal city, I'd rather not out myself quite so definitively."

I smiled. "Fair enough." I listened for a moment while a small group of people chatted, then heard the buzz of an elevator.

"Incidentally, do you have room for me at your place, or am I going to avail myself of the nearest Four Seasons?"

*I'm sure Mother could put him up if he wanted.*

"Because that would go over well," I muttered. Then sealed my lips closed. Depending on how they interacted, that could go a little *too* well. "You can stay with me."

*Where?*

I looked around. Covering the phone receiver, I whispered to Wednesday, "He can have the bedroom, I'll sleep on the couch."

*No! Then I'll have to sleep on the couch with you, and I like the bed better.*

"I can't put the King of the Faeries on the couch!"

*I'm not sleeping with your dad!*

"You know I can hear you, right?" Father's tinny voice said from the speaker, laughter shot through his voice. "*Both* of you?"

Wednesday froze, one ear twitching. *This is the most uncomfortable conversation I've ever had.*

"Your fault," I said self righteously, and put the phone back up to my ear. "We can take you, Father."

"Perfect," he said. "Now, let's talk face-stealing."

*I am leaving.*

"You might want to stay," I said. "I just have a couple questions."

"Fire away," Father said.

"Does it work on magical folk?"

"Not well."

"What happens?" I asked.

Father paused. "I feel like you're fishing."

"I am," I admitted, "But there's a reason."

I could almost see Father roll his eyes. "I hate fishing. What happened?"

"I'm worried that Rothbart stole Konstantin's face," I said. "But I haven't seen him for a day, and I don't know for sure. The last time we saw him it seemed like Konstantin, but something was...off."

"Then it wasn't face swapping. If it was Rothbart, it was probably an illusion spell using blood or something," Father said.

"How can you tell if it was Konstantin?" I asked.

"Did Konstantin speak?" Father asked.

I frowned. "Yes, he tried."

"Then it was Konstantin. Illusion spells rarely cover the voice. Case in point," Father explained. "Face stealing is a misnomer. It's more like full-on body stealing. The body and knowledge of the victim is taken over by the spell caster. The consciousness of the victim is ripped from their body and inserted into the former body of the spell caster and is left to die. It is always fatal. The spell caster receives everything—from how the client walks to how they address their mother. If Rothbart already knew all that and could become the perfect copy of Konstantin, why would things seem off?"

And why would Konstantin's voice still be damaged an hour later? "How is that different from how Wed—Giselle's spell works?"

"Giselle's spell takes more set up. She would have had to be imprisoned and kept in her alternate form for several months. During the first couple of months it is reversible, and so most often we see it used as a high-stakes spy spell. However, after any longer than a few weeks, the spell caster leeches so much of the victim's identity that the two merge and it's often difficult for them to separate themselves again. Without that willful separation, it's... less likely that the victim will survive. Merged too long, and it will be fatal regardless."

"And the face swapping case is always fatal?"

"Yes."

"So Konstantin is alive?" I asked.

"Most likely. The only other spells that would work on a shapeshifter are all non-fatal. Some require blood, but your friend should live."

I let out a breath that I definitely had been holding, pinching my eyes shut.

"Thank you," I whispered.

# 30

IN WHICH THERE ARE
WAFFLES AND
SEVERAL PHONE
CALLS

The rest of the day passed surprisingly quickly. Not trusting Wednesday to be left by herself, I bundled her into the car, grabbed a bit of dinner, and made a quick stop by a car lot to see the different options.

Maybe it was just the mood I was in, but there wasn't anything particularly interesting to me. So, we went home and went to bed. Around six thirty in the morning, I was woken up by a cold paw on my face, letting me know it was time for Wednesday to go outside.

I stumbled out after her, smoothing my messy hair back into a ponytail, and watched as she stepped over the threshold, the pinks and purples of the sunrise creeping up on the horizon. The cold from the clear morning hit my feet and I shivered ever so slightly as Wednesday stepped up through the door, pulling the hoodie a little tighter.

"Thanks for lending me this, by the way," she said, closing the door behind her.

"Of course," I said, heading over to the kitchen to get her a drink of water. The raspiness in her voice wasn't as bad as the first time she had transformed, but there was still a painful sort of sandpaper quality. She accepted the glass gratefully and, leaning against the counter, looked out the back windows at the pre-dawn light. "What do you want for breakfast?"

She looked up at me. "I'm not sure I'm hungry quite yet, but thanks."

I walked around the counter, and leaned up against the counter next to her. "Want to talk about it?" I asked.

She looked up in surprise. "About what?"

"About what's bothering you?" I poked her in the shoulder. "The only time I've seen you refuse food is...well, yesterday."

She thought about that. "I guess you're right."

"And?"

"Well, with you stuffing me to the gills every day, can you blame me for wanting to take a break?"

I pulled in my chin a little bit, but noticed the slight edge of a smile on her cheek. "Well, then, I'll leave you to your own devices tomorrow, then."

She stiffened and looked down. "There isn't any moon tomorrow. Well, there is but it only comes up after sunrise," she mumbled, her gaze dropping to her hands, which were half buried in her sleeves. "I'll be a cat until Monday."

I looked down at her. I wasn't exactly sure what my face was doing, but apparently it was mildly offensive, because she looked up at me and scoffed slightly. "Trillion, stop it."

"Stop what?"

"That," she said, waving her hand around.

"I literally don't know what you just gestured at," I told her flatly.

She looked away, frowning. "That—that look!"

"What look? This is my face!" I protested.

"The—I don't know!" she exclaimed.

"That doesn't help!" I replied, just as vehemently. It suddenly occurred to me that it we'd probably get a little farther if this didn't devolve into an argument. I took a deep breath. "I'm sorry. Please tell me what's wrong so I can fix it."

She glared up at me. "I don't like it when you're rational."

"Fine. Tell me what's wrong, so I can annoy you more."

She sighed, but couldn't help the slight smile that teased the edges of her lips. Rubbing her hands down her face she shook her head. "When you give me that expression—the one where it feels like you're pitying me—it makes me feel like things are a lot worse than they maybe are." I looked down at her, feeling my face get a little more serious. She looked up and sighed. "Yes, like that."

I blinked, and shook my head. "I'm sorry," I said. "I didn't realize that's what it looked like. I was just thinking that it was going to be hard for you."

"Yeah," she said quietly, pushing away from the counter.

"Wednesday?" I said, also pushing off the counter. Grabbing her gently by the shoulders, I turned her around.

She looked up, a dark, furious frown on her face. "It is hard." Her voice was hard and begrudging.

I blinked, a little curious at her vehemence. "Do you want me to—" I broke off, warning bells going off in my head. "What do you want me to do?"

The look on her face cracked, just a bit, and she dug her hands into her hair. She didn't immediately respond. "I—I don't know." It was a sigh. A puff of air with an inconvenient confession, and she looked away.

"Hey," I said, touching her chin gently. She looked back up at me, her deep green eyes unfathomable in the growing pink light of the sunrise. "I know you don't want pity. You don't want to be in pain, and you don't want to be facing your own mortality. But I never want you to think I'm trivializing anything. I will do my best to fix it, but you're in pain *right now*."

She blinked and shook her head. "I don't need pity. I can work through it on my own."

"Of course you can," I said, still holding her by the shoulders. "Would you mind if I walked beside you while you do?"

She looked up quickly, lips slightly parted, as if she hadn't expected me to respond like that. As she recovered she pressed those lips together and shook her head in disbelief.

"How do you always know what to say?" she asked, her voice barely above a whisper. I grimaced. If only she knew. Actually, I thought she did. All the teasing? All the speechlessness? Every single time I'd just stare after her open mouthed because I *didn't* know what to say?

"I don't." The admission was a little rueful, and Wednesday shook her head in response.

"It doesn't feel like that," she whispered. My hands trailed down her shoulders to her hands. They were small and smooth and seemed to fit perfectly in mine.

"Well, I guess that just proves you don't know everything about me. Even if sometimes I feel pegged worse than laundry."

"Does laundry get pegged?" Wednesday asked, a little confused.

I snorted. "It did about a hundred years ago," I said. "Perhaps I'm dating myself."

She laughed a little. "Maybe a bit." She paused. "Maybe a lot. Aren't you older than most American cities combined?"

"Hey—well," I broke off, thinking. "There's a lot of cities in America, and I'm only just older than Britain."

It was Wednesday's turn to snort, but the smile on her face was broad and genuine.

"Come here," I said, pulling her into a hug. She came willingly, her arms wrapping around my waist, and I smiled into her hair, closing my eyes. "It's okay to be independent, but let me know when you do need help, okay?"

She sighed, a puff of breath against my neck. "Okay."

We stayed like that for a moment longer. Finally, she pulled back and looked up into my face. "Can we have waffles?"

I laughed. "Yes, we can have waffles."

\*\*\*

Sunrise came all too soon, and the day plodded along. Father called a little before lunch and confirmed that his flight was leaving on time, and that left me nervous and restless. I was planning on leaving for the airport at about six in the evening, so in the meantime I cleaned, washed, ironed, folded, and vacuumed. Wednesday followed me, once again in cat form, lying on every available surface—usually the one I was trying to clean.

"Really?" I asked for the millionth time.

She blinked back slowly, her mouth curved into a grin as much as her feline features allowed. *Just enjoying the Feline Right of being in the way*, she said, rolling onto her back.

I rolled my eyes. "That's not a thing."

*Are you sure about that?*

Grinning despite myself, I kept on cleaning, moving on to mopping the floors. It was almost five, the sun just sinking below the horizon when my phone rang. Hopefully wondering if there had been some sort of freak wind, I picked up the cell phone from the counter. It wasn't Father, it was...the police station?

Konstantin.

"Hello?"

"Hello, this is Sergeant Barlow. This is Trillion Orris?" His voice was slow, and not particularly concerned.

"Yes," I confirmed quickly.

"Hello, I have the results of your request to ping Konstantin Vorkowitz's phone?"

"Yes, I'm ready." I nearly jumped across the counter to grab a notepad and a pen, practically laying on it as I pinned the phone between my ear and my shoulder. Wednesday walked up, a sense of confusion and disapproval radiating off of her, until I mouthed 'Konstantin'. Her tail swished in anticipation, and she jumped up onto the counter, close enough to where she could hear Sergeant Barlow as well.

"Yes, we found his cellphone by the lake on your property. Going by satellite images, it should be about five miles from your house. It's a bit fuzzy, but there's a structure there. It looks like...well, I'm actually not sure *what* it looks like. Maybe you know. Kind of like a half-circle, bunch of pillars?"

It clicked in my head and I frowned. "It's an amphitheater." I could almost see it by the lake, black hulking stone reflecting in the water. It was a beautiful structure, if a little imposing. "Sometimes the city borrows it for outdoor performances."

"Huh," the Sergeant said. "What kind of performances?"

"It really depends. Sergeant, when did you ping the phone last?" I asked.

There was the shuffle of paper. "Uh, it looks like a half hour ago. It was only approved this afternoon by the judge—"

"That's what I need to know. Keep pinging it every hour—more often if you can. If it changes, give me a call," I said.

"I can't keep pinging it forever," Sergeant Barlow warned me. "Besides, they could have left it somewhere, or it could be a plant."

"Or a trap," I confirmed grimly. "But this is the first lead we've had in two days."

Sergeant Barlow shifted a little, and coughed. "I don't want to tell you your own business, Mr. Orris," the Sergeant said in a low voice, "but be careful. I've read up on Rothbart. Some of the stuff that's in the file...Even someone of your skill set and pedigree has a good fight ahead of them."

"Thank you," I said, and I meant it. Taking a deep breath, I shook my head a little ruefully, looking over at Wednesday. "Apparently it's my destiny to rush headlong into things that aren't good for me."

"Pardon?"

"Nothing. Just keep me in the loop." There was a grunt on the other side of the line, and then a click as the sergeant hung up. A plan was percolating in my mind. I didn't think that Rothbart would be thick enough to actually keep Konstantin's phone, but I also couldn't go check it out without protection.

I didn't own a gun. I disliked the impersonal aspect of distance killing, and most faerie species were too fast anyway. Perhaps it was necessary, especially in modern warfare, but as much as I disagreed with killing on principle, I disagreed on faceless killing on a much more personal level.

Maybe that was why I had finally left the battlefield.

*Where are you going?* Wednesday asked, trotting along behind me as I made my way to my bedroom. Beneath my bed was a long, oblong box, one that I took out exactly every three months, and no sooner.

Until today. I put the box on the bed and looked at it for a long, long time.

Then, the phone rang.

Wondering at my sudden popularity, I rose to my feet from the side of the bed and ran back out into the kitchen. When I got there, my heart stopped. There, on the caller ID was the last name I expected to see.

Konstantin.

"Hello?" I said, "Konstantin?"

"Ah, Brother Mine." A sickeningly familiar voice sang sweetly into the phone.

"Rothbart," I growled into the receiver.

There was a short 'tsk' noise into the phone, and his tone turned mocking. "Aw, is poor Twillion not happy to hear from his baby brovver? It's been almost fifty years since we last spoke face to face. I thought you might be at least willing to say hello."

"Fifty years ago you slaughtered fourteen dryads because their leader refused to swear allegiance to you," I said roughly. "Forgive me for not wanting to cater to the insane."

"Mmm, pity it's never stopped you before. First Father, then every notable European warlord since Europe existed. Then, of all people, Stanislava Carabosse. Boy, between her and her daughter, they have you wrapped around their fingers." The sing-song voice came back.

My patience snapped. "What do you want?"

"I was just informed by a *delightful* little spell that my location has just been compromised. Come to the amphitheater. I want to settle this once and for all. Bring the cat, and I'll let your little dog friend live."

"You're not one to generally keep your word, how do I know he's alive at all?"

There were a short pause, and a strained voice came over the line. Konstantin's. "Trillion, we're at the amphitheater. Don't you dare come. It's an ambus—" The voice cut off sharply, and Rothbart came back on the line.

"Now, since you know I cannot do imitations worth beans, no matter the spell, you know it's your friend. The amphitheater *was* intended to be an ambush, but our good friends the police have negated that neatly. I'll have to pay them a visit once I'm done dealing with you."

"I wouldn't make plans," I warned him. "I plan on occupying you for the rest of your life."

"Ooh," he said, sounding aberrantly pleased. "That sounds like it could be very unpleasant. Any specifics for me to look forward to?"

"I'm a big fan of spontaneity," I said cooly. "Time?"

"By seven, Brother Mine," Rothbart said. "No need to keep everyone awake into the wee hours of the morning."

I looked at the clock. It was five-thirty. By car I would have to go the long way around—it would be thirty minutes. But trails dotted the entire forest, and by snowmobile it would only be ten.

"I'll be there by six," I said.

I could hear the grin on the other end of the phone. "Excellent," Rothbart responded, and disconnected the call.

*Trillion!* Wednesday's voice was breathless and strangled. I ignored her, making my way back to the bedroom, looking at the box on the bed. With more determination now, I ran my hand across the lid, and then opened it.

Gleaming metal shone back at me, and I could see a broken image of myself in the steel.

*Trillion!* Wednesday's voice rang in my head as I pulled the sword from the box examining it from hilt to tip. Undamaged, as always.

"Yes, Wednesday?" I responded matter-of-factly.

*You—Rothbart—*

"Yes, I'm going to see him."

*You said you would bring me to him. What in the—*

"No, I didn't," I said, pulling out the scabbard, and sheathing the blade. Rising, I walked over and grabbed a clean set of clothes from the special shelf of my closet. These were my work clothes—black, but sturdier. Blood resistant, tear resistant, and hopefully death re-

274 - REBEKAH ISERT

sistant. I had not worn the still-bespelled clothing in a long while, and it felt surreal to be putting it on once more.

*Uh, I'm pretty sure I heard you,* Wednesday said, following me to the bathroom door.

"No," I said, shutting the door in her face. "You heard me agree to meet him, there's a difference." I dressed quickly and brushed my way past her. She stared at me, and stalked back to the bed. I looked back at her, buckling the sword onto a baldric, and then slipping it over my head.

*But you're still going. Trillion, why not wait for your father?* Her tone was desperate.

"It will be too late by then," I said shortly, leaving the bedroom, "Father's plane lands at seven. I'm sure if I leave Rothbart to his devices too long he'll kill Konstantin."

Wednesday rushed after me, meowing furiously. *Yes, but that doesn't mean you should go rushing after him by yourself! For the love of sanity, Trillion, you'd be going against two sorcerers at once! No matter how badly you want to beat Rothbart, there has to be a better way to defeat him!*

I turned on my heel, staring down at her. "Like what?"

*I don't know! But you're killing yourself if you do this! There has to be a better way.*

I laughed, utterly without humor and shook my head. "This isn't the first time I've faced off against two sorcerers, Wednesday."

*Then you know how intensely st—*

"I won," I said shortly. She stared at me, fury lapping against my consciousness like waves of an ocean of righteous but mute indignation.

*You're not*—Wednesday still didn't have any words, but she trotted after me as I barreled through the house, flipping off lights as I went. *You told me that you cared for your brother. You also told me that care would kill you. I can't let you—*

"If I'm going to die because of care, Wednesday, it won't because of Rothbart," I said wheeling around to face her. "It will because I care for you, Konstantin, and my father. And I will tell you now, that I would rather die a thousand times for you than live for a million years knowing that I could have made a difference."

Wednesday stared up at me. When she finally spoke, her voice broke a little.

*And I would rather die myself than live a day without you.* I froze there, standing in my dark kitchen. Wednesday sat, her tail curling self consciously around her tiny, perfect paws.

*This whole time, I haven't been mad or scared because I've been afraid of dying, Trillion. It's because*—she broke off, looking up at me with luminous green eyes. *It's because I don't want to leave you behind. I love you.*

It was intensely odd, having love declared to me by a cat. But then, it was also Wednesday, my impossible girl. In an odd way, it made sense for it to be this way. I smiled at her, a small bead of warmth slipping into the cool patch of dread in my chest.

*Please, Trillion.*

Squatting down, I ran my hand over her head. She pressed her head into the palm of my hand and the moment seemed to slow. I squeezed my eyes shut for a moment, trying to remember this tranquility. I would need it. And then I spoke.

"Stay here. I promise I will come back to you, and we'll work this out. Together."

*Trillion.*

"I promise," I said solemnly, standing. And then, without looking back, I swept out the door into the night.

# 31

## IN WHICH THERE IS A GREAT DEAL OF FIGHTING

The forest stretched before me, velvet darkness broken only by stars. The moon hadn't risen yet—it wouldn't until after sunrise today— creating a blackness so close I could feel it pressing in against my skin.

I didn't want to turn on my headlights. The bright lights would be nice, but they felt like a beacon, pointing all attention in the forest directly to me. Thankfully, even with the darkness, the trail was clear and the snow still white. I wouldn't need much light to see as I drove, just enough to reflect back at me, so I flicked my flashlight on instead and gunned the snowmobile into the trees.

If I hadn't known the trails quite so well, or felt so much urgency, I wouldn't have dared to go fast as I did, skidding around the curves, flying up and down hills so fast I could feel it in my stomach. The freezing air blasted in my face. Even with my resilience against the cold, I could feel the biting frost from my nose to the pointed tips of my ears. It seemed distinctly odd to be running purposefully into a situation that I was almost sure was a trap. Simply the fact that he'd told me to bring Wednesday was a huge red flag—my Achilles' Heel was taking care of innocents. I knew that, and if our various encounters had taught him absolutely anything, he knew that as well.

Wednesday would have something to say about being left behind. Possibly for several hours. Or decades.

I hoped I would be around to hear it. Grimacing into the wind, I gunned it even faster.

I didn't park close. I dismounted the snowmobile a half a mile away, hidden deep in the trees. I couldn't hear anything. It wasn't particularly late—technically speaking, it wasn't even dinner time—but the winter chill had stolen across the park and there was no one, ranger or patron, wandering around now.

Not that I knew exactly what time it was. I'd left my phone on the counter in my rush to leave. That would be all right. Even if Konstantin was injured, if he was alive I could keep him that way until I got him to safety. No, the real worry was that Rothbart was nothing if not thorough at killing escape strategies, not to mention everything else. If I parked too close, he could hear me coming and be prepared. Yet another reason to park far away. And so I looped around behind the trees, trying to make it seem as though I came from an entirely different direction.

I finally walked through the trees coming to the edge of the amphitheater. It stretched down the hill, the polished black stone of the stage dimly reflecting the stars above in the sky, as though it was an extension of the lake behind it. Snow piled up around the sides and in the seats of the audience, but the surface of the stage itself was perfectly clear. And above it, as though scraping the tops of the trees, hung a full moon.

I frowned at it. It was an illusion, but was Rothbart so desperate to lure me in that he would... I looked down into the amphitheater. In the light of the fake moon, I could see three figures on the stage. One bent and bowed. One small and lithe. One pacing.

Konstantin, Odell, Rothbart.

I unsheathed my sword. The gleaming steel glowed a faint white in the darkness, and the pacing figure stopped, looking up at me.

"Ah, brother," Rothbart said, brightening the fake moon until it was a spotlight. "I see you made it. And with a King's blade, no less."

"I serve the King, Rothbart."

"Is that Excalibur herself, or the fair blade's cousin?" he asked.

I let the corner of my mouth twitch upward in a humorless smile. "You know the legends as well as I, brother," I said, descending the stairs one by one. "Only the rightful ruler of England can wield that blade."

"Perhaps the only responsibility that you do not take upon yourself." Rothbart's voice was mocking, and as I came down the stairs, it was almost a shock to see Siegfried's face glaring back at me. The neat brown hair of the dancer's body was disheveled, and he was searching my eyes for something as I arrived at the bottom of the stairs.

"Perhaps," I agreed. "I see no fault in looking after the welfare of others."

"Careful, Trillion," Rothbart sneered. "Looking after their welfare comes awfully close to *caring* for others. Heaven forbid you sacrifice yourself for someone of lesser worth than yourself."

I didn't respond, and I didn't move forward. Instead, I looked over at Konstantin. "You holding up, my friend?" I asked. Konstantin didn't respond, but nodded stiffly, as if he was fighting against something to do so.

"I have enchanted the dog that he may not speak." Rothbart strolled toward me, speaking conversationally, as if he was pointing

out an interesting feature of the amphitheater, or perhaps a particularly interesting plant. "I do not approve of animals that talk back."

"What a good thing you never officially met Wednesday," I said
mildly.

Rothbart looked around the stage. "Yes, where is the precious
kitty? From what I saw, she and Konstantin had become quite... attached. It's why I abducted him, of course. I thought she was in his
tender care. Turns out she was worming her way into *your* psyche
the whole time."

Again, I didn't respond, but looked over at Odell, who hadn't
moved since I had entered the arena. She looked vastly different
from the last time I had seen her, her build a little shorter and more
square than Giselle's, deep, dark eyes staring back at me across the
platform in the light of the faux moon, the shadows from the light
making the shadows under her eyes seem sharp and extreme.

"You don't have to support him," I told her quietly. "You haven't
killed anyone yet. If you could—"

"Oh, but she *tried* that," Rothbart said. Sweeping grandly over to
Odell, he put one arm around her shoulder, pulling her into a mocking, frightening half-embrace. "Two whole days ago now. Precious
little Odell tried releasing the spell over dear Giselle and nearly
killed herself in the process. For her own protection, I've had to keep
her under lock and key. She doesn't seem to understand the *consequences* of her actions." He threw a dark look down at her. She grimaced and looked away.

I looked at her more closely. What I thought were shadows were
actually dark marks on her face. Bruising? From trying to lift her
own curse?

Or from defending her choice to lift it?

"Now," Rothbart said, releasing Odell, shoving her slightly so
she teetered precariously off balance, unable to catch herself. She
squeezed her eyes shut, and I realized with a hot flash of anger that

this was not the first time that this particular thing had happened. "Where is the feline?"

"Why do you care?" I asked. "It wasn't your curse."

"Ah," Rothbart turned smartly, offering a slight curtsy, "you got me. Odell here's been doing most of the work. It's been quite nice, for all of her inexperience in the dark arts."

"Yes, I've always wondered why you haven't ever teamed up with some other practitioner," I said, looking over at Konstantin. He looked over at Odell, as if watching her carefully. I looked at her too. She remained unmoving, her eyes locked on Rothbart.

Rothbart shrugged, not noticing either movement. "I've thought about it. But they're so difficult to kill afterward." He glanced back at Odell. "Sorry, dearest. If it makes you feel any better, I think I'll actually regret killing you. Speaking of killing," Rothbart turned back to me. "Since you deliberately ignored my instructions to bring the cat, I have no reason to leave you alive. Thanks for nothing, brother."

With that, he waved his hand, and a bright green sheet of energy roared toward me. I brought the sword up, whispering words of power. The sword's glow sharpened, the inscription etched into the blade flaring to life as it sucked in the magic. The green brightened to white, burning a flash into my eyes.

"*Draconis*," Rothbart breathed. "You *do* come well-prepared."

I didn't respond, feeling the magic entering through my fingers, purified. Whole. Clean.

Ready for me.

"What now, brother?" Rothbart said, head tilting to the side in a swift, almost grotesque motion. "Will you kill me?"

"Do not tempt me, brother," I said quietly.

"That's what I've been doing for *ages*," Rothbart sneered. He spoke three words, each crackling with lightning, blackness streaking toward me with the speed and power of a train. I was already in motion, twisting, slashing across each of the black streaks.

"Really? And here I just though you enjoyed killing people," I said, taking a step toward him.

Rothbart thought about it for a moment, a comical sort of frown crossing his face. "You know? I think you're right." Looking back at Konstantin and Odell, Rothbart raised his arms. Odell recoiled, head tucked against the coming onslaught. I acted quickly. Releasing magic to make my steps light and swift, I slid in between them, sword arcing through another sheet of green.

"Protecting your prey now? How very soft of you. Of course, given your history, I could hardly expect otherwise," Rothbart said. I heard the smallest of whispers, the words soft and feminine. I knew that spell. Release. There was a rustle of movement.

"History would disagree with you," I said, stepping forward. I held the sword aloft in front of me. Part of it was for protection. Part of it was for the light. I could barely see Rothbart now, the moon dimming as he used more and more of his power to throw curses me, but with any luck, he wouldn't see Odell moving behind me.

It was right about then that the thought struck me that I hoped Odell wasn't playing both of us. Stabbing me in the back—figuratively or literally—wasn't going to do her as much good as she probably thought it would. But no. There was another small scuffle, and then footsteps receding straight back from me. Two sets.

Good. At least one of them knew about defensible positions.

And now there was no one to defend.

Only me.

And only him.

"And yet," Rothbart said, his voice silky, "it seems that history has forgotten you."

"And yet," I repeated his words, heart hollow, "there are many thousands of dead men for whom I will always be their last memory. Is that not a place in history? No matter how many people you have killed, remember that I have had a thousand years longer to wreak havoc on this world."

"Except for the last three hundred years," Rothbart mocked, a ball of black, writhing energy twisting around his palm. "You haven't killed me."

"Perhaps I never wanted to. Perhaps after a thousand years of killing, I found I didn't have much taste for it at all. Perhaps I was trying to help you. To save you from the same fate that I find myself in."

There was a moment of silence, and the world was still. Even the lake was quiet, the waves stilled by the deepness of winter. Then, the whisper of wind in the trees, the soft song soothing.

"You," Rothbart's voice was low but vehement, breathing so hard I could practically feel the cold air biting into his lungs, "have never been interested in saving anyone from anything."

"Rothbart—"

"You let my mother DIE!" Rothbart screamed, the black twisting mass around his hand shooting toward me with the speed of a bullet. I deflected it, and another, and another, *Draconis* shining ever brighter in the darkness. Magic shot up my arm, so quickly it was painful, and I expelled it with a shout, throwing my arms down toward the ground between us.

Clear sheets of ice shot up between the two of us, forming a circle around Rothbart, illuminated by an unearthly glow. Rothbart threw a spell at it, but the magic in the barrier held, absorbing it, and he paced along the full inside of the circle before looking back at me, grimacing in anger.

"The Baroness did not want to change." My voice was hoarse, and not a little desperate. The barrier would not hold out forever. "She did not want Father to change. He was willing to make that sacrifice! She refused him time and time again."

"YOU'RE LYING!" Rothbart yelled. "Mother loved Auberon. She wanted to spend the rest of her life with him. She would have been willing to share the time!"

"Rothbart, your mother *did* share the rest of her life with him. But she refused to share his life force. She believed that he could do more with an eternal life than live only a couple more hundred years with her. She refused him, even as she drew her last breath."

"You. Are. Lying." The growl was more animal than human, and pain sheared through my soul as I remembered a significantly younger boy with a different face.

"I swear it."

"On what?"

"On both of our mothers' graves," I said, gravel scraping in my throat.

Rothbart looked at me furious, his entire body trembling with anger. "Well, then," he growled, his voice shaking, "perhaps she might have been a little less selfish in making such a decision."

"Do you even hear yourself?" I demanded. "Do you know what you were asking of both of your parents? No one wants to see their parents die, Rothbart!"

"And you'll never have to!" Rothbart bellowed.

I narrowed my eyes. "Haven't I? Did it never occur to you that I have not lost one, but two mothers?"

Rothbart sneered, and turned his back on me. I looked down briefly. I could feel something, rising up through the floor. Some sort of power. Not necessarily a spell.

"And you?" Rothbart asked. "If you were in Auberon's shoes would you make the same decision? Would you be willing to sacrifice immortality to share your life with the woman that you love?"

A pair of green eyes flashed through my mind, and I bowed my head.

"Yes, I would." The coolness of the night hung between us. "But your mother had a choice, Luther. And she trusted you to trust her."

Rothbart's head came up, teeth bared. The power that had been seeping up under me flared red hot and I jumped back.

"DO NOT CALL ME THAT NAME!" Rothbart howled. "You have *no idea* what you are talking about! You could not *possibly* understand."

"Luther—" I whispered.

"Why won't you just *die?*" Rothbart screamed, and the ice prison shattered. I felt the frozen crystal rush toward me, impacting my armor and I swung the sword to repel as many as I could, razor bits of ice biting into my skin. Turning and twisting to avoid another salvo of a particularly nasty curse, I summoned my own magic, hurling it in a burst of white light, exploding like a firework across the stage.

Rothbart staggered, but I could tell the magic didn't take, splashing around him like a particularly solid splatter of paint. He rubbed his chest where the spell had hit him and looked up at me in disbelief, as if he couldn't believe I had caught him so soundly.

It was just my luck that he had elvish blood, stronger than most. Nothing short of a mortal curse or injury would take him. I didn't know mortal curses—they were all black magic of one sort or another.

Thankfully, I had never been all that unskilled at causing injury all by myself.

Rothbart hurled two pieces of writhing, gnashing magic at me, the heat of them blasting me in the face as I brought *Draconis* around to break the seals of the spell. Rothbart surged forward, pulling a long sword made from darkness itself and brought it whistling through the air.

I pulled my own sword up and around, connecting so hard my

teeth clacked. Rothbart of old had never been particularly powerful, but he had the skill. Now he had a dancer's body. Strong, powerful, graceful.

Funny, though, that no matter how much he looked like a complete stranger, I could only see my little brother. The curly-haired, ruddy-cheeked little boy that would run up the Great Hall being chased by me or his other brothers, laughing and giggling. The teenager, joking and teasing his family at every opportunity, learning magic simply to conjure roses for his mother. The young man, who trained with me every day for twenty years. Not Baron von Rothbart. Luther.

I couldn't kill him. I couldn't do it. He would escape here, free to cause more havoc and more pain. I was weak.

I cared too much.

I blocked another swing, deflecting it and shoving him away hard, my mind racing, wondering if I could trap him. The darkness moved around his weapon, repelling light, illuminating our surroundings almost as much as my own sword. The light glinted off the dark stone only a couple feet away. If I could collapse it, then maybe the stone could trap him. At least until I decided what I could do with him. He would protect himself. He would have to.

I allowed Rothbart to drive me back toward the stage. All things considered, I probably should have felt worse about demolishing a building, but in my defense, I'd been trying to get the State Park to demolish the eyesore for years and build something a little more environmentally friendly.

Stepping close to the building, I sent as much magic as I could to my elbow and struck the wall as hard as I could. The stone cracked, and the enormous structure started to slide. The stone started to slip off the building, crumbling like a landslide, pummeling down around Rothbart. He stayed in place, caught off guard, dropping the dark blade and covering his head. As the stones fell, I realized, breathing far harder than normal, that this could kill him. Out of the way of the falling stones, I forced myself to watch, gritting my teeth as the building gave way completely, sliding over top of Rothbart, a grave of dark rock. I couldn't hear him, but I could see him, his mouth open, his eyes squeezed shut.

He was screaming.

I took a step back, but allowed myself to go no further. I was responsible for his death. I would not run. I could not. For centuries that was the only care for my fellow men that I had been afforded, and though I was not human, it was the bit of humanity that I would never give up.

At long length, the rumbling subsided, and a small breeze blew the rest of the sound away, leaving only the cold chill of the December night. I swallowed, feeling the chill in my bones. Had I done it?

Had I just killed my own brother?

I stared at the pile of rubble, disbelief and pain ripping through my chest. I had done it. I had—

The ground shuddered violently.

I caught my balance, but just barely. A second shudder, more of a tremor, blasted through the ground, cracking the stone under my feet. I fell, my sword skidding away as I hit what remained of the stage at full force. The pile of rubble exploded, and I ducked, protecting my head against the onslaught. As suddenly as it started, the tumult died, and I looked up.

Rothbart stood in the middle of the pile of rubble, looked around at it with a mixture of disdain and downright fury. I didn't think he could see me, half buried in rubble as I was, but his eyes trained on me like a heat seeking missile.

I suddenly had the urge to move.

Letting magic fuel my muscles, I shoved the rocks that half buried me off with a strength that surprised even me, but I was too slow. Rothbart was on me in a flash, grabbing me by the front of my coat, hoisting me off the ground.

"*How dare you,*" he whispered.

I gasped a little, unnerved by the feeling of only my toes scraping the floor below. "Had..." I wheezed, "To give it...my best shot."

"Was that really your best?" he sneered. "I'm surprised you survived the fight for Britannia." He threw me away from him, sending me across the rubble. I felt several somethings crack in my ribcage, and another rock clipped the back of my head. Pain stole my breath away.

"I—told you," I gasped, trying to get up, but giving up a moment later, gritting my teeth. "I—I can't kill you."

"So you've said," Rothbart said, one corner of his lips curling. "Thankfully, I have no such qualms. Once you are dead, I will have no qualms going after your father. And that cat, too."

Cat. Wednesday. She was in danger. I renewed my struggle to get up, barely managing to rise to my elbows before the agony in my chest forced me back down. There was shifting in the rocks around me, and in the light of *Draconis* several feet away, I could see a mass of rocks gathering above my head.

I couldn't move. Pain lashed me in place as cold horror sunk into my soul. He was going to do to me exactly as I had done to him. I reached in toward the magic inside of me. I'd expended too much breaking apart the ampitheatre. Of the magic I had left, too much was going to my ribs, to my head. I tried to tear some away, to defend myself or to throw at him, to do *something*. The pain was overpowering, blackness threatening as I tried to pull it apart. I collapsed backward.

I was going to die.

Care will kill him.

That blasted witch.

I could see Rothbart out of the corner of my eye, arms raised high above his head, gathering the rocks to him. Above me. It wouldn't be long now.

I should have closed my eyes, but I couldn't. I didn't know why.

Would he look at me as he killed me?

And then he brought his arms down.

Nothing happened. I blinked. The rocks remained where they were, slightly shifting in the mass above my head. I looked at Rothbart, who looked back at me, shocked, as though he thought I was the one responsible.

I wasn't. But then, who—

I looked past him to the base of the stairs. I probably wouldn't have been able to see her at all, except for a light grey hoodie that stood out from the darkness. Her hands—human hands—were outstretched, and I could see her shaking from the effort of keeping the enormous load aloft.

Wednesday.

# 32

## IN WHICH I GIVE MY ALL

What in the name of actual sanity was she doing here?! I tried to push myself up, the pain lancing through me like a fresh stab wound. Straining, she pushed, sending the enormous pile of floating rock tumbling to the ground in a thunderous crash just out of reach. I couldn't look away from her.

She was human.

She was here.

She—

I looked up at Rothbart who was looked at me with a careful, dangerous look.

"Not you, then," he whispered. A cold smile crept up his cheeks. "Who then, I wonder?"

And then he turned. Wednesday was breathing hard, but still standing. How much energy had she just expended? Did she even know how to fight? Would it do any good?

"Leave her, Rothbart!" I shouted. It came out weak and painful as my lungs crushed against my broken ribs. Rothbart turned back, walking toward me, and with a quick, decisive motion sent his boot hard into my face. My teeth clacked together, and the world went fuzzy. I remember having the hope that none of my teeth had broken, and there was a short flutter of blackness.

My heartbeat thundered in my ears, and I heard a muffled shout, saw a flash of light behind my eyes.

Wednesday.

My eyes cracked open. I could see her running in slow motion along one of the tiers of the amphitheater, barely managing to cut up and back the other way as another white-hot curse shattered the dark stone behind her.

Rothbart was screaming. "Why won't you just die?" he demanded, and a faint thought in my head noted that he had asked me the same question. Wednesday stopped in the bleachers and she scowled at him.

"You should have killed me before I knew what you were!" she shouted back. "I remember everything! You were going to do to Trillion what you did to me—you just didn't know the effects it would have on elvenborn."

"You know nothing!"

"I heard you in my own kitchen! At my own birthday party! I overheard you and Odell. You were going to kill Auberon. And I was going to act." Wednesday was clutching her side, and I could see her pale and shaking. Whatever had happened—how she could be human when there was no moon—had taken its toll on her.

What had she done?

"You always were getting into things that you shouldn't have," Rothbart said, prowling toward her. "If you hadn't started to remember, we wouldn't have had to turn you into a cat the second time. Or kept it long enough to be ingrained in your soul. You're dying, aren't you?"

"That's none of your business," she spat, straightening.

"Sure it is," Rothbart said. "Trillion certainly cares. Seeing you die would be the greatest of tortures for him. I wonder, should I kill you outright or make him watch you suffer?"

"You'll have to catch me first."

"Then I'll kill your boyfriend," he said, gesturing back at me with his sword.

"He's not my boyfriend," she said, looking down at me. A fond look flashed across her face. "You forget, I'm a cat. He's my staff."

"You're ridiculous."

"And you're psychotic. And you can't dance worth beans. I'm sure Mother only kept you on because of your face."

Was—was she trying to bait him?

Moving slowly, I rocked myself onto my side. If I could just get in reach of my sword—

"Silence!" Rothbart roared, and hurled another curse at her. She was fast, but the force of the blast knocked her forward. She skidded forward onto her hands and knees, an audible gasp of pain ricocheting around the arena.

He was going to kill her, and unless I moved I would be doomed to watch.

Something woke in me then. Pain tore at my insides, but as the world slowed to a crawl, I could feel something else build within me. Maybe I had been unconscious longer than I had thought. Perhaps magic was building up inside me, healing me.

But I didn't feel healed. I felt energized. Something else was powering me, and I was willing to bet anything that it had something to do with Wednesday.

Gritting my teeth, I forced myself to stand. Everything protested, and I let out a yell as I propelled myself forward and up.

One step, and I bent down to scoop *Draconis* into my hand. Another and I was on my way, rushing toward Rothbart in the light of the blade.

My footsteps thundered in my ears as I sprinted toward him.

One step.

Two steps.

I could hear Ædda's voice in my head, feel her old wizened hands rest on my young shoulders. *Care will kill him.*

I screamed in defiance.

So be it. If it was for Wednesday, so be it.

Rothbart turned and I swung viciously at him. He jumped back, deflecting my sword, but I was already pulling away and swinging around the other side. He deflected that strike as well, dodging my blade as I struck again and again.

He tried to use his magic, sparks dancing across his hands, but I kept him far too busy for that. All I could hear was Wednesday's gasp of pain as she hit the ground. He'd hurt her. He'd hurt her like he'd hurt hundreds of people before. I hadn't allowed myself to care too much for them. The guilt would have permeated every waking thought. Still had permeated every waking thought.

I was as responsible for them as much as he was.

No longer.

Not Wednesday. Not anyone else.

Never again.

Rothbart shouted back at me, anger and determination written on every line of his face, as I was sure it was written on mine. He was fighting for his life. But I had Wednesday.

I pushed forward, hacking away at him, his arms moving slower and slower as I drove him back across the rock-strewn stage. I had him. Energy filled my limbs anew and with one swipe I shattered the sword of darkness, and then buried my sword to the hilt in his chest.

Rothbart stopped, shocked into stillness. He looked down at the King's sword in his chest, which emitted a bright white light, casting shadows ghoulishly onto his face. My hand was still on the hilt. He took my hand in both of his, and pushed me away. The sword slid out easily, far too easily, and Rothbart dropped to his knees, blood soaking his front.

Cold realization of what I had done gripped my heart, and I stumbled forward, dropping *Draconis*. Catching Rothbart in my arms, I lowered us both to the ground, clasping him to my chest.

"Rothbart?" I gasped. "Luther?"

His eyes were already flickering. The strike had been perfectly placed. One that could have only been done by one with a thousand years of experience. I gripped the fabric of his clothes, gritting my teeth and bowing my head against his shoulder.

"I'm sorry." I gasped the words into his shoulder, something searingly hot and ice cold dropping from my chest to my stomach, cracking something deep within. "I'm sorry, Luther. I'm so sorry."

Rothbart didn't reply, and when I raised my head to look into his face, he stared back at me, something deep and unknowable behind his eyes.

"I love you, my brother," I whispered to him, reaching up to stroke his hair, something cold and wet trickling my cheeks. "I am so, so sorry."

Luther looked around the amphitheater, opening his mouth as though to reply. He couldn't quite catch his breath. He looked almost sad for a moment, and then he sighed a long, deep sigh, his eyes losing focus. His body relaxed in my arms, face tilting up toward the dark, starry sky.

"Luther?" I said, giving him a little shake. "Luther!"

He didn't move, and we stayed there. I could feel the deep magic within him melt away back to the earth. I squeezed my eyes closed, sending up a howl that bore my entire soul. Pressing my face into his shoulder, I sobbed and sobbed, rocking my little brother back and forth.

There had been no other way. I knew that, and yet it offered no comfort to the pain in my soul. It burned, raging and blistering its way through me. It was torture. It was as though I was standing on the edge of death itself. And yet through the sobs, the trembling, the ache that I knew would never fully fade, I could not shake the feeling that I had been given the glimpse of something very precious. Pulling back, I lay Luther down on the ground, gently closing his eyes. Wiping my tears on the back of my hand, I stood, staring down at him.

"Our final farewell, my brother," I said quietly, studying his face in the dim light from my sword. "May you at last know peace."

Silence reigned for a moment as I looked down at him. His features were relaxed, calmer than I had ever seen them, and although they were not the features that he had been born with, it struck me that it was not an expression that he had worn for quite some time. I bowed my head.

"Trillion!"

My head jerked up, looking up the steps of what remained of the amphitheater, visible in the light of a pure white sphere that was rising into the sky. Four figures stood on the top steps. The tallest figure, I recognized immediately.

"Father!" I burst out, and tried to jerk myself into some sort of shambling jog. The other man moved quickly, jumping down the stairs, long russet hair flying back as he ran to me. I tried to keep moving, but my body suddenly remembered the beating that it had been through mere moments before. My chest tightened, pain blasting through me, and I stumbled. Strong hands caught my shoulders, and I was pulled into a firm but gentle embrace, somehow avoiding my ribs.

The scent hit me first, memory slamming into me like a freight train. Cedar and sandalwood, mixed with green and home. I gripped the back of his jacket for dear life, burying my face into his chest.

"It's done," I gasped. "He's gone."

"I know," Father said, running his hand over my head. "We saw."

"How did you get here?" I asked pulling back and looking at him. "Who told you?"

"Well," Father said, "it's not every day I get a voicemail full of screeching feline yowls." He placed his hand on my shoulder and glanced behind me at the fallen body behind me. "You should go to her. She's in rough shape. I will—" He looked away for a moment, eyes the color of an autumn sky shining with tears. "I will be with you in a moment."

I turned and noticed the other three figures had huddled over a fourth.

"Wednesday," I breathed, and stumbled to the stairs. My ribs didn't hurt quite as bad. Had my father done that? Picking my way over the rubble, I came to the second tier, where the still-human Wednesday lay in her mother's arms, eyes closed. Konstantin and Odell stood staring down at the couple on the ground in worry, looking a little the worse for the wear. My heart jolted painfully. Stanislava looked up at me, concern in her face as I knelt, letting me take the young woman from her.

Wednesday's eyelids flickered, and then cracked open.

"Oh," she said, her voice raspy, "It's you."

"Hey," I said, one side of my mouth involuntarily twitching. "I just saved your bacon."

"Did you—" she broke off, taking a deep breath, "—just call me a pig?" I stared at her for a moment, absolutely speechless, and she smiled. "Have I ever told you how cute you are when you don't have a clue what to say?"

I couldn't help it. I smiled, looking over her in concern, my hand running over her hair. I couldn't lose her too, not today. "No, you haven't."

"You're cute a lot."

"*Hey*," I protested gently, still smiling despite myself.

She huffed out a laugh, and a sad sort of tired look pulled on her face. "I'm so sorry, Trillion," she whispered. "I thought by breaking the spell... I thought it would fix things. Me. I think... I think I broke me instead."

"No," I shook my head.

A frown pulled at the edges of her lips and she tucked her head against my elbow. "I gave everything I had," Wednesday whispered. "It was the most worthwhile thing I've... I've ever done. I would do it again." Desperation crackled in my chest.

"No, Wednesday. You will not die. Not today. I can't—" My voice cracked and I cleared my throat. I heard footsteps behind me in the rubble and I looked back to see my father. "Father, is there something that can be done? It—she—" I tore my eyes away from him, looking down at Wednesday. Her eyes had drifted closed again.

Father walked around me. In the white light from the sphere above our heads, I could see the slight reddening around his eyes. A look of pained compassion crossed his face as he looked down at us and he crouched down, placing a gentle hand on Wednesday's head.

"She is very far gone," he said quietly.

I looked up at him. "Anything, Father. *Anything*."

He looked at me, and I could see the struggle there. Auberon, King of the Fairies, looked down at Wednesday and shook his head. "She has worn out her life for you," he murmured. "She will die, unless—" he broke off, swallowing, and looked down.

"*Father*," I whispered, hollow to my soul. "Please."

He closed his eyes and sighed. "It is only fitting, I suppose," his sad voice quavering, "that this would be our only option." Then he looked up at me, his voice becoming low and rough. "If you were to give her your soul to share… she… she would have a chance." Looking into his eyes, sitting in the aftermath of such a decision, I felt I knew what it cost him to suggest such a thing, while simultaneously knowing that I could never possibly understand.

"I don't know how," I whispered.

He smiled, or attempted a painful excuse for one, and moved his hand from Wednesday's head to my shoulder. "I do. If she is willing, I will help you."

I looked down at Wednesday, where she lay with her eyes closed and breathing shallow. It wouldn't be long now.

"Wednesday," I said, my voice low and husky, running one hand along her cheek. "Wednesday, can you hear me?"

"Yes." The word was the barest whisper.

"I can save you," I whispered to her. "I can save you, if you will share your life with me. I can give you part of my life to live out with me."

"You'll die," she protested.

"One day," I confirmed. "But not without having lived a very long time. With you."

"You would?"

I took her hand, clasping it to my heart. "It would be my greatest honor. I love you."

She cracked open her eyes. She seemed to search my face for a moment, and then her eyes slid closed again. Her body relaxed.

"Yes," she murmured.

"Trillion, she's slipping," Father warned.

"You will?"

"Yes," she whispered again, her voice the reediest of threads. I pulled her a little closer and looked up at Father with nothing short of desperation, and he nodded, squaring his shoulders.

"Say her full given name."

"Giselle Carabosse," I said, looking down at her face.

"Repeat after me," Father instructed, and began the spell. It didn't take long, repeating the Old Faerie words, but I could feel her light fading, her breaths coming so short and faint that she may as well have not been breathing at all.

But she was.

"That's it," Father said. "Seal the enchantment."

I looked up in confusion. He smiled a gentle smile. "How else would you seal a spell of true love, my son? With a kiss."

Looking down at her, I ran a hand down the side of her face. She stiffened for a moment, but not at my touch. This was the end. If not now, then never.

Cradling her gently in my arms, I leaned down, and gently pressed my lips to hers.

# 33

## IN WHICH IT ENDS

I could feel the magic buzzing around her and me, flowing between us. At some point, something that I could not describe seemed to leave me, but was replaced by a sudden knowledge of something else. Someone else. Wednesday. I could feel her. Inside and out. Back and forth. Now and forever.

For a moment, Wednesday did nothing, simply hung limply in my arms. The next, a pair of slender arms that could have only belonged to one person wrapped themselves around my neck and into my hair and pulled me even closer, suddenly very alive. I responded in kind, completely losing myself in Wednesday's kiss until I realized some moments later that we had an audience.

A very... parental audience. I broke the kiss and drew back, finding myself met by a pair of alert green eyes. Wednesday smiled back at me, and I could feel my heart melt.

"Well." Stanislava's voice was dryer than the Arabian Desert. "You seem to have made a lasting impression on my daughter."

Father snorted. And I looked down, an uncontrollable smile

crossing my face. "It worked, then," I said softly, running a finger down Wednesday's cheek. She met my eyes, a sweet smile building on her cheeks. I felt my father's hand on my shoulder, and dragged my gaze away from her up to his smile.

"It worked," he confirmed. Wednesday sat up under her own power, blinking in the artificial light, and shivered, pulling a little closer to me.

"It's going to get colder," I noted, feeling the nip on my cheeks a little more keenly than before. "We should head home. I'm sorry, I only brought my snowmobile. I can run back and get the car, but it's going to take—"

"That's okay," Wednesday said quickly. "I brought yours."

I stared at her, blinking furiously. "You—what?"

"How else did you think I got here? I've only ever been here for performances. It's not like I'd go running after you in the snow."

To be perfectly honest, that was exactly what I'd thought she'd done, but I knew better than to actually say anything.

"Were you..." I tried to think of a delicate way to put it. "...human?"

"No. Well—" she broke off, shrugging. "It kind of... happened in the middle of driving."

"You changed while driving my car?" I demanded.

"It's a rental," she soothed. "Besides, you're acting like I don't drive distracted normally."

"Do you?"

"Of course not! That would be incredibly dangerous." Her smile was impish, and despite my frustration, I had the sudden desire to kiss it.

"That's not comforting, Wednesday." But I was grinning at her. A thought struck me just then, and the smile calmed on my face.

She noticed. "What is it?"

"How did you break your spell?" I asked.

She looked down, her lips pressed together. "I'm not sure," she admitted. "I've tried to break it before. Especially at the beginning with you, I tried to will myself back into being human. I think," she looked thoughtful, and then glanced up at Odell, who looked as though she wanted to fade into the background, or simply disappear altogether. "I think it had something to do with you."

"Me?" Odell asked. Even from the last time I'd seen her, as she and Konstantin had been held captive on the stage, she looked more like herself. A smattering of freckles crossed her nose above brown eyes, and her brown hair had a golden sheen to it. "But I haven't—I mean, I don't—"

"Odell?" Father's voice broke through her protests, and she looked over at him. "You said when you found us that you had been trying to lift the spell, is that right?"

She looked down and nodded.

"You *found* him?" I demanded, frowning incredulously.

She didn't look up. If nothing else, she seemed to want to sink into the ground more than ever. Swallowing, she nodded again.

"Why?"

"Because..." she said, eyes locked on the snow-strewn rock beneath us, "I was wrong. Rothbart he—he made promises. Promises that, as I got to know him better, I knew he was never going to keep." Her voice broke a little and she shook her head.

"He said it would be a temporary curse. That I could stop it whenever I wanted. All I wanted to do was dance like her—to know what it felt like to do it properly. To do it perfectly... I was never going to keep it forever. And then Rothbart said that if I didn't keep it going—I didn't know what else to do. I was heading to your house, to maybe find someone or something to help but His Majesty and the Councilwoman were already on their way here. We ran into them on the trail. He was following your path through the woods."

I blinked. "So soon? I thought you were supposed to land at seven?"

Father looked distinctly uncomfortable. "I may have been a little... earnest to get here."

My frown deepened. "Did you manipulate the Jet Stream? Father, that could have severe ramifications on the environment!"

"I'm fine, by the way," Konstantin finally broke in. "Little banged up, lost a couple pints of blood at my house, but no more the worse for wear than usual."

I looked up, a little speechless for a moment, and then rose. Wednesday came with me, but stepped back as I pulled my friend into an embrace, hugging him tightly. "I am so glad you're okay."

"You are acting very emotional," Konstantin said uncomfortably, gingerly patting me on the back. "A nice 'Good Job, Konstantin' is more than adequate."

"You were imprisoned for several days," I said.

He shrugged nonchalantly, but he was smiling. "Actually, I was left alone most of the time. Without you chattering in my ear, it was almost like a vacation."

I squinted. "There's something wrong with you."

"Probably," he said flatly. "But you've most likely got the same problem."

"That's fair," I laughed.

"If I could beg your pardon," Father said, interrupting us gently. He turned back to Odell. "I should like a bit more perspective on what happened."

"But must we freeze in the meantime?" Stanislava asked. She turned to me. "Would you mind us invading your house for a little while? I, too, would like a few answers, and yours is the nearest acceptable establishment."

"Of course," I said. I looked between all of us, and then down at Wednesday. "Where are the car keys?"

"I have them," she said, smiling, and started to stroll toward the nearest set of stairs. I followed her.

"I know that. I would like to drive." I held out my hand.

She moved a little faster. "You've driven the whole time I've known you. It's my turn."

"You don't have your driver's license on you!" I protested. "Besides, you've been a cat."

"Irrelevant," she said smartly, and started up the stairs. After two or three, she turned back, a serious look of realization on her face. She looked solemnly down at the stage, and I knew in an instant what she was looking at.

Following her lead, I turned, looking back down the stairs to the nearly obliterated stage. There, where he had fallen, a clear dome covered Luther's body, protecting it. I looked over at Father. He was slowly making his way over to us, but his eyes lingered on the body. He looked up at me, and I couldn't look away his deep sorrow piercing my soul.

Arms wrapped me from behind and Wednesday, on the step above, leaned her head against mine.

"You know, I'm grateful to him," she whispered in my ear.

I looked up at her. "Why?" I asked.

She met my eyes, deathly serious. "Without him, I never would have met you." She paused, and kissed me gently on the cheek, one hand running through my hair. "And I think he was the first one you ever realized you cared for. Which let you care for me. Come on, Trillion. Rothbart is safe for now."

She took my hand then, leading me up to the car. Feeling just a little drawn out, I let her walk me to the passenger seat, I paused, looking in the windows. "Wednesday?"

"Yes?"

"There are six of us," I said.

She looked around, one eyebrow raised. "Yeah?"

"There are only five seats. There won't be enough seatbelts." Wasn't it obvious?

Wednesday clicked the car open and slid into the driver's seat. I could fairly feel her truly impressive eye roll as she settled herself in comfortably. "Trillion, has anyone told you that the more tired you are the more ridiculous you get?" she asked, her voice muffled by my closed door, pressing the ignition button. The car started with a hum and I frowned, opening the door as our ragtag group crunched up the gravel of the parking lot.

"I'm not tired," I grumbled, sliding into the passenger seat. She reached over, the nicest expression of incredulity I'd ever seen crossing her face, and took my head gently, caressing my cheek.

"It's been an odd day," she said soothingly. "I'm sure they'll be fine squishing in. Besides, if push comes to shove, we'll have Konstantin shift, and we can put him in the back."

"No way," Konstantin protested.

"What are you talking about? People put dogs in the back of cars all the time."

"Two words: Doggie vomit."

We all grimaced.

Father slid into the car easily, "Don't worry. We'll all fit."

I looked back. "Are you sure? I mean—"

"Yes," Father looked faintly smug, "We will."

I lit the fire when I got home. It wasn't strictly necessary, but even after blasting the heat the whole way home, I still didn't feel quite thawed through. Or maybe I felt drawn out. Or maybe I just wanted to distract myself from the fact that my father was holding an impromptu trial in my living room.

"I hope you understand that what you've done is quite serious," he said, sitting opposite from Odell on the couch. She sat, eyes and head down, hands clasped together so tightly her knuckles were white.

She nodded.

"You've employed black magic, and in the eyes of magical law you could be sentenced to death on precedent." Father's voice was matter of fact but somehow still inviting. Inviting questions. Inviting explanation.

Odell nodded again, face almost grey in the dim light of the room.

"I don't think that's necessary," Father said, studying her face.

She exhaled sharply and looked up at him, eyes filling with tears. "What?"

"Despite your unfortunate choice in ally, you were not a true partner to his crimes. As far as we have been able to trace it, he killed Siegfried Handel before you met or became involved with him, and when it came down to it, you were integral to the success of Ms. Carabosse's breaking of her own spell, eventually aiding her recovery. And then there is the matter of Rothbart's scheme."

Odell glanced up at me. I looked at both of them in confusion. Wednesday slid off of the barstool and came to stand next to me, hand interlacing with my own.

"What's this?" I asked.

"Giselle was a trial run," Odell explained to me softly. "Rothbart thought if I could live under the spell as Giselle and Stanislava didn't know, he could do the same to you. Take your appearance, fake whatever deaths he had to, and return in glory to his father's halls. And then kill King Auberon in secret."

"It might have worked," Stanislava stated uncomfortably. "The focus of the spell was on Giselle. Odell held little to no magical residue on her person. If His Majesty was caught unawares..."

"Which only confirms my decision," Father said quietly. Straightening a little, he nodded deeply to Odell. "I thank you that you chose to right the wrong that you had created. Unfortunately, choices have consequences, and I think you know that."

Odell nodded, lips pinched together. Father continued.

"I will give you a choice. You are a sorcerer by education, and you have shown great skill and love of the art. You are also a fantastic dancer. A human who can rank herself in a ballet company made up almost entirely of those of elven descent is a force to be reckoned with—a fact that is confirmed by Stanislava. You have told me that you studied magic to lengthen your dancing career. We know that it has led you to a lot of wrong choices and serious problems."

Odell's face had tilted up to look at Father, as if she was holding her breath. He studied her carefully, gauging her reaction. His face was solemn, but firm.

"You must choose between the two. You may practice magic under the guidance of a competent master. If you are ever found to be practicing black magic again, we would not be so lenient. Studying magic, you may spend your extended years studying to your heart's content, but the gift of dance will be taken from you—the knowledge and the skill.

"Or, you may choose to dance. You would live to the age of a tree—one hundred and twenty years—and be young and strong, dancing until your dying day, if you wish, but the powers of sorcery and enchantment will forever be removed from you." The room was silent as we all looked at Odell. Father stood. "These are your choices. I will leave you to deliberate."

# EPILOGUE

I never found out what Odell chose. Wednesday knew. I didn't have much inclination to ask, and Wednesday never told. Odell moved away scant weeks after the new year. I never heard from her again.

After a few weeks of reconditioning, Wednesday finished the ballet season with a bang, dancing principle in the ballet *Cinderella* as the titular character, *Sleeping Beauty* as Aurora, and lastly as *The Firebird*. Shortly thereafter, she announced her retirement. We were sitting on the floor of Orris Investigations eating pizza one day late in May when she looked up at me a little contemplatively.

"I'm not going to go back to the company this fall." She said it conversationally, leaning back against Konstantin's desk, tipping her head back to look at the ceiling. I looked over.

"What?"

She shrugged. "I think it's time to move on."

"It—what—are you okay?"

She looked over at me, and shrugged again, with one shoulder this time. "All the mess with Odell got me thinking. Am I taking someone's place in the ballet?"

"Of course you aren't," I said. "You earned your place there. You've done the work, put in the time—why are you shaking your head at me?"

"Sometimes I kind of miss being a cat," she admitted with a laugh. "I think my mental translations are better than what my tongue can do. I mean... what if by leaving I can open a door for some other dancer to grow? To become better?" She shifted a little. "I've never admitted this to anyone, but those last couple of months before everything happened, I wondered if there was something else that I should be doing. I love to dance. I've done it since I was six. That was eighty-seven years ago. I think it's time to let someone else take center stage."

There was a quiet moment where Wednesday smiled sadly down at her pizza, lost in thought. Then she blinked and shook herself. "We also need to talk about your promotion."

It was my turn to blink. "My what?"

"I was informed by a very reliable source that you've been a loyal staff member for the last five months," she said, a small smile crawling up her cheeks. I thought about it for a moment, and I fought back the smile that threatened to overcome me.

"I've done my very best to serve, Wednesday," I said as seriously as I could manage. "It hasn't always been easy, but I trust that you're satisfied with the results."

She smirked briefly, and nodded. "So I am, so I am. In light of that, I would like to promote you."

I looked at her contemplatively. We'd chosen to take it slow. Despite the deep connection that now existed between our souls, the simple truth of the matter was that we'd only known each other for two weeks. We'd been through so much together, but we wanted to take it slow. Become bonded by something other than trauma. So, she had moved back in with her mother, and we had small things like this—eating pizza together, me going to all of her ballet performances, and any other small, fun dates that we could think of to help us get to know each other.

Father had thought I was insane. I could understand why. To

him, years were like seconds, the decades like minutes. Why would I waste time when I had so little left? He'd never expressed any disappointment, but I knew he could feel the loss already. He was already planning another trip back here to visit.

A balled-up napkin hit me in the nose. "Trillion, are you listening to me?" Wednesday demanded.

"What?"

"You're doing that stare-y off into spacey thing," she said. Then she sobered. "Do you not...want to yet?"

"Want to what?" I asked. She sighed and reached forward, punching me in the arm.

"Ow!"

"You *weren't* listening. I swear, Trillion, if I had claws, I'd walk across your lap right now," she told me sternly. "I want to marry you." Her voice dropped in volume toward the end and I probably would have missed the entire statement if my hearing hadn't been quite so good.

"Come again?"

"I want to—" she broke off, looking up and seeing my grin. "Oh, come on!" She wiggled a little bit as I grabbed her and pulled her toward me. "No lifting!"

"Fight me," I said easily, setting her down in my lap. Once there, she looked miffed for a moment, but then settled there in my arms and looked into my eyes.

"If you're not ready, Trillion, it's fine. I—"

I kissed her. Soft, slow, deep, making sure she knew exactly what my answer was without saying a word. Pulling back slightly, she rested her forehead against mine and sighed.

"That had better be a yes, Trillion, because if it's not—"

"It is," I confirmed, unable to stop the smile crossing my face.

"So what now?"

I pulled back. "Apart from wedding planning?" I asked.

She shrugged. "Actually, I was kind of thinking we could elope."

"Do you want to bring my father's fury down on our heads?"

She grimaced. "I can't really gainsay the King of the Faeries, can I?"

"Probably not a good idea," I confirmed. "How about happily ever after?"

She laughed, but her eyes were soft. "For real?"

I grinned. "Of course."

THE END

# ACKNOWLEDGEMENTS

If I am perfectly honest, the person to blame, ahem, I mean *thank* for this adventure is W.R. Gingell. In the spring of 2020, mid-Pandemic, she gave us 200 words to write a story that included the words "Wednesday" "Brownie" "Everywhere" and "Email." I bit, wrote a teeny tiny excerpt that asked more questions than it answered, and I totally didn't win. But Trillion and Wednesday—albeit in much more dramatic form than they are today—were born. So thank you Ms. Gingell, as always, for your never-ending inspiration, even if you mess up my publishing schedule. ;)

Additionally, thank you for the INCREDIBLE amount of mentorship and help that you have provided as I've learned to navigate the world of writing and publishing. In the simplest terms: *I* adopted *you*, and I can never thank you enough for your seemingly never-ending kindness and patience for my literally never-ending questions.

I'd also love to thank my wonderful sisters, Jesse and Sarah, and my Mom.

Sarah, thank you as always for walking me through my plots and asking the *right*, if inconvenient, questions. Also, thank you for dropping absolutely everything when I decided to go from first draft to publishing in twenty-eight days. That part was technically *your* idea, but THANK YOU. I can never thank you enough. Thank you, thank you, thank you, thank you, thank you, thank you. (Times a million.)

Jesse, thank you for falling in love with Wednesday as much as I did, and being the inspiration for the use of Swan Lake. Your love of ballet inspired my love of ballet, and as ever, you guided me in the right direction. Thank you for wanting a copy for Christmas—it got me in the editing mindset, and pushed me in this direction. I hope this is at least a semi-acceptable Christmas present. I'm sorry it's not a proto-copy. ;)

Mom, thank you, thank you, thank you for so many things. For giving me life, for encouraging me to study English and, in this case, for teaching me how to do things, even—or especially—when they're hard. I wouldn't have been brave enough to do the hard thing of learning how to PUBLISH A BOOK without your constant love and understanding.

I love you all SO MUCH.

Also, thank you (as always) as to my Alpha Group: Jesse, Sarah, Cate, Caylie, and Stephanie. You're the best audience to write to, and it's fun to make you scream in frustration.

Also, thanks to the Royal Ballet, adjunct to the Royal Opera House. The unprecedented access to your performances and life behind the scenes due to the 2020 pandemic made it SO easy to research, and enjoyable research it was. Major kudos and thanks to Marianela Núñez, who is now my favorite ballerina of all time, and also who I see in my mind when I picture Wednesday. Y'all have NO idea who I am, but I'm so grateful that I know who you are.

# ABOUT THE AUTHOR

Rebekah Isert lives in the West, but unfortunately not with the elves. She spends a truly exorbitant amount of time writing (much to the dismay of her sleep and exercise schedule) but can also being found traveling, cooking doing jiu-jitsu, and reading anything that sounds interesting. The author is a Christian, and is endlessly grateful to her Heavenly Father for the light and inspiration that she receives, even when she feels like she doesn't always deserve it. She can be reached at rebekahisert.author@gmail.com, or you can touch base with her at her author pages on Facebook or Instagram (@rebekahisertauthor).

This is her first published novel.

CPSIA information can be obtained
at www.ICGtesting.com
Printed in the USA
BVHW051108100323
660173BV00014B/700/J

9 781737 336303